D0671867

The
Student Conductor

The
Student Conductor

Robert Ford

G. P. PUTNAM'S SONS
New York

This is a work of fiction. Names, characters, places, and incidents either are the product of the author's imagination or are used fictitiously, and any resemblance to actual persons, living or dead, business establishments, events, or locales is entirely coincidental.

⊪P

G. P. Putnam's Sons
Publishers Since 1838
a member of
Penguin Group (USA) Inc.
375 Hudson Street
New York, NY 10014

Library of Congress Cataloging-in-Publication Data

Ford, Robert, date.
The student conductor / Robert Ford.
p.   cm.
ISBN 0-399-15037-4 (acid-free paper)
1. Americans—Germany—Fiction.   2. Teacher-student relationships—Fiction.   3. Conductors (Music)—Fiction.
4. Defectors—Fiction.   5. Germany—Fiction.   I. Title.
PS3606.O745S78   2003   2003046514
813'.6—dc21

Printed in the United States of America
1   3   5   7   9   10   8   6   4   2

This book is printed on acid-free paper. ♾

BOOK DESIGN BY STEPHANIE HUNTWORK

FOR MY PARENTS

The
Student Conductor

1

Barrow woke to the hard yank of an oncoming train and caught the whisper of the last orange car as it passed. Outside, the German sun flung itself in all directions, glanced from the rails, perfected clouds. It was the kind of day they polish steel for.

An elderly woman sat across from him in the compartment—gray hair, black raincoat, and striking blue eyes. "Pretty sun," he said in German. *Schöne Sonne.*

"*Ja.*"

Her eyes did not leave the empty headrest to his left.

He tried giving himself over to the clip of passing utility poles, their near-rhyme. The intervals were not quite fixed, which only fed his anxiety.

He glanced back at the old woman. "One sees the Rhine on this trip?" he asked, still in German.

"Where are you going?"

"Karlsruhe."

"No."

She turned to stare out the window. He noticed the severity with which her hair had been clawed back into a bun, the particular gray of her skirt. She could be a nun. He considered her profile, pictured her as a little girl—and older, at the age of her decision, her commitment or whatever they call it, standing before the altar at the head of a long line of other girls, her blue eyes angled down so as not to astonish the priest.

He wandered between awake and stupid, the kind of stupid induced by trains. Farm fields chased by his window, some harvested and trailing smoke, fires running lengthwise in banked rows—he'd read somewhere that ash was good for the soil.

Inches from his cheek, the safety glass was warm from the sun. When the conductor announced the Karlsruhe station, he was half asleep.

Another spark from the intercom—*Nächste Station Karlsruhe Hauptbahnhoff.*

He was on his feet, pulling down bags. The nun's murmured "Good luck" surprised him, and he muttered something back. In the station he pondered food, but his stomach rejected the idea. He found a locker for the larger of his two bags, bought an English-language newspaper and a map, and worked out a walking route to the Karlsruhe Festplatz.

A wide boulevard called Ettlinger Strasse led to the heart of the city, and he strode its tree-lined sidewalk, working his calves to muscle out the excess adrenaline. Tram tracks split the broad avenue, and he sought distraction in the geometry of the electric lines slung overhead, the quiet *shim* of passing streetcars. The Festplatz came up. He checked his watch and walked for another three blocks, doubled back, and dropped to a bench by a circle of fountains surrounded by flowers bright as lemons. He surveyed the brick-paved acreage, followed the lazy progression of a two-baby family attired for a stroll through the city zoo.

It was his accursed gift to know that his heart rate was just over 116 beats per minute. He stared into the fountain and closed his eyes, thinking to lose himself in the steady smack of water on water—the consolation of pure noise—but it didn't work.

It was too early, but he got up, adjusted his pack and headed for the massive limestone building that held down the far corner of the square. The Konzerthaus. Wrecked by war, and now, forty-something years later, back on its feet. A verandah of trees hid the rear quarter of the building, where Barrow had been assured over the phone—a brief word with the people at the music school, the Badische Hochschule für Musik—that he'd find a certain door unlocked. It was unusual, they had said, but the maestro liked to audition his pupils in the concert hall.

Inside, a guard directed him to a stage door across from the men's toilet, where he retreated, a place to limber up his arms in private. Glancing in the mirror, he regretted an earlier decision not to change out of his jeans. He'd meant to shave on the train—another oversight. His face looked paler than usual, older than thirty—brows too dark, cheek bones and forehead too prominent. Jet lag, he thought. He had a tie and he slipped it on, retucked his white oxford shirt. With wet fingers, he combed the hair out of his eyes.

The stage door opened into the left wing of a large stage set for full orchestra. His eyes went to the conductor's podium, its black safety rail shiny under the dim light. He gazed at it.

Get the fuck out, he thought. Walk away.

He checked the knot of his tie.

A couple of rolling lamps marked the edge of the stage. Burgundy seats, row upon row, disappeared toward the back of the hall in a weak fluorescent haze. The rear of the house was invisible. He approached the podium, knocking a couple of metal stands together with his backpack. The brittle retort bespoke the vastness of the place.

His forehead burned. There was a growing confusion between the outer recesses of the hall and the inner recesses of his own skull. Sound, stored above the catwalks, approached and receded. Leftovers from a thousand concerts—a full-voiced Beethoven chord, the thin-clad opening of Mahler's First. He couldn't stifle the need to float his right hand forward, test the thick wedge of air between the soft flesh of his palm and the acoustically disciplined back wall of the stage.

From far up in the seats behind came a short volley of words, shot through with command.

"*Nehmen Sie es!*"

Take it.

He blushed and stepped up to the podium. A plank creaked under his left foot, some imperfectly cinched brace in the substructure.

"*Kein Taktstock?*" A perfect baritone from forty yards back, maybe fifty, straining against the traces of its upper range.

Barrow shrugged off his pack, bent to unzip the compartment that held his baton, his *Taktstock*—get used to that word. When he straightened, the blood rushed his head and the stage took a swift turn before his eyes. He rooted himself to the podium, safety lamps flanking him on either side—things to navigate by. The tip of his baton rested on the sloping desk in front of him.

Again, the voice, in German: "First symphony, fourth movement."

Beethoven's First—it had to be. The coincidence struck him. His last time before an orchestra, it had also been Beethoven's First.

His wrists shook. The hall was a cavernous void, nothing but a place to breathe. He raised his arms, left palm up, stick delivered straight forward. Conjure orchestra—

"You're shaking!"

Thanks, he thought. He'd crossed an ocean for this.

His arms opened to embrace the solid trunk of the fourth movement's opening *fortissimo*, and with a simple flick of the wrist he indicated an upbeat, released the opening sonority. The thick chord sprang up in his head. Full orchestra. *Tutti.* He held it, widened the embrace just so much, swiftly cut it off.

"*Halt, halt, halt! Wie gross ist das Orchester?*"

He would not have thought to ask—

"How large is the orchestra?" the teacher demanded, in English this time.

"I understand," Barrow shouted back in German, noting the shrillness in his voice. "Modern orchestra. Eighteen firsts, sixteen seconds, viola twelve, cello—"

"*Aufstellung.*"

The English, the English—

"*Aufstellung?!*"

Arrangement.

"Traditional. Firsts here, seconds here, celli ..." Barrow indicated the placement of violins to his left, celli to his right—

"Continue," yelled the teacher in German—it would always be German, German from here on in.

The opening six bars consumed thirty minutes of harassment. The correct length of the eighth note, the gradations of soft, softer, softest; their precise indication with his hands. A good conductor would never rehearse a full orchestra this way, this stopping and starting; they would mutiny. He would call out suggestions, cajole in passing, return only later to pick up what was missing.

Barrow began the new tempo, the *Allegro molto e vivace*—

"Too loud, too loud!"

There's no fucking orchestra!

He fought the impulse to turn, face his accuser. He didn't have to. The teacher had advanced to the lip of the stage, and it was Barrow's first look at Maestro Karlheinz Ziegler. A slight stoop and a large head added to the impression of great height. His thinning white hair was overlong, rash and unkempt at the sides, perhaps studiously so.

"Bow the cello part for me, please," the old man said, his voice softer, "from bar twenty-three."

Barrow dragged his baton back and forth across his left forearm while Ziegler sang under his breath, eyes fixed on Barrow's hands. The old man's skin ran bright pink with agitation under the dim light. His blue-gray eyes never met the American's; set deep under a tall forehead, they danced between meanness and delight.

"Now a slow movement from one of the concerti, any slow movement." Barrow hesitated—there had to be a correct choice. "You stop to think. Do not."

"Third piano concerto, second movement."

"Begin." Barrow looked for some response, a nod of approval on his selection. "Begin," the teacher said.

He imagined a piano to his left, a gaping concert grand, and a new set of eyes, the pianist's, twelve feet off. Ziegler was a background blur in the same direction. A long piano solo began the movement, and because it was not his job to conduct the soloist, he skipped ahead and started beating one full measure before the entrance of the orchestra. He nodded to "the pianist," beating lightly through the soloist's closing two measures, transferring the tempo to the players.

"What is that?"

"I am starting where—"

"You would carve the Madonna without a head?"

"No, I—"

"Start where Beethoven starts."

Barrow stood, head bowed. His eyes swept the empty stage, the assembled chairs, and settled on the pianist. He dropped his chin in what was meant to be a subtle nod, marking the start of the movement. He and Ziegler shared a minute and a third of silence, the same tune supposedly trailing through their heads. Barrow lifted his arms to ready the players, delivered a simple upbeat.

Ziegler broke in. "Who is your soloist, Liberace? Too shitting fast."

"I'm sorry."

"Pick someone else."

He picked himself.

Rochester, New York. Eleven years before—1978—and a certain all-night session alone in a practice room. He'd played the opening measures of the second movement on the piano again and again without thinking. A gross self-indulgence, but weren't these the saddest sixteen measures ever constructed? *A desperate whisper for redemption,* some teacher had said.

He made the mistake of meeting Ziegler's eyes.

"Where are you?"

"Pardon?"

"This is not church."

For two hours, Ziegler called out movements and sections of movements, observed Barrow from the house and from every part of the stage. He interrupted—or did not—there was no pattern. Correction or scrutiny, the effect was the same: to strip Barrow of what little certainty might be left after eight years away from the podium. Again and again, Ziegler asked him to make his own selection. Each time, Barrow scrambled for the least obvious choice: the first movement of Beethoven's Eighth, or the second of the Second. In the end, it didn't matter, because he'd begun to understand the old man's message, even as he watched its deliberate, sleight-of-hand insinuation. The most ancient spell of sorcerer over apprentice: *How little you know, how much I can teach you.*

A pair of musicians drifted in from the wings, possibly students. Barrow paid little notice. His clothes were soaked through with sweat, his soul borne up by a sense of possibility, because the more Ziegler drove him the luckier he knew he was. The other half of the old man's intended message: *How lucky you are, how lucky that I should even spend the time.*

There was a low "snap" off in the wing, and light flooded the stage. Ziegler stood by the podium. "I will teach you," he said, and he slipped Barrow a small card with his address.

"Thank you," Barrow said.

"For the first month we meet every day."

"On the weekend?"

"Every day," the old man said. Barrow nodded, beating back elation. "This is to bring you up to minimum standard. Bare minimum."

"Yes, Maestro."

Minutes later he stood under the trees behind the Konzerthaus, allowing his eyes to adjust before wandering out into the direct sun.

This, he thought, is what a ghost feels like his first day back.

2

He took an attic apartment in the tiny Karlsruhe suburb of Ettlingen. For three weeks, he kept company with a small borrowed table and his musical scores. He passed days and nights conducting cassette tapes from a stool, existing on boxed soup and *Käsebrötchen,* the addictive cheese-encrusted rolls he bought fresh.

His lessons were a revelation. Ziegler was a sculptor, endlessly observing and adjusting his student. He had no apparent program, no rote course of study; he selected, at random, from the entire symphonic canon. The connections he drew were unexpected, ingenious, his knowledge fathomless, and Barrow filled the margins of his scores with the maestro's wisdom.

There were, occasionally, extra-musical points of contact, a single question stiffly put. "Do you like to hike?" "Yes." On with the lesson.

Or—the old man had conducted once in Chicago years before—"You swam in Lake Michigan?"

"I grew up in Cleveland."

"I see."

At such times, Barrow's spirit soared. Such was the ridiculous state of his isolation.

At rehearsals of the student orchestra, he met the other graduate conductors and two or three of the players, but he dodged their friendly advances and they soon learned to keep their distance.

He was haunted by the need to make up for lost time. His only lust was utter concentration.

⁓

Early in his fourth week a hairline crack developed in his routine.

Perched on his stool for an hour, maybe two, he sensed a presence in the attic and turned to find the little boy from downstairs—one of his landlord's kids—standing on the top step, imitating his movements. "Bin dein Schatten," the kid said, hands flitting about in the sun from the sky-light. He must have been four or five, a blond cherub with excessively pink cheeks. "Yes, yes, very good," Barrow said, uncertain of the word Schatten. The boy beamed and scampered down the steps. A reprimand filtered up from two floors below, hushed and motherly, Johannes!

Barrow stared at the spot under the skylight, so packed with life mere seconds before. He took out his dictionary. I'm your shadow, the boy had said.

He pulled on his sneakers and descended the stairs. All was quiet— the second-floor bedroom shared by the two children, the living room with its Ansel Adams print over the couch. The boy and his mother must have slipped out.

He'd not entered his landlord's kitchen in three weeks—not since closing the deal on the attic. In the first week, he'd been invited twice to join the family for dinner, and twice he'd declined. He had not been invited since.

The refrigerator's compressor kicked on. A brief shudder, a sustained hum.

"You're a monk," he whispered, and for once he did not like the sound of it.

✍

Two days later he was crossing the Festplatz, heading for the Konzerthaus an hour before rehearsal, collar up against a damp wind. He was going through a score in his head, so he didn't see her until it was almost too late—the young woman standing under the trees, maybe twenty meters back from the personnel door.

He slowed his pace.

She wore a yellow scarf over her head, a dab of color against the gray morning, and she hugged something to her chest, possibly a clarinet case. He thought he recognized her from the wind section.

He considered a quick retreat to the café across the street, where he'd been chugging coffee for the last half hour—but a few minutes alone on stage was all he needed, if only to take the edge off dread. Ziegler had assigned him a score the night before, with the distinct implication that he'd be asked to conduct it this morning—his debut before the orchestra. He needed the stage time, and, if necessary, he'd negotiate for it.

He mapped a wide angle, came up well behind the clarinetist, and lingered under the trees. The personnel door must still be locked, or she'd already be inside. He noted that a few strands of dark hair had blown free from her scarf and taken to the air currents above her head. She looked at her watch and he grew worried, until she pulled out a paperback and restationed her clarinet case between her feet. He pulled out his score of *Tristan und Isolde*.

Within a minute, the door opened.

Caught up in her book, the clarinetist fumbled the moment, unaware that Barrow had been waiting. He outflanked her, got himself through the door, and without, he hoped, seeming obvious, was well down the corridor before she'd even arrived at the door. Her hushed *"Guten Tag"* to the guard followed him down the hall. He noticed the specific lilt of her voice, but didn't look back. Two turns, a jog down another hallway, and he was at the stage door.

Oddly, two industrial-sized fans had been erected in the wings, directing air toward the stage. He dropped his coat and bag and walked out to the podium. Rehearsal lights were up and the empty hall yawned before him. He faced the array of stands; it was necessary fuel, this understanding that could only be found by standing on the lip of the stage, the hall at his back. He closed his eyes, and in the low white noise of the offstage fans—because he'd been up all night studying it—he heard the opening sounds of the greatest love ballad of all time, *Tristan und Isolde*.

When he opened his eyes, the clarinetist was standing in a field of music stands, her hair tucked indifferently behind the wings of her glasses. She must have slipped in under the noise of the fans. She slung her coat over the principal oboist's chair. Underneath she wore a deep brown, vertically ribbed sweater.

She placed a plastic cup of reeds on her stand—oboe reeds—and he found the discovery that she wasn't a clarinetist vaguely disorienting. "*Morgen*," he said—or heard himself say—"morning" in German, also "tomorrow."

She looked up sharply and adjusted her glasses. "*Morgen*." When Barrow said nothing, she continued in German. "They say the ventilation is being worked on all morning."

He hesitated.

"And thus, the fans," he said, injecting a bit of a flourish into his tone, feeling instantly foolish.

She had fine brown eyes, and for a moment they stayed on his, assessing him in some way. Perhaps he'd picked the wrong German word for fans. She smiled—just at the corners of her mouth—looked down, and began assembling her oboe. He wondered what he'd already revealed of himself, here on the podium, one hand resting lightly on the conductor's desk, the other slipped nonchalantly into his pocket. If only he had his violin, how much easier to be warming up with a few scales somewhere back in the violin section.

"I was hoping for a few moments alone," he said.

She looked up. "I'll leave."

"No, I'm ..."

"I thought you were just ..."

"No."

She had already removed her reed. She was blushing.

"Why don't you stay?" he said. "It doesn't matter."

She made a clatter at her stand, gathering her instrument and her things. The sudden shift from woman-at-home to woman-in-flight took him by surprise. Her balancing act with case, music, and fully-assembled oboe, her hair messing about her shoulders. Her reddening cheeks.

"I'm sorry," he whispered. But she was gone, having disappeared into the wings, leaving her coat draped over her chair as a remembrance.

✎

Ziegler snapped out two or three commands the moment he saw the fans. They were unplugged and, when that wasn't enough, removed altogether. The temperature soared under the rehearsal lights while he took the orchestra through a close reading of Brahms' Second Symphony, first movement. Barrow rolled his sleeves above the elbow, followed the score, and leaned forward in his chair to keep his shirt dry.

Precisely fifteen minutes before the end of rehearsal, Ziegler closed his score and glanced at Barrow—as predicted. Barrow turned to the two grad conductors who huddled next to him. They nodded.

He arrived at the podium and dropped his score to the conductor's desk. The students were restless. "*Tristan und Isolde,*" he announced, without looking up. When he did raise his eyes—because sooner or later he must—they went first to Ziegler, who stood behind the percussion section with his back to the orchestra.

"*Tristan,*" Barrow said, louder this time, "first movement," which was, of course, idiotic—worse than idiotic—since there was only one movement and therefore no movements at all, really. He'd meant to say *prelude*, but it was too late to correct himself, and he traced the wave of stifled laughter that breezed through the orchestra. He smiled weakly, attempting to join in on the joke.

So it went, his reintroduction to the podium—a short passage after all, from hermit to public spectacle.

He looked up a second time, directly into the eyes of the principal oboist; his thoughts were in such disarray. Mechanics, he thought, lifting his arms. He whispered it. "Mechanics." Nothing else to hang on to. The first sound—a dry, slightly out-of-tune unison in the celli—shocked him as it had years before, his first time before an orchestra. He hid his amazement.

He'd built an edifice in the night, and he entered it. An architecture of discoveries, all about *Tristan—the way his mind could work when he wanted it to*—the exquisite unity of the piece, the relationship of all parts to the whole, and here, atop the podium, he watched the walls fly up, the arched ceiling, the nave stretching out before him, everything lining up. He lost himself in the design.

His first real error.

A foreign sound, not in the score, not Wagner, sailed over the orchestra. *"Danke, danke."*

It was Ziegler.

The music fell away, the edifice flew apart. Barrow glanced at the two grad conductors seated behind the orchestra, foreigners like himself, both looking for cover. They'd all been through it.

Ziegler's voice cut through the uneasy silence that had settled over the orchestra, regulated and sure. Businesslike.

"Herr Barrow. The engineering school is across town."

Barrow fought to maintain some measure of dignity. "Excuse me, Maestro."

"We want more *bowel*, Herr Barrow."

Some of the players looked away. Others watched to see the American's reaction. He cocked his head in such a way as to convince his fellow students that he was not above honest criticism.

"Rehearsal over," Ziegler said, and a low murmur rose up from all corners of the stage.

Barrow could not relinquish the podium—such a glorious height—his five minutes' residence there, gone. He closed his score, hands and wrists numb. He glimpsed the principal oboist, who had not yet begun to break down her instrument. She leaned forward, chin on her knuckles. Her covert grin seemed meant for him—stirred him unexpectedly—and he looked away.

3

The *Tristan* humiliation had the same effect as a hazing. Before the incident, the students rarely looked at him; now the more outgoing among them made a point of smiling, saying hello, often throwing in some crack about intestinal difficulties. The timpani player stopped him in the hall, a tall black man from Boston. "Hey, Maestro," he said. "Can't wait for the second movement."

At the same time, Barrow's perfect run of discipline began to falter. He would lay in bed until well past seven, replaying his encounter with the principal oboist—whose name, he had learned, was Petra Vogel. In rehearsal, he paid extra attention to her playing. Her tuning note would soar across a quarter-acre of lacquered wood, ebony, and brass, and land like the first duck on an evening pond. She was good—her tone, a marvel of suppleness.

He accepted a standing invitation to join the other two grad conductors for coffee. They seemed to have mistaken his aloof behavior for shyness, a welcome misapprehension on their part. At the first opportunity, he slipped Vogel's name into the conversation and discovered that she was a defector from East Germany—or DDR as everyone seemed to call it. She had escaped from East Berlin the year before. "Ironic, no?" said Antonio, who was from Milan. "Today she could simply take the train to Prague, and *whoosh*, out."

Barrow asked if he knew anything else about her.

"Personally, I would stay away," said Berndt, a tall Belgian, with light gray eyes.

"Personally, you are married," countered the Italian.

"But *he's* not," Berndt said, and they both looked at Barrow.

"That's not why I ask," Barrow said.

In rehearsal that day, Ziegler dispatched him to inspect a discrepancy in the second horn part of the Mozart they'd been sight reading. Returning through the stands, he glanced at Petra. Her face was flush from playing. He risked a second glance, over his shoulder. On his third—this time from his seat—she was looking right at him.

After rehearsal, in his most daring act in recent memory—even more daring than auditioning for Ziegler—he approached her. She was taking apart her oboe, so she didn't see him come up. He hesitated, hovering over her shoulder. "After letter C?" he said, heart pounding.

"*Ja?*"

"I am wondering about your choice to breathe."

It didn't matter that her passagework was already immaculate.

"Of course."

"I mean, here," he said, pointing to a specific measure in the music. He sensed that his manner was too brusque—brusqueness having been the closest mask at hand.

She removed her glasses and said simply, in well-schooled English, "I swim on Fridays." A single phrase, and she dismantled him. "Bad Herrenalb," she said, "the swimming baths." He found no words to ask, for example, What time?, so she helped him with that too, "From six to seven." She returned her glasses to the bridge of her nose, close to the tip. "So what is this phrasing?"

He panicked. How could he have been so forward?

He woke early on Friday, and for over an hour he stared blankly at the skylight over his bed. Snow had been falling since before dawn, an utter fluke for late October, and he gazed at the wandering flakes, dismayed at his lack of resolve and how it was eating into his precious study time. He remembered a piece of wisdom dispensed by an old roommate. "You aren't the only one who spent puberty in a practice room. Pick up the goddamn phone."

He devised a plan.

After lunch he tossed a swimsuit into his pack, along with a score and an extra sweater, and headed up into the hills behind Ettlingen, the northernmost reach of the Black Forest. He had to make twenty kilometers—roughly twelve miles—by six o'clock, and while the tram covered the same distance in under half an hour, the hike suited him more. The idea of earning an audience with Vogel, paying in advance.

The temperature dropped as he climbed. He crossed the paved road to Busenbach, which was shiny with snowmelt—all familiar ground. He had imposed himself on the place a dozen times, drawn to its unbounded tangle of trails, its Bronze Age–forks in the road, drawn also, he thought, to the feeling of being known, even understood, the same feeling he found when studying a score by Beethoven or Mahler.

But everything was different this time. His world had been invaded by the principal oboist, and his mind returned to her again and again. How would he find her at the pool? Would she even be there? He pictured her aboard the mustard-yellow tram as it sliced through the woods, far below. Was she alone? Had she failed to mention, perhaps, a boyfriend?

He scripted and rescripted his final, stuttering approach—a hopeless exercise.

He distracted himself by going through a score, mentally rehearsing

Brahms' Second Symphony. It was the perfect antidote and his mind leapt to the task. He trudged through the snow, his third eye traveling in steep sine waves across page after page, tracing in notes, absorbing sound. Stuck—unable to visualize some voicing, usually in the violas or second violins—he would go back, get a running start. It happened once with a short passage in the violas: he listened, hummed parts, and nothing. He tried subterfuge, concentrating on the woodwinds, hoping the violas would filter through in the background. Nothing. He tried visualizing the players, their bowings, watching them saw away to his right, just below the podium. Nothing.

He had the score in his pack, and he took it out, removed his gloves, and leafed through to the trouble-spot. He checked a few other places before it struck him that he'd stopped walking.

The sky above the trees was clear, and the snow glowed gas-jet blue under the moon. He'd left his watch behind—another bright move. How much time had gone by?

He stuffed the score in his pack, grabbed his gloves, and began jogging down the vague indentation that was the trail until his toe caught a root and he stumbled, hopped once and hit the ground, gloves flying out of his hands. Lying on his side, he breathed heavily and yelled his frustration to the empty woods.

They fell silent—and the whole pitiful sound came back to him. He'd found an echo.

He rolled to his knees. "Rehearsal over!" he shouted, and the words came hurtling back. "Rehearsal fucking over!" and they played back, three words seizing up all the silence for miles around. He sang a major-seventh arpeggio and it came back a chord. He sang it again, "La-la-la-la!" surprised at the anger in his voice. He stood up. He yelled and sang until his throat ached.

His fingers were numb and he slipped them under his shirt, straight up to his armpits. He winced. Far above, a stiffening wind rattled the topmost leaves in the canopy. He cinched his scarf, dried his face with the end of it, and retrieved his gloves from the snow.

He was an idiot not to have taken the tram.

∽

At the ticket window, a woman asked if he needed something called a *Badekappe*. The clock over her shoulder read two minutes past seven. The woman held up a rubbery blue bladder. A bathing cap. Of course. Idiot. He shoved the money across and she counted out his change in English.

He found the men's locker, suited up, and found his way to the *Schwimmbad*, a cavernous area with steamed windows and tropical plants and at least two separate pools. The place teemed with Friday-nighters all sharing the same oppressively humid air.

He felt a tap on his shoulder. "Hey, Maestro."

It was Stefan, a student cellist from Austria, one of the players who had warmed up to him after the *Tristan* debacle.

"You have not gone in yet?" Stefan said in English.

"No."

"That one is quite hot." The cellist's hair was flat and streaming. "You should go in this one first, followed by that one. I think that's quite a good idea."

"Okay."

"I am just departing, it's too bad."

"Too bad."

Stefan crossed to a tiled ledge and slipped his feet into a pair of plastic sandals that had been lined up neatly with a dozen others. He turned back, grinning broadly, and called across in English. "By the way, that oboist is here. Petra Vogel."

Barrow managed a salutary wave from the hip, the sort of small gesture he might use to soften the viola section. *Does he know?*

He retreated to a short set of stairs flanked by a couple of leafy restaurant plants. Normally he'd have hung back at this point and let fate or some other grand operating principle take over. Hadn't the important moments, the key advancements in his life, all crept up on him like that? From behind? A tap on the shoulder? Marty Weissberger up in Rochester, his first conducting teacher, "Ever thought about conducting?"

He didn't see Petra anywhere in the lukewarm pool, so he laddered down into the hotter of the two and pushed off from the edge. The water, not quite chokingly hot, pressed back and freed the muscles of his abdomen. Disembodied heads glided by, blue eyes and steadfast solitude. He stroked past three girls bent in the tight circle of their own world. The oboist was not among them. At the far end of the pool a set of black tire-flaps gave access to an outside extension. He swam for the passage and pushed through the stiff flaps to the night sky—steam everywhere, rising and swaying above the water's surface. An elderly German sat on one edge, framed by a melting bank of shoveled snow, one leg crossed over the other, his glistening, elderly skin stretched tight, steam peeling off into the night. *"Abend,"* the man said.

"Abend," said Barrow, his voice pitched a good fifth below normal.

At first he didn't see her. He kicked to the center of the small pool, which glowed aqua from the light of a single underwater head lamp, the bite of frigid air in his nostrils.

There was a subtle splash to his left, followed by the sound of her voice.

"Guten Abend, Herr Conductor."

God, he'd forgotten its low timbre.

He turned. A twist of dark hair had escaped her *Badekappe* to loop across her forehead. Her face was round and every shade from white to crimson. He took a quick pull of air—it came laced with ice and he coughed against it, out of control. Before he could clear his eyes she had swum across, slid an arm around his chest, and towed him to the side. He felt the burning imprint of her shoulder strap, the shock of her fingers across his ribs as she released him to the buoyant water.

"You are okay," she said in English. "You breathe the mist too quickly and ... well, you know..."

"The mist," he said, wishing he could sink to the bottom, stay there, live for a century—

"Come on," she said. She hoisted herself to the edge of the pool, and he did the same. She pulled off her *Badekappe* and tossed it to the snow. He glanced across the water, concerned at her infraction of the rules, but the old man was gone. "It is not for them to care," she said. Her matted hair shone in the pool's refracted light.

He peeled off his cap and pulled himself out of the water.

She lay down and rolled in the snow, moaned against the pain, and the sound undid his knees. He was kneeling next to her, scooping up a pile of the loose stuff; it was hot charcoal against his chest. She made him roll to his back, where he lay, unnerved at the sound of his own groaning. She laughed and laughed, and he could see stars through the steam. "Come on," she said, "I can't stand it." She stood on the edge of the pool, and he gazed at her—the shimmering, backlit *composition* of her, how her suit clung to her breasts, the frank outline of her nipples, how the water coursed over her lean-muscled arms and legs. He forgot the cold, the exhaustion, the hoarse ranting in the woods.

"Come on," she yelled, and he pushed himself up with both arms, one foot slipping out from under, and all the way up to stand at her side. She grabbed his hand and looked straight into his eyes, inches away, and there came a corresponding release, a profound inflation of his lungs, and they both jumped out—out from the edge, through the steam, over the water, screaming full out until it all blew up in brilliant relief.

⚬⌀⚬

"Tell me about Maestro Ziegler," she said. They sat across from each other in a café, speaking in German.

"Like what?"

"Just little things."

He lifted his elbow from their shellacked, wood-top table and it rocked noticeably to the right.

"For example, does he speak English to you in lessons?"

"Only when he thinks he knows some English expressions. This morning he says—we're looking at a scherzo, and I ask if he conducts it in one or in three—and he says, 'In three? They will laugh their shoulders off.'" Petra looked confused. "Laugh their heads off. It's our saying. Laugh their heads off?"

"Mm-hm. Does he smile?"

"Never. He smiled once."

"Really? He smiled?"

He had the fleeting thought that all this—the swim, the whole evening—was merely about getting dirt on Ziegler. Petra had volunteered to divert the American for an evening's chat, a fact-finding mission. She would collect her data and fade back into the wind section by the middle of next week.

He started folding a napkin to prop under one of the table legs. "His cat attacked the end of my baton. One lesson."

"His cat."

He looked at her. "You've seen it?"

"No, of course. He has a cat?"

"Yes. He smiled then."

She seemed delighted. "Herr Maestro Ziegler has a cat?"

"It's gray. It's just a gray cat."

She looked across at him—she wanted to see if he caught the humor. He hesitated. She produced a small *meow*, and they both laughed, even though it wasn't that funny, laughing to laugh.

Barrow ducked under the table and shoved the napkin wedge between a heating grate and the guilty table leg. He glanced over at Petra's feet—her jeans tucked into thick wool socks, her boots gray with light green suede, the laces orange.

Her face appeared. "What's the matter?" she asked, and he responded by banging his head into the table, clattering silverware. She groaned sympathetically and started to reach across, but a voice interrupted, slicing through the warm hubbub of the café. "*Zwei Gulaschsuppen?*"

They surfaced with the landing of two large bowls and the sweet smell of stewed meat. He caught her eye and they slid their spoons in simultaneously. He scooped out a delicate cube of beef just as a blast of hot dry air started out from the grate at their feet. There was a musical phrase to tuck around the moment, but he couldn't think of it.

"It has been a question," she said in English, "of some, should I say, significance, of who would see you laugh the first."

"Oh?" He had always felt incapable of stirring questions of significance.

"Yes. Of course, I was quite sure it was at least *possible.*"

"*Natürlich.*"

"Alexandra disagreed with me."

"Alexandra?"

"My roommate. Principal viola, on the Brahms?"

He remembered Alexandra, tall with two sheaves of blond hair that swung in perfect symmetry when she played.

"In Südstadt. We live there. You know, this neighborhood next to the music school." He nodded. "You are here for one year?"

"Unless I can get an appointment with an opera, or somewhere."

"You will get an appointment."

He tried to read her face, studying her next spoonful, the way she bunched her napkin to wipe drips from her chin. A woman in a green loden coat raised a glass of wine at the next table, red and deep. Life, he thought, in a glass. He would order a bottle.

Petra had followed his gaze. "Yes," she said.

"What?"

"I think we should."

He hesitated, thinking through the arithmetic. He had lost his deposit on the *Badekappe,* having left it in the snow.

The toe of her boot touched his calf. "I get the wine. I have this stipend, too." She smiled again, and it was one lovely smile too many. She turned for the waiter and Barrow followed the fineness of her neck muscle as it flexed below her ear and disappeared beneath the frayed collar of her sweater. He felt too much heat in his face.

"Excuse me," he said. "I have to ... I'm ..." He stood up.

She looked into his face. "Yes," she said.

The restaurant was a blur of candlelight and brass plate. There was a bar with possibly every flavor of schnapps and next to the bar an alcove with a phone and a couple of promising doors with curled iron thumb-latches. He pulled open the one marked *Herren* and stepped in. The latch dropped behind him. One stall. He slipped in and pushed the door closed, his hands gripping the top, forehead pressed to its cool metal. Still he could not fill his lungs. A hand came to his face, thumb and forefinger pressed into the hollows of his eyes. Part of him, the part that watched, remembered his first encounter with the second movement of Beethoven's Seventh, and he thought, How ridiculous that I should be remembering this from a Schwarzwald toilet. He was twelve. An Otto Klemperer recording. The music yanked and twisted him, wedged him into the impossible space between his bed and the wall.

He was pulling down long gulps of air when he heard the latch flip and someone enter and go to the sink. He flushed the toilet and dropped the seat noisily. He assembled a pile of toilet paper singles and blew his nose, waited until the other man left, and went out to the sink. In the mirror his eyes were red, his dark hair matted to his forehead. He splashed water in his eyes, dried his face, and with his fingers combed back his hair. He stopped to look at himself, smiling weakly. It's been too long, he thought. I've been starving myself.

His eyes were red. She would know something. So be it.

When he arrived at their table, she tilted her face to him, smiling. Low voices eddied in the corners of the restaurant. A tall green bottle stood open on his side of the table, with two glasses.

"I have not had wine in a while," he said.

At thirty, a man who had never poured wine for a woman. He did so, and she held her glass high, her free hand touching the edge of the table. Her hair was lank and artless, her cheeks still pink from the cold. A certain smile, one he'd already begun to commit to memory, just touching the corners of her mouth.

"Prost," he said, unable to invent anything else.

"Prost," she said.

They drank and he was surprised by the rash acid of the liquid.

"Pretty good," he said in English, not knowing.

"Ja, 'pretty good,'" she said, and the sound of "pretty good" coming from her mouth, the way it couldn't just roll out, thrilled him.

She took another sip, and some private thought seemed to pull her glance to the far corner of the room. Pause lengthened to silence. He wanted her to talk so he could watch her, look at her hands, her dark eyes, not think. From behind the bar came a crash of silverware and a burst of laughter, a woman's birdsong, several men *basso*. Subsidence.

"Is it true," he asked, his voice dangerously shaky, "that you defected from East Germany?"

She threw him a look, an expression impossible to read.

"Tell me," he said, taking a chance. On impulse—a good impulse—he topped her glass, the purple streaming over its side, clinging to the tiny globe, pooling around its base. She giggled, anchoring the wet stem with her fingers, lowering her lips to the rim. "Like the cat," he said, "the way you are drinking," and she sputtered, spraying more wine. When she lifted her face, lips apart, there was wine on the tip of her nose. She wiped it with her finger, licked clean the knuckle.

"Please tell me," he said again, mopping, setting his napkin under her glass. He leaned forward, resting his chin in his hand.

"It was a year ago," she said. "September. Nineteen eighty-eight. The Concours Internationale de Paris. I was lucky to obtain a special travel visa to enter the competition. I was with some other young musicians, East German, and after we dropped off some things at our rooms, I separated from them." She hunched her shoulders, dropped them.

"That's it?"

"Other than I avoided a certain friend, a bassoonist, who I was certain was the Stasi informant in the group."

"Stasi informant?"

"Secret police, you know. Best friend of the state. There is always at least one, probably more, even in a little group like ours, if you are going out of the country. To keep an eye out. Take notes on what we do, whom we meet." She looked at him—he could tell she was trying to gauge his interest. "Even at home," she said, "every group has someone, an informer. I have heard it called in English a 'plant.'"

"Yes."

"You know about Stasi?"

"I've never known how much to believe."

"Believe everything."

She took another sip. She seemed, he thought, a degree or two less reluctant. "You've had to tell this a million times," he said.

"At first when I came, yes."

"Don't stop."

She smiled, and he waited.

"I was lost three times on the way to the West German embassy—I have terrible French. There were no chairs left when I got there, and I sat on the floor in the lobby. I was shivering and I had only my oboe case and I would not move until they promised me asylum. Of course they did. According to law they have to. That's it."

"So you dropped out of the competition."

She shook her head. "I won fourth place. I could have done better if I wasn't so nervous all the time. When I told my teacher—he was judging the competition—he shouted at me, in the lobby of the Comédie-Française, in front of all these people. 'They will not even *listen* to you in the West,' he said."

"But you're very good."

"Maybe."

Her fingers traced the bottom of her glass. The fingers of a boy—square, untapered, a little raw with play. There was a single red nick at the tip of one, recently healed, perhaps from her reed knife.

"You say that I am good, and that is because I practiced hard. Extremely hard. But not from any kind of liking for the music. Only to get away from the East."

"And now this," he said.

"You mean, what a waste of time that I defected? Suddenly one can get out through Hungary and no trouble?"

"Or Prague."

"Prague, sure." She glanced at something across the restaurant. "I don't care," she said, adding in English, "I have killed something that those people will never have such opportunity to kill."

"By defecting, you mean?"

She reached for her glass. "Yes."

It seemed to be a difficult topic for her, and he decided not to push it.

She rescued them from the lull that followed. "You went to Juilliard?" she asked, forming the word with a touch of wonder. Juilliard. El Dorado.

"Eight, nine years ago. I didn't finish."

"Why?"

It was his turn to shrug. "A defection of sorts," he said, instantly embarrassed at his choice of words. His retreat up the Hudson River, private battles that once seemed earthshaking—what were they in the face of political defection?

"So now you've come to Karlsruhe."

"My old teacher hooked me up with Ziegler."

"Ziegler is that special? To come all the way here?"

"Maybe."

"You came for 'maybe'?"

"I had no choice," he said.

"I don't understand. You could not choose?"

"No. I could. What I meant was"—he didn't know what he meant—"I was teaching. A little town. Outside New York City. It wasn't a lot."

"Teaching?"

"Violin. I used to play." She was paring down his resistance by her mere proximity across the table. "And playing in a small orchestra. A group, really. For weddings. Bar mitzvahs."

"Please tell me," she said, quoting him back.

"Things happened," he said, and something about the café, the shrill laughter from the bar and the clink of utensils, took him back. A large April wedding in Poughkeepsie, a renewal of vows, and a particular long frown from the master of ceremonies—a look of impatience with Barrow, his first violinist—wanting more effort or something, more *elbow* was the word he used, the bright light reflecting off his white dinner jacket, his dyed red hair brushing the collar, the sloppy arrangement of "All the Things You Are" they were playing at the time. In that split second Barrow had seen his own death. By white dinner jacket. He finished the gig and in the morning called Gil Shanahan, his old conducting teacher in New York.

"Weddings and bar mitzvahs," Petra said, chin pressed to her fist, somehow delighted and sympathetic at the same time. "I understand everything."

✍

They sat across from each other on the tram, the wide rubber scuff mat between, lulled by the low whine of wheel against rail. Outside, stars shone through the trees. She asked him something inconsequential about his birthplace in Ohio. He asked a corresponding question about the suburb of East Berlin where she grew up. Before she could answer, the tram operator announced Barrow's stop in Ettlingen. Petra pressed her lips together in exaggerated fashion, playing the stubborn girl with a secret.

He liked it. He liked everything she did. As the tram came to its neatly calibrated stop he, too, said nothing. He waited until the last possible second before springing from his seat and slipping through the accordion doors. As they whispered shut, quick and impatient, he thought he heard her laugh. He finished a perfect phrase by not looking back.

4

Lying awake that night, rummaging through the topics of his life, Barrow realized that he'd never fully appreciated Gil Shanahan. To leave a message with someone after eight years and hear back in less than twenty minutes—that had to be rare. Rare too was the obvious affection behind Shanahan's first words to him on the phone, "What're you out of your fuckin' mind?"

It was late August before Barrow met him face to face. He dropped by Shanahan's Upper West Side apartment one blessedly sub-ninety-degree evening. They strolled into Central Park while his old mentor enumerated the accomplishments of Barrow's former classmates, all of whom, unlike Barrow, had finished their degrees and entered the profession with splendid force.

They had stopped to watch a couple of company teams face off in a game of slow-pitch softball, when the subject came around to Karlheinz Ziegler.

"Here's what perplexes me," Shanahan said, nose in to the chain link fence. "Ziegler's got a pedigree like the Queen of England. He worked with Klemperer, Weingartner, and—who knows, he never mentioned—probably Furtwängler. We're in Salzburg, for example, back in the sixties. Someone gets him talking about himself, which is impossible—unless you get a good lager in his hand, get him drinking, at least in those days—and he goes on and on about Nikisch, how he saw Arthur Nikisch conduct when he was a kid in Hamburg, watched him from every angle, sneaked into the goddamn children's chorus for some performance of Mahler's Third—got himself hypnotized by the guy. That's what he said, '*Wahr hypnotisiert*,' he said. Richard Strauss himself makes a pronouncement over him while he's still in high school, the thirties, you know, *Gymnasium*, whatever they call it, 'Watch out for this one,' kind of bullshit. Then nothing. The war. Black hole."

Shanahan hadn't changed from the days when Barrow was a member of his innermost circle of students. Same wide-body jeans from the late seventies, same pale-blue short-sleeved shirts. He had started life as a longshoreman and proved it by storing his old union card under the front flap of his wallet. Local 809, Boston. Paid up.

"So you figure, okay, *Nazi*. This guy's got Nazi written all over him; he drops out of the picture after the war, no one hires him. But what the hell, look at Karajan for chrissakes—he practically makes an *asset* out of having joined the Nazi Party, saying, you know, 'I'm not political, I did it for the music, had to continue my art,' all that bullshit. And a million others. Karl Böhm? Nazi. Liz Schwarzkopf?—God bless that voice—Nazi. Did *their* careers suffer? Not a lot. Even Furtwängler, I mean what a messed up guy *that* was, total political idiot, never joins the Party but basically sleeps with Hitler and Goebbels all through the war, and again it's 'I had to preserve the German soul,' and *he* still has a career, right? Dusts himself off in 'forty-five, does Bayreuth, does London—they banned him in Chicago, big scandal in 'forty-nine—but the Brits loved him, a lot of people loved Furtwängler. So, unless Karlheinz Ziegler was a guard at Dachau or something, Party affiliation is *not* going to hold him back. So what's the problem?"

"Maybe he *was* a guard at Dachau," Barrow said.

Shanahan apparently hadn't heard. "Look at that," he said. "You gotta admire that. The cigarette people there, they got the spirit of the thing. They field a team, half girls, meanwhile they're stuck in the field for two hours while these Sony people, all guys—all basically imported from Rikers Island—they're cleaning up."

"So where does Ziegler's reputation come from?"

"You having some doubts?"

"No."

"'Cause it's your only shot."

"I know."

"Ten years is a long time in this business."

"Eight."

"I stand corrected."

Shanahan hadn't once questioned the manner of Barrow's departure, his less than graceful exit from Juilliard, how he'd dropped from sight by retreating upriver to Fishkill. It looked like he might be about to.

"Did you ever see him conduct?" Barrow asked.

"No but you shoulda heard Bernstein on the subject. I mean, you wanna see religion."

"Bernstein saw him?" Keep the old man on track.

"Europe somewhere. Dear old Lenny, you know how he'll get. He's gotta be head-over-heels in love all the time. This is—again—this is back in the sixties sometime. 'Gil,' he says, 'Gil, you *must* see this man conduct Brahms.' Here I've already met Ziegler myself, you know, in Salzburg."

"But you never saw him conduct."

"Didn't have to. I watched him analyze a score for some students, hands in the air half the time. Fucking brilliant. Had me ready to chuck it all in. Irony is, a couple years before—I'm in Austria—I overhear Ziegler slam Bernstein right outta the park. Doesn't even mention his name, but we all know. 'Mister Broadway,' he says. Has poor ol' Lenny up on all counts. Grandstanding. Overemotionalizing on the podium. The ego, the slow tempos, all the old complaints. Ziegler's jealous out of his gourd. And that's the thing—he never captured a damn thing for himself, after all those expectations before the war. He's nearly offered Pittsburgh, but Steinberg gets it. He's guest conducting all over the place in the fifties, but he never lands a post. No Vienna, no Berlin. Leipzig, Hamburg, Cologne, Hannover, nothing. None of the radio orchestras—why the hell is that? You gotta think maybe the guy never wanted it in the first place."

There was a *doink* of aluminum, and they turned to watch a short infield fly find its miraculous way into the third baseman's glove.

"Which about brings the subject around to you, doesn't it?"

5 The question of Ziegler's past never came up in his presence. Barrow daydreamed whole conversations— about wartime Berlin, about necessity and personal failure—but they never happened. The old man commandeered moments, managed proceedings, on the podium and off.

There was, for example, an established routine for approaching his apartment on Lessingstrasse. One knocked on his door at precisely the appointed hour, waited for it to swing back a few centimeters, allowed the passage of at least thirty seconds—no more than forty-five—and went in. There would be no greeting, a tedium obviated by the rite of entrance. One took one's station on the gunmetal stool and the lesson commenced. When or where this protocol originated, no one knew. It had been dubbed *das Klopfen*, or "the knock," by his students, and it was the common wisdom, conveyed student to student, perhaps for decades.

On the Monday following his hike to Bad Herrenalb, Barrow missed *das Klopfen* by five minutes. Ziegler's door remained closed, even after several tries. Barrow waited for several minutes in the rain, knocked again, and left.

Admitted to his next lesson—he'd graduated from seven to two per week—he sat on the stool and issued his excuse. There'd been a problem with the tram. The passengers had been dumped at the Hauptbahnhof.

"There is no excuse for your action," Ziegler said, "so do not make one."

"Pardon?"

"You must anticipate any breakdown, any dysfunction of the tram, of the weather, of the universe. You were a mere six minutes late, so there could have been a way—a taxicab or something—and you failed to anticipate it. Even in the event of a likely excuse, you will find I am not interested."

It had been raining like hell on Monday. No cabs at the train station, nor at any point along the two-mile route to Lessingstrasse. And yes, he'd run—he'd run the whole way.

"My expectation for your future fits in a rat's ass," Ziegler said in English. "You have the *Intermezzi?*"

Barrow sat, dumbfounded.

"Begin."

He'd been assigned a Brahms piano piece for in-depth analysis, to be imagined symphonically. He flattened the anthology against his stand, adjusted the overhead lamp, and began his analysis. Within a minute Ziegler had launched his first question, "How are the two themes related?"—followed by another, and a third, until impatient, on his feet, Ziegler began answering his own questions, disclosing the composer's mind, tearing him down for parts, extracting ambiguity, pulling in comparison after comparison—scores piling up like trash on his desk—voicing the piece for full orchestra, for string quartet, for choir. He made Barrow sing five or six figures from the *Intermezzo.*

"*Nein, nein, nein. Sehnsucht, wo ist die Sehnsucht?!*"

Where is the what? Barrow didn't know the word.

"Because, big surprise, there is no English. *Sehnsucht* is 'yearn' and, what, 'mania,' in one word. This old man, he is sixty when he composed this *Intermezzo*, but inside he's nineteen—wanting what he never had—nineteen, manic. Do you know the life?"

Barrow hesitated.

"The life of Brahms. The *life*."

"Yes."

"Do you know that Clara Schumann fed her husband wine from her fingertips? In his final days he could not move, so he took the wine from her fingertips?"

Barrow nodded.

"Where was Brahms? Was he in the room?"

"I don't know."

"When Robert Schumann was dying. These last moments with his wife. At the sanatorium. Was Brahms in the room?"

"I don't suppose—"

"No. Of course. But—mark me—he was in the building. He was, what, in the 'waiting room.' And what was he thinking?"

"I don't—"

"She is mine. He was thinking, Clara will be *mine*. He is twenty-three. Do you not think he longed for her? This is the longing I am talking about. *Sehnsucht*. Do you not think he longed for her?"

Barrow was too stunned to respond. In thirty or so lessons, Ziegler had rarely departed from the music itself, from the score, from close, chilly attendance upon the written note—

"Brahms was thinking, This man Robert Schumann, to whom I owe my career, my soul, all that I am, this man who discovered me, who has announced me to the world, elevated me to stardom—I want this man's *wife*. Robert Schumann is dying and I love him and I want his wife."

Ziegler stared at Barrow, his eyes filled with inspection. He grabbed a volume from the shelf behind him and flipped to the thicket of photos at its center. He shoved the book across the desk, one long finger singling out an illustration. "Here."

Barrow had never seen this one. A hurried sketch of Clara Schumann, greatest pianist of her generation, in her middle years. Almost certainly an idealized likeness.

"Would Brahms not want that?" Ziegler asked.

Clara's eyes were liquid with the Romantic sensibility, her high cheekbones, her fine chin and slender neck. Her breasts, voluptuous with the making of eight or ten babies.

Ziegler's voice dropped to a whisper. "Brahms walked away from that."

Clara had kept a diary with her husband, secret symbols for every time they made love, and when Barrow came back to her eyes he could see it all—the genius and the sexual intercourse—the way the dark pupils peered out from the deep cover of her brow.

"So," the old man said.

"Yes?"

"You are fucking the oboist."

Barrow stared in disbelief, flipped the sentence into English, back to German. Tested for irony. He had not seen Petra since the pool and the tram. He hadn't touched her—and how could Ziegler know anything about it?

"No," he said.

Ziegler stood and shifted the stepladder behind his desk. From the second step, he made a show of looking for a score, slid out an old cloth-bound edition, and remained on the ladder pretending to inspect it.

"Your mother."

"My mother?"

"Whom you say was a piano teacher?"

"Excuse me?"

"Your mother, whom you have mentioned."

Barrow stalled, his mind racing. "Yes, Maestro."

"Was she any good?"

"Yes. I believe so. Why are you asking?"

"I do not mean as teacher of pupils."

"Excuse me?"

"I mean as pianist," Ziegler said.

Barrow found himself distracted by the cheap operatic staging. The score as hand prop, the giant skull grazing the ceiling.

"I don't know," he said.

"You did not hear her play?"

"Yes. Naturally."

"And could she? Could she play?"

"Yes."

"But was she good?"

"Yes."

"Are you sure?"

"My mother studied with Leon Fleisher."

"And so?"

"She must have been good."

"And you heard her play."

"Yes."

"What was your opinion?" his teacher asked. He still held the cloth-bound score.

Barrow hesitated.

He could describe how as a four-year-old he would curl up at the base of his bedroom door, ear pressed to the half-inch crack where the volume was greatest; how he would surf the Chopin Ballades, the Polonaises, the Mazurkas that Ellen—he was instructed to call her Ellen from an early age—played incessantly, the Scriabin he discovered years later in the piano bench; how, in turn, they wracked his stomach; how throughout early childhood he displayed an astonishing array of abdominal symptoms—"Nothing wrong with the boy," the pediatrician said time after time, Ellen's face passive, betraying no feeling, not once, not to the doctor, not to the son.

"So," Ziegler said. "She was terrible."

"She stopped practicing."

"She was terrible."

"I don't think so."

He would sometimes crack the door, watch the racket come out of her, transforming her from the least demonstrative of personalities into a ten-fingered monster capable of shattering brutality, even torture, and all delivered from a sustained trance that rendered her completely unavailable, arms suspended over the keyboard for hours, whole afternoons, till Dad came home and the piano lid went down. One day she stopped altogether—not the teaching, but the playing. Years later he asked her why. She shrugged her shoulders and brushed back a loose strand of hippie-straight, prematurely gray hair. He pressed her. "Did you ever want a concert career?" "I enjoy teaching," she said without conviction.

"You cannot say, can you? She is your mother, so you lose all judgment."

"I honestly don't know how well she played."

"No—?"

"Or plays—"

"How can that be? You who have so fine an ear for music—or so others have claimed on your behalf—you cannot identify for me your mother's talent?"

He stared at the old man's profile, the gray sweater dragging at the pockets. He should pound his fists on the old man's desk; rage should fly him out the door and into the rain. He'd long since gotten Ziegler's message: *Beware affection, familial or otherwise. And beware of dating the talent. You will not hear straight.*

If that *was* the message.

Ziegler stepped down from the ladder—another blatantly scripted maneuver. "You know Reger? *Symphonischer Prolog?*"

"I have heard it."

"Take this." Barrow stepped forward to receive the score. "It's yours for tonight. Study it." He seemed to reconsider. "No. You will look at it now. I am doing something in the kitchen." He retreated down the short, score-lined corridor and disappeared into the back.

Barrow glanced at the Reger, clearly chosen for its title, *Symphonic Prologue to a Tragedy*. More bad farce. Ziegler's characteristic blue and red marks were etched above the first measure. The score would be filled with them. Every page in every score in the apartment, hundreds of scores, maybe thousands—more music than Ziegler could possibly have conducted—scribbled through with blue and red marks.

So, you are fucking the oboist.

No, Maestro. I shall, of course, apply to you first.

He stared at the score, the illegible Gothic typeface. It was *all* theater. Ziegler must script every lesson beforehand. Even now he must be back in the kitchen, chuckling over his bloated tea bag. *So, you are f'ing the oboist*—that was the punch line, front-loaded. Barrow shifted his weight on the stool. For his part, he was probably meant to have long since fled the studio.

From outside came the on-again, off-again treble of tires channeling wet pavement. He took a quick pass through the Reger and began a slower reading of the piece. Ziegler did not emerge. There had been no sound—maybe the old man had fallen asleep.

He finished his second pass through the score, and still the old man had not returned. Barrow had no feeling for the apartment's layout beyond the door, though he knew the kitchen came first. He pictured Ziegler asleep at a small dinette, a cup of stone-cold tea next to his large head. He moved into the hallway and stopped to gauge the light under the door. Without warning, it lurched open and Ziegler, impossibly, stood before him in a block of light, holding something. "*Allo,*" he said, apparently as surprised as Barrow. "I am going to Brussels in the morning."

"Yes."

"You will rehearse Brahms with the orchestra. Third and fourth movements."

"Maestro." Barrow was shocked. He could think of nothing appropriate to say. *Thank you,* seemed unbecoming.

"Use my score, of course." Ziegler held it out with both hands. Barrow's were frozen at his side. "Take it"—and when Barrow still could not raise his arms—"Take it, for godsake. It's not the Talmud."

∽

Seated on the tram home—the blessed, dry heat building up between stops—the feeling grew, the rush forward into space. A gaping suspension of the kind left open for miles by a composer like Mahler or Bach. The stubborn *appoggiatura*. Gutsy, painful, and stupendous. In one mystifying act, Ziegler had handed him back his life—ninety minutes on the podium with Brahms' Second and a completely fine, *fine* orchestra—and now Barrow could not remember why he had ever left it, left New York, left Juilliard and the possibility, the certainty, of success at the one thing he'd ever loved.

He arrived breathless outside the townhouse in Ettlingen. His landlords had shuttered down for the night, and he bore his secret up two darkened flights to the attic and there flipped on every light, the neon over the stove, the bathroom overhead, the bedside, the sconce by the table, and he cracked open the Brahms to movement three.

6

Twelve hours later he sat at the desk in Ziegler's Konzerthaus office, staring at the five Polaroids taped to the wall above, all of Ziegler's cat—on the bed, leaping from the kitchen table, at the food dish—a day in the life. Ziegler appeared twice, his gray-sweatered torso as backdrop, his hands enfolding the cat in a cage of fingers. Barrow, unhinged by lack of sleep, contemplated the massive hands. Who had snapped the picture if not Ziegler himself? Who had such access to the old man?

He recocked the gooseneck lamp, pulled the score of Brahms' Second Symphony into his lap and swung away from the desk. Out on stage the orchestra warmed up in a chaos of Brahms, a sound that normally filled him with excitement, but now spelled catastrophe.

He'd been set up.

I'm going to Brussels. You rehearse the Brahms.

He'd put it together sometime in the middle of the night, around the same time he realized how unprepared he was, even to *rehearse* the Second. Brahms was beyond him and Ziegler knew it. Better to ride a horse into battle, no saddle and no sword.

He'd been seduced by the idea that the old man had identified some hidden reserve of talent. But reality was more compelling: Ziegler had spent sixty years studying Brahms' Second, Barrow a week and a day. Never face an orchestra unprepared, that was the rule, and here he was, already fighting a deficit of monumental proportions after the *Tristan* horror. He should have lodged his protest, no hesitation, staked it right there in the old man's studio, feigned illness, feigned death.

The office door opened. Barrow didn't look up—he needed every last minute for study. But when the door closed, he came to. "Hans!"

Hans returned, a good-natured flute player who doubled as orchestra librarian. Barrow thanked him and handed over the conductor's score.

From his years in the violin section, Barrow knew the myriad ways that players scour for advantage over a conductor, especially a young conductor, especially a young *student* conductor. For example, does he appear unduly attached to the score? Disdain him. Advantage, players.

On the other hand, does he let on that he knows more than you? Hate him. Advantage, players (again).

Barrow put his shoulders through a series of swim stretches. At a minute before nine, he strode down the hall to the stage, arriving just in time to hear the orchestra manager announce Ziegler's absence—and the noisy wave of relief that followed. The manager was carrying her French horn; she shrugged her shoulders, glanced at Barrow and strolled to her chair. He gave the players a minute to enjoy the news, chatting with the timpanist, the African-American from Boston. Students shot him glances from various angles. His substitute role had not been announced, but the blocking told everything—the orchestra manager's look, Barrow's own stance, arms crossed, hanging back in the percussion section apart from the other student conductors.

The timpanist's easy manner had won him a coterie of friends. He said something funny and Barrow made a point of laughing loudly. He glanced at the grad conductors—Berndt and Antonio—and the three or four undergraduate conducting students who regularly attended rehearsals. No one looked at him. They wouldn't.

He shook the timpanist's hand and started for the podium, expecting some lessening of volume; there was none. He glimpsed Petra, who was marking something in her music, a reed tucked into the corner of her mouth. He continued to pan the wind section, the brass. He stepped onto the foot-high podium and mustered a smile for the principal cellist. A smattering of faces looked in his direction, but the volume had cranked up yet another notch. A second violinist far back in the stands was twisting through a chromatic scale. A huge joke in the horn section had him look down at his fly. The conducting students avoided his glances—all except Berndt, the Belgian, who smiled back.

Barrow looked down at the Brahms and opened to the third movement, Ziegler's assignment. Still the noise. He had maybe ten seconds left before he would have to rap the desk for quiet, and he definitely did not want to do that. Respect should arrive with him at the podium. Besides, it would be disastrous if he rapped the desk and they ignored him.

Just to his left, an urgent series of taps rang out. The concertmaster was rapping his bow against his music stand. Precisely four times and the noise dropped rapidly off. The entire orchestra was still, and Barrow felt a surge of gratitude; he suppressed an impulse to flash the concertmaster a thumbs up, settling instead for a quick nod. The concertmaster nodded back—a dark and compact man, probably in his early twenties. A Romanian, Barrow had heard, and the second or third best fiddle player in the school.

The concertmaster raised an eyebrow. "Another A, perhaps?" His English felt even more soothing than the bow taps.

"Ja," said Barrow, "natürlich."

He listened to the orchestra assemble itself—Petra's warm, acorn-brown note followed by the lavish sound of sixty-four A-strings blooming into open fifths, the whole thing spreading before him, centuries in evolution, a million student-hours of practice. He folded back the corners of the first few pages of the third movement, glancing down at the opening measures. The tuning strings faded to the background. The gift of concentration was large in him; it had led him to conducting. The power to take a moment and make a diamond of it. He flipped to the first movement just to have a look.

I know this music.

Hearing the players open their parts, the familiar clatter of pages, he felt bolt after bolt of confidence.

"Brahms," he said.

His voice felt steady. The crime—and the possibility of getting away with it—rushed up to greet him.

"First movement," he said.

He was a burglar with one foot over the sash.

He heard himself say, "We take the first ending," and it was too late. He was going to read the whole damn symphony.

Peripherally, he noted the conducting students, their attitudes of alarm. He suppressed a smile, and they disappeared completely from his concern. The horns were already wetting the tight funnels of their mouthpieces. He called across, "Half up, remember." They raised the wide bells of their instruments above stand level.

His eyes swept the rest of the wind section, most of whom would enter four measures later. He had their attention.

And the strings. First home. From the age of six, up through a full violin scholarship to the Eastman School of Music, and Marty Weissberger inviting him to be his first undergraduate conducting student— late night sessions over scores and bottles of Latrobe, early graduation and an airtight recommendation to study with Gilbert Shanahan in New York.

The lower strings waited, bows raised. He lifted his left hand, signaled caution, the soft, unhurried opening. A simple upbeat with his right, and the thing was aloft.

It was that simple; the whole goddamned thing was moving. The *Tristan* debacle had been forgotten. Two phrases in, something loosened in his chest, some element undisturbed in eight years. The strings leaned into their instruments. Other faces, many others, checked in with him—they were coming along. He smiled twice, three times, in the direction of the celli. Someone smiled back. He kept his gestures modest. Let the players come to him. Establish tempo, glance out the entrances.

The first movement stirred and channeled through the hall. He heard it behind him. When it grew—as it did, in piles, horn on brass on *tutti* strings—he stood down from it, kept small. He was the listener. It was a review session. The bassoons missed his signal in the off-the-beat thirty-second-note passage; no matter, he would take it up later. He was discovering that this was his way—perhaps it always had been, he couldn't remember—to smile at mistakes, at most to raise an eyebrow. He could feel the response; the beast shifted, relaxed, stretched, he thought, perhaps a little further.

They reached the first-movement recapitulation. It was going well. There would be no mistakes on his part.

∽

After rehearsal he tried to catch the concertmaster's eye to thank him, going so far as to grab his shoulder as he walked away. The gesture was a bit rough and the smaller man's neck tensed as he turned around. *"Vielen Dank,"* Barrow said, catching a glimmer of hostility in the Romanian's face before it broke into a tight smile.

"Ja. We had a nice time," the concertmaster said. He turned away and joined the crush of players throwing on coats and leaving the hall.

"Are you hungry?"

It was Berndt. The Belgian was tall and gaunt, with light gray eyes and a large head. Of the three graduate conductors, he was the one most likely to resemble Ziegler in fifty years. "Let's have lunch, shall we? With Antonio?"

Barrow, defenseless and riding on ninety minutes of sleep, felt his face melt into a grin. "Yeah. Let's go."

"You were lucky to be asked, I think."

Yes, Barrow said.

He'd been scanning the hall, realizing only after several passes that he was looking for Petra, hoping for a parting glimpse.

"Come," Berndt said. "You need beer."

7

The following evening Barrow took the tram from Karlsruhe to another of its outer suburbs and ate supper in a pizzeria across from the tram stop. Around the corner, he found the red-sandstone church he was looking for, one of the few in the region not blown to bits in the war. He walked in and stationed himself in the rear pew.

He counted more than seventy in the audience, and more arriving by the minute—not bad for a weeknight in the suburbs. Everyone sat up straight and no one spoke above a pre-sermon murmur. A Bach audience. His eyes picked out a woman with blond hair in the second row—Petra's friend Alexandra—and, next to her, a man who appeared to be her boyfriend.

He was unprepared for the first gentle report of Petra's oboe. From somewhere off to the right, the vestry maybe, she ran lightly through a single, mid-range octave, and his heart jumped. He flattened the concert program across his knees.

She didn't know he was here. He considered it a risk, in fact, to have come at all, since the one time he'd seen her all week she'd been speaking with someone else, oblivious to Barrow hovering in the background. He'd replayed their single evening in Bad Herrenalb—her touch in the pool, the bottle of red wine, the easy conversation—and found no evidence to support his dumb hope that she might feel for him—*exotischer Amerikaner*—anything more than a faint, wine-induced sense of curiosity.

The musicians were tuning offstage. Besides Petra, there were several strings, a soprano, and the soft-palate warmup of a high baritone.

Barrow drew his hands up into the cuffs of his jacket. The lights in the church faded to a single spotlight on the altar, a boulder of oak with whispering saints carved into the side. The spill from the light took in a harpsichord and eight wire stands, each preset with music—elegant sentinels against the dark religion of the place. Up in the second row, Petra's friend inched closer to her man.

Without warning, a door swung open and the performers strode out. They hit their marks, ignored the applause and leapt straight into the music. Barrow sat bolt upright. He understood the choice of venue—the tiny church was perfect for Bach. The old composer's flawless counterpoint seemed to crave the space, with its brick walls and its king-sized tapestries.

A couple of arias went by, the singing scrupulous and unpompous. Barrow gazed at Petra as he never could from the podium or jailed behind the trombone section with Berndt and Antonio. She wore earrings, a single pearl dancing below each lobe—tiny stabs at elegance. Her regulation black concert dress dropped smooth below the soft contours of a charcoal sweater, sleeves pulled to the elbow. Her bare wrists, the supple architecture of her neck, all in service to the oboe. Her face was pure thought, lines converging on a single prospect, a sound, a certain way through a phrase. She turned to the singer, to the violinist, and Barrow felt a surge of jealousy—not for her, but for the religion they shared, the straining after perfection.

Maybe he'd start up again. Practicing. His violin lay flat on its back in the apartment in Ettlingen, the brown canvas cover, the corner where the zipper always caught; inside, the dank must of old felt, undisturbed since his departure from Fishkill, New York.

The applause was solid. Petra bowed with the others, though she looked uncomfortable with the gesture. That will change, he thought, and in those few seconds—in the space of the first applause—he saw her long career unfold, the steady orchestra job, the abundant chamber work, recordings, teaching, her increasing presence as a soloist. At fifty she'd still be beautiful to watch, profoundly beautiful to hear. He could not imagine his own edition of fifty, not on the podium, not anywhere; he could only imagine the next day, the next rehearsal, the music itself, measure on measure, carried to him in leaky buckets by his own weak brain.

Another singer appeared, a large man with a wide face and a thick blond beard. He took the spot next to Petra and muttered something to her. She laughed, said something back. The audience settled down. The harpsichord player laid out the first few chords of a *recitativo*, and the new man started in, words rumbling deep in his chest, "*Wachet auf, ruft uns die Stimme ...*"

⌘

"Mister Barrow?"

He turned on the steps outside the church to see Alexandra holding the hand of her thin-bearded companion.

"You are going?" she asked.

"*Abend*," he said.

"*Abend. Hier ist mein Freund, Wolf.*"

Wolf was two inches shorter than Alexandra. His smile said, I'm sorry I speak very little English. They shook hands.

"It was a quite good *Konzert*," said Wolf, pleased.

"Yes."

"Petra is putting on her other clothes," said Alexandra. "We will go and have some wine or other things, and so ... maybe you will join us?"

She and her boyfriend wore matching oversized sweaters. A pair of warm woolen mittens, Barrow thought. "Inside," said Alexandra. "Come. It is cold. Then we have a car."

Barrow hesitated. The audience had begun leaving the church. They could be commuters disembarking from a ferry—no less ordinary, an evening of Bach exquisitely delivered. He recognized a face in the crowd—the concertmaster from the Hochschule orchestra. The Romanian was pretending not to see him.

"I'd like to just ..."

"We are waiting on the inside," said Wolf. "You can come in some minutes."

The Romanian crossed the road and disappeared down the next street. Barrow made for the same corner and nearly collided with his quarry, who stood cupping a lit match, a glove jammed under each arm pit. *"Entschuldigen,"* Barrow said.

In a tiny act of composure, the violinist finished lighting his cigarette. *"Bitte,"* he said, taking a second stiff hit. He reached the cigarette across to Barrow.

"Nein, danke." Barrow indicated the church. *"Alexandra und ihr Freund, sie warten auf mich."* His eyes caught something that caused his words to trail off. *"Vielleicht ..."*

The violinist held his cigarette between his third and fourth fingers. There was no index finger on his right hand.

"You like the Cantatas?" he said in English. "It surprises me somehow. I only came to hear *'Ein' feste Burg.'"* His accent was vaguely Midwestern. He settled the cigarette in his mouth and began pulling his gloves on.

"I'm embarrassed that I don't know your name," Barrow said.

"Tano. I am Tano Popescu. And we all know yours, of course."

"You do?"

Two women from the audience led a small boy down the opposite sidewalk, held him swinging between them. *"Doch!"* the boy said, reveling in the strength of his own voice. The women laughed.

"These *Bundis* are so happy all the time," Tano said. "Are you noticing this?"

"Bundis?"

"What the East Germans call the West Germans."

Another glance at Tano's glove.

"I guess it's the Wall and everything," Barrow said.

The right forefinger was an empty jab of thick black leather. How could he control his bow? How could he even play?

Tano must have read his mind. "I use this long finger. The second one." He indicated by pressing his right middle finger through the glove with the thumb and index finger of his left hand. "It becomes very important. For *sforzandi* especially."

Barrow looked up, embarrassed. "Vogel and her friends, they are going somewhere to drink wine."

"But I am going home." Smoke from Tano's cigarette shot through the steam from their breath. His lips carried a slight smile. "She is a lovely player."

"Yes."

"Good night."

✍

Alexandra repeated the words "Chagrin Falls"—emphatically, to no one in particular, testing inflections—while seated behind the wheel of her late-model Citroën. The car skidded though the back streets of Karlsruhe.

"But what is 'Chagrin Falls' in German?" Petra demanded, both hands gripping the headrest in front of her. "What do you think?"

"I don't know," said Alexandra.

"Die 'Verdruss Fälle.' Das ist die Name auf Deutsch!"

Alexandra laughed wildly. Even Wolf joined in from the passenger seat. It didn't seem all that funny, but Barrow marveled at the attention.

"You have to excuse us, please," said Alexandra. "We are so, what, *entzückt* to have the American director in the backseat."

"Delighted," said Wolf, whose English was turning out to be excellent.

"*Conductor*," said Petra. "Not director."

"Excuse me, Herr *Conductor*."

Wolf stole a glance at Barrow. "I would like to ask something."

"No, no, no," Alexandra said.

"A little argument we are having."

They'd made him the center of attention, and he found he enjoyed it. "Sure."

"What is your opinion of Kurt Masur?"

"He's a fine conductor."

"Of course, of course, but what of these other events?"

"No politics!" cried Alexandra. She sped the car around a traffic circle and ramped up to the autobahn, *Direktion Stuttgart*.

Wolf enumerated with his fingers. "That he used his reputation to save the East German revolution. That in Leipzig he averted another Tiananmen Square. That last Monday there was near half a million in the Leipzig demonstration—"

"He conducts with his bare hands," said Alexandra, "and what would Maestro Ziegler say about that?"

"He should be the next premier of DDR," Wolf said.

"He should not."

"*Why* not?"

"He is a *musician*."

"So much the better for politics." Wolf looked at Barrow, apparently hoping for some backup.

Barrow, hopelessly underequipped, in turn glanced at Petra, who had dropped out of the conversation entirely.

"Don't worry about her," Alexandra said. "She is busy missing her days in the Free German Youth. Communist kindergarten, you know?"

Petra ignored the joke. "It doesn't matter," she said, her words clipped and rapid. "There will *be* no premier because in a few months, in a year, there will be no DDR, no East Germany."

"Maybe."

She turned to her window. Barrow watched the headlights play over her cheeks as the Citroën raged against the highway. She was a defector, and wise beyond him. She had said, *I have killed something that those people will never have such opportunity to kill,* and he was one of those who had never had such opportunity, not with his wedding jobs in Poughkeepsie, his pointless insecurities. Sitting in the backseat of the Citroën, it was, he felt, an impossible gulf between them.

∽

Alexandra parked on the sidewalk outside a darkened *Apotheke,* and Petra led the pack through Stuttgart's red-light district, a precinct of mannequin johns and prostitutes under glass. The zone was overlit and obvious, explicitly marked for the seedy side of life, yet somehow unable to give over to its spirit. The Turkish March in Beethoven's Ninth, minus the cymbal crash on the second and fourth beats. Barrow caught the glance of a rake-thin woman with brilliant orange lips, her turned-out ankle displayed on a milk crate. He smiled, embarrassed when she smiled back.

A narrow descent dropped them to a semi-enclosed acre that pulsed from all sides, various musics spilling out to the pavement whenever any of a half-dozen doors were opened. A small crowd waited outside one club in a typically German line, neat and self-possessed. An understated sign read DAS WUTHAUS, which Barrow translated as "The Anger House."

Petra parked them at the end of the line and disappeared inside. A man with dyed-black hair and a tux jacket emerged—a concert pianist gone mad. He motioned for the three of them to come forward, and they passed to the front of the line.

Alexandra went in first. Barrow held back and the metal door swung shut. It was pitted with BB-sized dents and coated with flat black paint. On the other side there was a sound like a row of idling trucks.

Barrow turned to Wolf. "I have never been to one of these."

Wolf, who seemed bound to grin for eternity, nodded energetically and pushed him through the door. The darkness hit. And the noise—a hard thrumming noise, which he felt first in his lungs, then throughout his body. Blasts of treble jammed his ears. He ducked, almost lost his balance.

He heard someone's voice. It was Petra. She slipped a mug of beer into his hand. *"Ich muss ausgehen,"* he yelled.

"Was?"

"Ausgehen—" and he motioned over his shoulder in the presumed direction of the door.

Her response was to slide her arm around his waist and pull him close, a practical measure given the surrounding crush of bodies. She put her mouth to his ear and shouted something in German. She shouted again, in English, "You will get accustomed to it," and he felt her lips brush his neck and linger there. Under the spell of her breath, he found himself turning his face to hers and meeting her lips, which were already wet with Pilsener. They kissed, beers aloft. Her mouth was soft, softer than in his imagination, and she opened it wide, her jaw working against his, testing for something. His right hand, with its full mug of beer, pressed her to him, trying to help. Everything was the press of her ribs against his, and all sound, all other sensation, was in another room, another hemisphere until her lips slid away. She relaxed the full length of her body into his and allowed the softness of her brow to rest against his mouth. He felt the rapid inflating-deflating of her chest.

"Come," she said and he nodded. But neither moved.

"Come," she said again.

"I've spilled some—"

But she looked up at him, and even in the dim purple of the room, her eyes found light.

"Look at you smile," she said. "You like this music?"

"Music?"

He laughed.

She grabbed his arm, causing more beer to spill, and towed him deeper into the club. People adjusted their cigarettes as they passed.

"Who is this?" he asked. Her hand in his was small and damp.

"Stevie Ray Vaughn," she said, her V's coming out F's, her eyes trained on the small stage, rapt by a music he'd ignored all his life.

Because of her, the music swept him up. He would not know precisely why or when—though there were things to notice, things to account for. This Stevie Ray Vaughn, rarely settling on the beat except by surprise, teasing the strings, his wide vibrato curling around all those flatted thirds and sevenths, curt flashes of color, harmonics, then nothing, a checked temper, and all of it building—no real evidence for this, just a suspicion—building with an extra note here, a whiff of intention to break out in the next measure, never an excess, no bad calls. And the whole time facing straight out, eyes closed under the broad brim of a black cowboy hat, a single stream of sweat—ignored, steady—guttering from the tip of his nose.

The song was over and the crowd yelled, and for the third time in a German week—the echo in the woods, the roll in the snow by the pool—here in the presence of the girl from beyond the Wall, Barrow opened his mouth with no thought for what might come out.

∽

He tried to hide his panic, but he was in a sock. Walking back to the car he could hear nothing, though Wolf assured him that it would be temporary. Petra mouthed the word in his face, "*Ist* temporary," just her lips. He cracked a smile, and she laughed.

Wolf drove while Alexandra slept. Petra's head lay against Barrow's leg, her feet on the seat, eyes closed, and he thought he could stay like this for the rest of the night—the weight of her head on him. That for all he cared Wolf could drive to Hamburg, switch off with Alexandra, drive on to Denmark, ferry to Sweden.

He stared at her ear, marveled at its delicacy. He'd had a dream about her; she was smoking her oboe reed like a cigarette, her face veiled in smoke, and some part of his sleeping brain had tried to voice the image for brass choir.

He didn't know when, but he'd begun to dream like a conductor again. In his dreams, every aspect of life was notated in a score and was therefore conductible. A measure to climb the tram steps, a *fermata* to pay the fare, three measures to find a seat. A change of key when a cloud passed over the sun.

By way of control, he thought.

He allowed his hand to drift down and ride the small of Petra's waist.

His teachers had always stressed preparation, and through preparation, total control, which—extended in all directions—became mastery. Preparation suited him perfectly. It started as habit and turned into physiology. Four hours a day for eleven years—seven hours a day on weekends—alone with his violin. That's the thing about practicing, he thought. You are alone. Alone you can control how everything goes. An hour for scales, forty-five minutes on thirds, twenty on octaves, fifty-five memorizing Paganini. The rest, the dessert, memorizing some violin concerto.

Conducting, too, was all about preparation, and he was damn good at it. "Too good," Marty Weissberger said once, early in his second year of study at Eastman. "You're too goddamned good at it. You're all about contingencies. You're all about 'What if this happens?'—but it's not 'What if this happens?' it's *Now this happens.*"

He glanced down; Petra's eyes were open. "Are you warm enough?" he asked.

"I'm fine." She closed her eyes, pressed the soft curve of her neck into his leg.

"Vaughn was good," he said. "I wouldn't have thought."

"Yes," she said, quieting him.

The Citroën had found its groove on the highway, its own steady hum, and when he spoke his voice felt off-key. "That first day in Paris?"

"Mm ..."

"Did you ever think about changing your mind?"

Moments passed—maybe she hadn't heard.

"By Gare de l'Est," she said, "I had already decided not to think."

He waited for more, but she had drifted back to sleep.

In a rare accident, the tram ahead of Barrow's hit a bicyclist. The ensuing disorder ate up the half-hour cushion Barrow had come to allow before his lesson times. He sprinted from the tram stop at Mühlburger Tor straight to Ziegler's door. It was 9:04. Seven hours earlier he'd been stumbling through the streets of Stuttgart, stone deaf.

He knocked. Head pounding, hands on his knees, he shot lungfuls of fog to the sidewalk. The door fell away its four inches and he groaned his relief, waited the regulation thirty seconds and stepped inside.

The old man was on the phone, the receiver somehow out of place in his hand—too modern—the way he balanced it in his palm, bent his neck to it. The tone of his voice, too, was out of place—the kind reserved for close family. The old man puckered his lips, "*Also, ja, ja.*" He towered behind his desk and glanced over at Barrow, who was still scarfed and holding the Brahms. It was not a hostile look; it may even have carried a trace of humor. Barrow wiped his feet and removed his coat.

"Ja, ja, natürlich ..."

Other things were not right. The gunmetal stool held a stack of mail. A plate of food graced the clutter on Ziegler's desk, tears of bread, soft chips of bratwurst. Trapped in the dense wool of Ziegler's cardigan were crumbs and stray fragments of cheese.

Ziegler caught him staring. "What's the matter?" He'd hung up the phone.

"Nothing."

"You have my score to the Brahms?"

"Yes."

"Tell me everything you did."

"Yes."

Almost everything.

The old man sat in his chair on the front side of the desk, and Barrow cleaned off the stool, handing over the mail and the score. He began talking Ziegler through the rehearsal—all but the wasted half-hour, the criminally self-indulgent half-hour. Ziegler nodded gravely, seemed to follow every nuance. Barrow talked through the tempo relationships in the third movement, the multiple handoffs between string sections, the difficulty of keeping the students together in this or that passage. He offered justification for a separate string rehearsal.

Only once did he diverge from the outline in his mind, to note a recurring intonation problem in the winds. The principal flutist's upper register was consistently sharp in pitch, and the octave passages with the oboe were particularly brutal-sounding as a result. He hazarded a metaphor. "Worse than a bad streetcar brake," he said, and Ziegler obliged him by smiling.

There was a short period of silence during which the old man folded and unfolded his hands.

"It is the oboe," Ziegler said.

"Pardon?"

"Our principal oboist plays always flat, you don't notice this? Not the flute. You must take care in the woodwinds, if there is a badly tuned vertical, take care to identify the fault. A flat note lower down, and the top note sounds sharp. This is kindergarten."

"Of course," Barrow said. He hesitated. "Nevertheless in this case I am certain it is the flute."

"Mm." Ziegler lifted a pale cube of cheese to his mouth and slipped it between his lips. Barrow took the opportunity to run his mind back over the exchange, skim for any betrayal of personal interest in the oboist. It was the flute in any case; the old man would see that for himself in rehearsal.

"Continue."

He did. He described his handling of the fourth movement, the sordid task of holding the orchestra together through staccato passages, further tuning problems, technical dilemmas with the stick, how he'd resolved them, one or two others he might want some advice on. Ziegler merely nodded. Barrow talked for ten straight minutes without interruption. It was a day of firsts.

When Barrow had no more to say, the old man, without explanation, picked up Brahms, cracked it to the first movement—the illegal movement—and began a page-through. While he did, the gray cat appeared from the kitchen. He leapt to the desk, caught up a nipple of bratwurst and jerked it down.

"How long is this Symphony Number Two of Brahms," Ziegler asked.

And so it arrived—with the certainty of a snapped tibia, instant and life-changing—the realization that Ziegler knew everything.

"You do not know this? How long is this symphony?"

"Yes," Barrow said.

"Well?"

"Forty-six minutes. If one follows the markings exactly."

"And who would not do that?"

Barrow hesitated, sniffing out the trap.

"So. No answer."

"There can be arguments either way."

59

"Naturally." Ziegler took another cube of cheese. "And after working these passages as you have said, these passages in the third and fourth movements, only afterwards did you read straight through. The third and fourth movements."

Nur hinter—only after—why exactly was Ziegler drawing this out?

He retranslated the old man's question, sifted for another interpretation, a glimmer of humor, some clue to the maestro's intentions. Fucking German—in English you could play all kinds of innocent. Was this pleasure for Ziegler, to know that his student had not rehearsed to begin with? That he had, in point of fact, flushed thirty minutes of a ninety-minute rehearsal down the toilet, wasted it on a play-through of the entire goddamn symphony—and that it had been wildly fucking exhilarating?

Ziegler knew; he knew or he wouldn't have asked the question. Ziegler knew outcomes.

"So. Again no answer." The old man scanned the Brahms score at arm's length, as if considering a purchase. "Or perhaps you do not understand the question."

Barrow cleared his throat, attempting unconcern. "We read it through first."

"Read what through."

"The symphony. All four movements." He waited for the explosion.

Instead, there was silence. The cat reappeared. "This is one approach," Ziegler said. He tapped his knee and the cat jumped into his lap. "Was it for your pleasure, or for the orchestra?"

"What, Maestro?"

"That you did this."

"For the players," Barrow said. "To review your work from the last rehearsal. And to get a sense of the whole."

The old man glanced down at his cat. His left hand hung loose, veins loaded. "And did they?"

"Did they what, Maestro?"

"Get a sense of the whole."

"I don't know."

"This symphony—by whom? Who composed this?"

"Brahms."

"This Second Symphony by Johannes Brahms, which none of our players, being German of course, will have encountered."

Barrow smiled, unwittingly, out of nerves.

"And you reviewed our work from last rehearsal?"

"Yes."

"How poorly did they do, you did not mention this"—Barrow cleared his throat, but Ziegler did not wait—"For example, at the B-major section, first movement, the cross rhythm there. Did they get this correct? You did not mention."

"No." There was little point in lying.

"They never do. The students. Even the second time. Unless they studied the score. Like you. Did you?"

"Yes."

"For more than ten minutes?"

"I was up all night."

"Astonishing. And when you heard them misread this place, this one spot, you stopped to fix it? To alert them to the error?"

"No, Maestro."

"But surely you came back to it."

"No, Maestro."

"Why?"

"We went directly to the third movement. Per your instruction."

It was not the thing to say.

"Never do that."

"What, Maestro?"

"Never use my instruction to excuse your self-indulgence."

Barrow couldn't speak. He returned the old man's stare, stayed and stayed with the face, the long gray-pink cheeks, the brilliant eyes.

"So you read movements one and two for review, yet it did not occur to you to touch this particular spot for three minutes perhaps, and so they played it once, and this once was wrong? Is this what you tell me?"

"Yes."

"Which is the same as learning it wrong."

"I tried to give them—"

"No."

It was certain. Ziegler had known in advance, even of the mistake in the B-major section. He had known everything in advance of this lesson.

He continued the drill, unhurried. "They performed it correctly last week, and they performed it incorrectly yesterday. Which will they remember in rehearsal this afternoon? The brain learns these things. It carves a path either way, right or wrong. It carves a path. It does not know. The brain is gray and stupid—you, American, do not know how gray and stupid is the brain—so the next time they come to this passage, which way do they go? They have learned both ways, which way will they choose? Who knows which way?" He waited. *"Which way, Herr Barrow?"*

Barrow stared. It had begun to rain outside, a loud downpour.

"There is something you have in English." Ziegler's eyes, his face, did not change. "'A toss over the head,' something. Tell me. *Tell me.*"

"A 'toss-up.'"

"'Toss-*up*,'" Ziegler said, reversing Barrow's emphasis, correcting him from force of habit. "It could already be learned, but now I have to work it again, this afternoon. I have to work it to unlearn this mistake at the B-major section. I could be rehearsing something else, a sonority, some transitions, some *Brahms*, but now I must waste everyone's time with this, all because our American visitor, before doing the work of a symphony conductor, must steal time for his own purposes. For purposes of what, of masturbation? I think yes."

The old man's eyes returned to his cat. With his index finger he rubbed its chin. Lesson over.

9

He stood in the lobby of Schloss Gottesaue, the music school's main building, shedding rainwater on the honey-planked floor.

Reeling from his lesson, desperate, he thought back to a moment ten years before—his first time in front of an orchestra. He had stopped after three measures, laughing impulsively, feeling foolish but endearing himself forever to his fellow Eastman students. The gesture of control, of leadership, had caught him by surprise, so similar in preparation to the lift of a violin bow, so completely different on delivery. Violin strings sent back tremors through the forearm, fusing body with instrument. There was density under the bow; the violin was another being, pressing back. But with an orchestra—a vast, keyless piano—there was no such resistance. It had struck him that the exercise of conducting was the practice of illusion. That's why he laughed: that there should be no physical resistance, yet canyons of sound.

He remembered the scene vividly. He had recovered from the giggling, begun again. Illusionist—fancy name for magician. One preparatory beat, in tempo, and armed divisions arrived with him. He'd been hooked for life.

And now he would never conduct again.

So fucking brittle, the way back.

Hands shaking, he loosened his scarf and felt around in his pockets for a piece of Kleenex.

Someone called his name—the first bassoonist, who stood before the bulletin board where orchestra assignments were posted. The first clarinetist stood next to him.

"Do you know why is this?"

They were as far away now as they would be in rehearsal.

The clarinetist spoke. "Why is Petra Vogel no longer principal on the Brahms? Do you know why this is?"

The bassoonist was more openly hostile. "What did you say to him?"

"Excuse me?" Barrow had one glove off and he gripped it like a lifeline.

Fire the oboist, a perfect consequence. This must have all happened within the last half hour.

"You complained to Ziegler? Is this it?" It was the bassoonist again. And of course, what other conclusion would they draw? The American wastes two minutes in the last rehearsal trying to solve the tuning problem in the winds. The American reports back to the maestro, and Field Marshal Ziegler yanks another general from the front, Petra Vogel this time. Who would be next? That was their question, wasn't it? Such power the American has with the maestro.

I equal zero, he wanted to tell them. The maestro is toying with the American, teaching him something. Be patient; there is a reason.

Besides, I'm leaving the country.

"What happened?" the bassoonist demanded.

It started as a sensation, a signal to the palm of his bare right hand, followed by an urge of the wrist joint to rotate back, lift, float hand to the level of chest. He followed the urge. The duo looked at him, seeing only a gesture, perhaps, before speech. But Barrow knew better; he knew it was the need to reestablish tempo in the lobby. He looked down at the hand, watched as it reached across to remove the other glove.

"I don't know," he said.

⁂

He jogged to the Konzerthaus, rain pelting his face.

Word must have reached Petra, because she sat, one of three players on stage, reading through her new part, assistant second oboe. Unbelievable. She was that dedicated—or defiant. He dropped to the chair behind her.

"I don't know what happened," he said.

She was changing reeds.

"It must be a mistake," he said.

"He is here," she said, her words clipped. "Don't you see him?" Ziegler was at the far end of the apron, discussing something with Hans, the librarian, and, yes, it did occur to Barrow that he shouldn't be seen talking with her.

"I'm sorry," he said.

She said nothing, well into the throes of humiliation.

Back at their seats, Berndt spoke in a hushed voice. "What is this? Do you know what this is?"

"Ziegler thinks she tends to play flat."

"I think not. She is a beautiful player."

"It's what he thinks."

"But she is *always* principal on the big pieces. She will get a big job, an 'A' orchestra. That's what they say, have you heard?"

"It's what Ziegler thinks."

"But why it is changed after three rehearsals?"

Barrow shrugged, pulled a newspaper out of his pack, and pretended to read.

More seats filled and the room bloomed with discord. He dreaded the moment when Ziegler would take the podium and cue the winds, thus cementing the new order. Perhaps there'd been a mistake; the old man would arrive, notice the switch in the oboe section, make a big frowning fuss, and in a clatter of music stands restore the proper hierarchy.

Antonio arrived. "He has changed the oboes."

"He says Vogel is flat," said Berndt.

"Ah. Yes. Perhaps in her playing." The Italian winked at Barrow, who looked down at his *Herald-Tribune*. "I have always thought she was out of tune. A little bit with the flute. How are you, Barrow?"

The chaos of sound fell away; Ziegler was approaching the podium. Barrow looked up in time to see him comment privately to Tano. The concertmaster smiled back dutifully and turned to the new principal oboist, whose small, workmanlike A sputtered and caught. An elegant enough tone, and when it emerged from the swollen noise of the winds and brass, it had gained some strength for the strings. Barrow watched Ziegler for any unusual behavior. He scanned the orchestra; no one seemed to have noticed that the world had turned upside down. Even Petra seemed oblivious as she made last minute adjustments to her reed with a stubby cane knife, intently shaving its tip.

Normally twenty years younger on the podium, Ziegler looked old, older than that morning, the top of his wide forehead more than usually flecked with dry skin. The maestro glanced down at the closed score on the conductor's desk, the same score Barrow had conducted from two days before. He wondered if the old man would open it, knew the two next to him wondered the same.

Seconds passed and Ziegler still looked down. It seemed too long. What went through his mind? Was he listening, recalling a sound, some sonority? Was it prayer, or was he plotting, hatching new tortures? Was he with the music or with the students who were his charges, Petra, Barrow, the terror-stricken new principal oboist?

Abruptly, Ziegler looked up, directly at the cello section. So there would be no rehearsal, no "three minutes," no review of the dotted sixteenth-note figure—it would be the first movement, from the beginning, the very act he'd reprimanded Barrow for. *I can do this, you cannot*—that was the message. He signaled the size of what he wanted from the celli, tensed his cheeks in a smile. It was almost mischief. He glanced at the horns, who waited, bells half up. His right hand rose, the score stayed closed. It was an illusion, the age. Ziegler was a boy born to fly kites. His eyes were bluer than ever. A flip of his hand and the Brahms began, washed through the vast hall. Sixteen measures on and Barrow understood more than he ever had about the motion of waves, merely watching a man whose left hand, the hand of expression, stayed at his side. Ziegler didn't need it; his mere presence let in the sea.

10 Ziegler made no further mention of Barrow's indiscretion, nor of Petra's demotion.

A week passed. At an hour before dawn, on November 10, Barrow lay in bed listening to the BBC. "Late last night, Herr Günter Schabowski, spokesman for the Central Committee of the East German Communist Party, let it slip that pending a new travel law East Germans might come and go as they pleased. And they did; they most certainly did."

Another report followed, taped sometime in the night, the female reporter's voice pitched high:

"I'm standing here, just by Brandenburg Gate. Minutes ago—and I am watching, and it's really phenomenal, really, *really* phenomenal—minutes ago, a man, I'll describe him as a young man, possibly in his twenties and presumably from the East, an *Ossi* as they call them here, somehow got himself atop the Wall, walked back and forth like the cock-of-the-watch—really incredible—until the East German border guards shot at him with a power hose, watered him down with a hose, and, really, he just kept going, parading back and forth up there until he emptied the water out of his knapsack in sort of an act, really, of insolence, and within, I would say, ten minutes there were literally hundreds of people up there, on the wall itself, dancing and clasping one another, and they had flasks of wine and were kissing each other, Easterners and Westerners, *Ossis* and *Wessis*, and now, at this very minute—it's incredible—actually chipping away at the Wall itself, at the concrete, with hammers and chisels, appearing, really, from nowhere, taking the wall apart. Incredible. I can't believe my eyes."

On his way out, Barrow heard his landlord in the kitchen and ducked in to say hello. "You heard the news?"

"Yes, of course," said Helmut.

"It's pretty amazing."

"It is a big day." The ex–soccer player, father of two, bent over his espresso maker. A sleek new Braun.

"Not working?" Barrow said.

"I will get it."

In the street, he was met by a sharp urge to see Petra, to celebrate the fall of the Berlin Wall. He imagined their passage through Brandenburg Gate, the crowds surging back and forth between the two Berlins, forced to grab hold of each other to avoid being separated. She would show him where she once lived. They would cross Alexanderplatz, the famous city swirling around them, flights of pigeons.

Since her demotion, he'd waited for her twice after rehearsal, under the trees behind the Konzerthaus, hands in his pockets, backpack at his feet. She'd appeared once with Alexandra and once with a band of wind players. Both times she'd seen him and looked the other way. He had her phone number, but that would have required courage.

⁀ॐ

"Separation of the church and the state. You have that, no, in the U.S.? It should be the same, I say. Separation of the *arts* and the state."

Antonio thrust his broad face across the café table. Even in English, he could squeeze an astounding number of words into the space of a minute.

"Hitler was an artist—a bad artist, so what—he *thought* he was an artist, he had the *vision* as an artist, *inspired*, what have you. And that is where all the dangers come from. Sure, I like Kurt Masur, sure I would like Kurt Masur to be my uncle, but, no, why would I want him for premier, or even just mayor? It's crazy. Conductors should conduct. Who knows, he can be available for the next revolution."

Berndt leaned back in his chair. "South Africa, Beijing—"

"No. Understand. With Hitler—please tell me if I am wrong—the world would have been so much better off if only Hitler had had the gene to be a truly great artist, a painter or a librettist or something else—famous, and therefore very, *very* busy—thus he would have stayed away from politics. So much trouble saved. Politicians are best to be bureaucrats only."

"Perhaps it's only that we don't want to be governed by *bad* artists," said Berndt.

"So what. Wagner was a good artist."

"Questionable."

"Why, because he hated Jews?"

"Because he lacked a sense of proportion."

"Bullshit. Wagner was a genius, and you would want to be governed by him? *Presto*, move up the Holocaust sixty years. Eighteen-eighty."

"Which would have been good, would it not?" Berndt said. "Less technology. Not-so-good trains. No Zyklon B."

The Italian's free hand flew up. "*Scheisse!*"

"*Bitte.*"

"I am serious!"

Berndt got to his feet, his empty cup dangling from his pinkie. "Anyone else?" The others shook their heads, and he slouched off in the direction of the serving counter.

Barrow took another sip from his cup while Antonio leaned back in his chair. "One wonders," the Italian said, "what Fräulein Vogel thinks of all this very good news."

A twitch at the corner of his mouth was Barrow's first clue that Antonio might have guessed his feelings toward the oboist. Perhaps it had been Antonio all along. Antonio, gathering the stray details and reporting to Ziegler.

"One wonders if perhaps she will go back," Antonio continued.

Barrow attempted a strict modulation of his voice. "Why would she go back?"

Antonio shrugged. "Friends. Unfinished business." He broke off a quarter-sized chip of crust and popped it into his mouth. "This is unreasonable?"

"What sort of unfinished business?"

"They do not let them out of the country, the East Germans, without some—like with a loan? A big loan?"

"Collateral?"

"Sure. Collateral. Or a favor. Something in exchange."

Barrow took another sip of coffee, still feigning disinterest. "Would she go back to continue studying?"

"If she wants to be stuck forever in some orchestra in Magdeburg, some dead end." The Italian had studied music composition in the States and owned a fat repertoire of American idioms. Each usage was a mini performance.

"Probably for a visit," Barrow said.

"What?"

"She'll probably go back for a visit."

"Yes," said the Italian. He had not stopped looking at Barrow. "You've been seeing her?"

"Not really."

"You're a funny man, Barrow. Very private for an American."

Barrow shrugged, even as it occurred to him that he should plunder this man-of-the-world for advice. But the Belgian had returned, holding up his mug in a toast.

"Wall gone," he said.

The other two lifted their mugs in response. "Wall gone."

✍

"What is that?!" Ziegler's voice shot out from the back of the orchestra, arresting the string players, their bow arms dangling, midair.

Berndt was on the podium.

The bows came down in twos and threes, and Barrow exchanged glances with Antonio; they both knew the Belgian's mistake. The three of them had discussed the trap while walking over from the café. "I can't help it," Berndt had said. "It is habit. It is just so ... how do you call *einge-fleischt?*" "Ingrained," Barrow guessed. "I*ngrained,*" said Berndt.

"What *is* that?!" Ziegler thundered a second time, illustrating with a hard chop of his right hand. The players did not turn to look. Berndt stood, his long neck bent forward, his gaze level.

At issue was the first beat in bar forty-five of the second movement— the *Adagio*—of Brahms' Second Symphony, one of those breathless, silent beats that becomes a kind of focus, a gathering point, where the music disappears briefly below the surface. You do not conduct such a beat. They knew this; Berndt knew it, but it could be tricky. The body's musculature, from sheer habit, demands a strong first beat. It was not the sort of thing that gave Barrow any difficulty, but Berndt had picked up a lot of bad habits from his years of conducting the Belgian equivalent of a high school band.

Berndt dropped his head and began fumbling with the page corners of his score. Ziegler was a one-strike-and-you're-out sort of schoolmaster in the best of circumstances. This morning he was in a horrible mood—clearly he had not read the papers, or perhaps he had. Either way, Barrow knew the next beat in Ziegler's little play. Antonio hadn't survived the third measure. Berndt had done well to reach bar forty-five.

"Barrow!"

Still on the podium, Berndt hesitated. *"Danke schön,"* he said under his breath to the orchestra.

That's grace, Barrow thought, hating his teacher, hating him for making a contest of Brahms, hating him for poisoning November 10, 1989, the morning after the Wall fell.

"*Herr Amerikaner!*"

Barrow took a breath and held it. Parts of his upper body trembled, but no one watched. No one dared engage so much as a neck muscle.

He rose from his seat behind the lower brass and tucked his score under his arm, holding the place with his finger. He passed Berndt, who chose not to look at him. Most of the violinists still had their instruments under their chins. He sensed that the players, while looking vaguely in the direction of the podium, were focused entirely on the real seat of power behind them. The real conductor, the real *Dirigent*, was in the back of the room.

Barrow was at the podium when he realized that he'd forgotten his baton, which lay on his stand twenty meters away. He thought of not using the stick. It might be appropriate. Kurt Masur never used a baton. Neither did Pierre Boulez or Charles Münch, but they were French. Ziegler would howl him off the podium.

But by retreating to his stand, he would lose the slim wedge of command he held over the moment.

"*Stimmen Sie, bitte,*" he said quietly to Tano, who read him instantly, stood, and nodded to the first oboist, a slender girl with hunched shoulders, for a tuning note. Next to her sat Petra Vogel, directing her gaze at Barrow, her eyes bloodshot and puffy.

He looked away—he mustn't think about her. He slid his score onto the conductor's desk and strolled back to his seat, listening to the beast tune itself, bracing for another protest from Ziegler. Antonio slipped him the baton—bless him. He waited for a comment from Ziegler. He strolled back to the podium under the collective gaze of the orchestra, and by the time he stepped onto the platform—still no commentary from Ziegler—the celli were ready, ten bows hovering.

He looked out over the Konzerthaus stage, held his stick in both hands. Ninety *Studentenmusiker*, waiting, terrified for the American conductor, for his mistake, for the coming devastation.

Their eyes on me, their attention on the back of the room. Say something.

"*Es ist ...*" The words caught in his throat.

"*Es ist der zehnte November,*" he said, "*ja oder nein?*" A slight stir, as through a startled herd.

November 10, yes or no?

He added a note of urgency. "*Ja oder nein? Der zehnte November.*" He was thinking of the Berlin Wall, the BBC reporter, *incredible ... dancing on the Wall ... flasks of wine.*

He was greeted by utter silence. And with it, a sensation—it was the blood leaving his face. Perhaps his words had yet to reassemble in their minds. He fought to keep his eyes level, the temptation to glance at the score. He could not remember a time when he'd said anything the least bit extra-musical from the podium, and he was astonished to feel thus stripped of confidence.

I know the music. I should not make pronouncements.

It is November 10, yes or no?

Dumb idiot.

Marty Weissberger had told him once, way back at Eastman, "You will never be a conductor until you learn to trust your instincts." He'd never understood what that meant, but he suspected he was in that territory now.

No one moved; he could not read them. The seconds crept by. *Seconds.* Far too long. But he risked another beat of silence and, in a slow sweep of the room, took in the players, picked out a dozen or so faces, avoided Petra's.

The moment stretched, but he would not take the next step without their collective nod.

He saw it—Alexandra, principal violist, watching him in pale earnest. He felt a rush of adrenaline. To her left, the assistant principal violist's eyes rimmed with red.

Shit.

Others, two or three, on the verge of great emotion. If that was possible. Elsewhere, readiness.

His hands shook and there was nothing to do but Brahms.

Inwardly he tried smiling away the panic—I am the illusionist. He flattened his score against the conductor's desk and cast a final glance at Ziegler, who stood behind the percussion section, back to the orchestra, long hands in his pockets, waiting. In rapid succession Barrow caught the bassoonist's eye—*tempo, tempo*. And the tuba player and celli—this was *their* opening, this passage. It would be their second time this morning, the fiftieth in their lives, but he, American though he was, would have it be their first.

He raised his right hand, the hand with the stick. The opening lyric was a twelve-measure span, and when Berndt had taken them through it earlier, Barrow had noticed a slackening in bar six. But he would not allow that. *"In einem Atemzug,"* he said to the celli, a hoarse whisper. *In one breath.* He held back to get the opening color in his ear. Ziegler had not spoken in ages. There was a stillness he had never encountered between the walls of Konzerthaus. He thought, Now we can create this world.

A breath, a conjoint pivot of the hand, and there it was. The opening timbre.

Startling.

That there should be sound at all.

And such a curious beginning, almost mid-sentence, as if there had once been two or three measures before this, which Brahms, in a fit of temper, had ripped from the manuscript, the celli crossing down through the bassoons, hiding under a shimmer of winds, resurfacing. For once they had lost their smooth-chinned earnestness; in its place, a grown-up sensuality. At the sixth bar, he touched the beat with his right hand and drew back his left in a motion similar to pulling taffy; they let up just enough without interrupting the *sostenuto*.

It was so fine, he felt the blood rush to his face. Concentrate, he told himself because privately he knew that Brahms had written not a phrase of six or even twelve bars, but a narrative without seam, one hundred and four bars that wanted never, never to let up. This was not Beethoven's Ninth, not man approaching God, but man approaching man, this surge of Brahms, who at nineteen, on his first concert tour, took to the hills on foot, engagement to engagement, Hamburg to Lüneberg, crossing the North German countryside, music on his back. Brahms, who lived alone his entire adult life, adored by other people's children, occasional visitor to the people he loved, the widow Clara Schumann his sweetest thirst.

Bar forty-four, the empty beat, Berndt's undoing—he relaxed the tempo a hair, froze his hands upon arrival at the apex of the fourth beat, allowed the first beat of forty-five to sit unmarked in the room. It was a longer beat than those coming before or after. No one breathed. The kind of hush poets crowd around.

Beat two, and all arrived by perfect agreement.

Little to remember after that. Letter E, where for the space of three or more measures he closed his eyes—this place, the soft warm hollow of the movement, the tension of three against two, the nostalgic return of the opening subject, the organism's response to a higher pitch in the strings; later, some eye contact with the American timpanist six from the end; the clarinet's quarter-note solo in the penultimate bar; eight full counts on the last dotted half. Off.

∽

The string players held their bows in the air, the arch of their supple young backs; the winds sat forward in their seats. They waited for him to break the moment. He closed his left hand and returned his stick to the desk. The score remained open to the first page of the movement; he'd never looked down. It had been no big deal, there had been no self-indulgence; Ziegler would be content. Someone far back in the second violins began to tap his stand. Two or three others joined in, but the gesture failed to catch.

The orchestra seemed quieter than usual at the close of rehearsal. Even grave. He gathered up his baton and score, glanced to the back wall where Ziegler should be—but wasn't—and made his way toward his station behind the trombones. A cellist stood and offered his hand. "It was good," the cellist said in English. Barrow had no response ready. But to another cellist he said, "You all were excellent. Really excellent."

"I think it has been our best," the cellist replied. "It is the day, as you said. November tenth."

"*Natürlich*," Barrow said.

A double bass player stared as he approached, but turned away at the last minute. The ordinary noise of departure returned.

He supposed it must have been good, though his mind was blank. Ziegler would have a report.

"Barrow, you were very good, thank god." It was Berndt, hand outstretched at chest level; they shook, high and quick.

"Where is Ziegler?"

"Gone. Nobody has seen him leave, only it was before the end. His coat, it is gone."

"How about Antonio?" Barrow asked.

"He has gone to look for a message. For class."

"Is Ziegler sick, do you think?"

"I am believing not. You believe so?"

Barrow shrugged. The old man never mentioned health. He wouldn't. He was the sort who would stomp to the edge of his grave, bark at the priest, and climb in.

He watched Petra disappear into the far wing, her canvas pack hitched to her shoulder. It had been a week since her mumbled "good night" in the Citroën—since he'd received a small folded piece of paper from her sleep-warm fingers. It felt like a month.

Berndt was saying something about health matters.

"Please excuse me," Barrow said, disobeying the call of instinct—the reflex that said *go after her now*—and instead backing toward an offstage closet where a pile of broken music stands and a two-meter-wide push broom hid a toilet that no one ever used.

Before shutting the door, he caught Berndt's grin. He felt for the light switch, reached for his wallet. The week-old fold was still crisp;

the handwriting loose and fast. *"Bitte anrufen,"* it said. Please call. And a phone number. And a penciled arrow shot to a crudely drawn stick figure with a bulbous head and the German word *bald,* three times—*bald bald bald*—crowning its scalp.

Soon soon soon.

11

That afternoon he stood in the Schloss Gottesaue lobby, stalled before the tin-gray doors of the elevator. In the first-floor recital hall, a wind quintet rehearsed a piece by the American composer Samuel Barber—lush, tuneful, and far from home. He waited until he could determine that the oboist was not Petra.

"You are a string player, I think."

He turned.

"Cello?"

It was the concertmaster, Tano Popescu, descending the stairs, violin case in hand. Natural light from behind caught the loose weave of his overcoat, lent him a faint aura.

"Violin," Barrow said.

"Your left hand, sometimes it makes the *vibrato* when you conduct." Tano rattled his hand, in close to the collar bone. "Especially in *espressivo* passages." Barrow had never noticed. "You shouldn't worry, Toscanini did the same." The Romanian stopped to button his coat just as the elevator doors slid back. "You are planning to go up to the library?" Barrow nodded. "Don't bother, it's closed. A fatal coincidence between our librarian's birthday and all this Wall hysteria."

They left the building together. Tano stopped on the landing to light a cigarette; a cold gust tore away the smoke. He suggested coffee, and they descended the steps and headed toward Durlacher Allee.

According to Antonio, Tano Popescu had escaped from Romania on foot, carrying only his violin case from Timisoara to Budapest, where he conned his way onto a Vienna-bound InterCity train. No one could remember hearing the story directly from Tano's mouth, but his very silence on the matter seemed to lend it credence.

The afternoon sun reflected off the glass front of the café in a dazzling broadside. Upon their entrance, the freckled girl behind the counter looked up and smiled, and Barrow resolved for the tenth time in an hour to call Petra. Next phone booth, he told himself. The girl put their coffees in separate paper bags, and he pointed to a cruller that had been reduced to half price.

"I live on the other side of the Schloss," Tano said. He hid his cigarette behind the palm of his hand, smoke trailing up his arm. "You like to walk?"

"*Sicher. Bis dem Schlossplatz.*"

"We should speak English. That way at least one of us speaks his own language."

It was an afternoon of unspoiled air and low, fast-moving clouds. They struck a moderate pace through the shopping streets of downtown Karlsruhe, chatting intermittently about the morning's rehearsal, events in the East. They stopped to take in a window display of chess sets, and Barrow asked him where he was from in Romania.

"I am from Cluj."

"Transylvania."

"You know the country."

"Not really," said Barrow. "It's where Ligeti studied composition."

Tano turned. "You know Ligeti?"

"I conducted the Double Concerto once. The flute and oboe."

Tano seemed surprised. "In America?"

Barrow nodded.

"And you like him?"

"I do."

"So why do you waste your time with Brahms?"

Barrow chuckled.

"No," Tano said, lighting another cigarette. "Actually. You like Brahms?"

"Of course."

"I hate him."

They passed through a bank of moist air wafting from the open door of a flower shop, and again Barrow thought of Petra, the near physical urgency of the repeated words, *soon soon soon.*

"Ligeti owes him a lot," Barrow said.

"That's ridiculous."

One of those lonely dogs, always chasing down the next fight.

"Anyone composing today owes a lot to the past," Barrow said, apparently grasping at blandness.

"*Beethoven* affected every composer after him. Brahms affected Brahms."

Barrow could not resist the provocation. "Schoenberg loved Brahms."

"Yeah, and you know when Schoenberg wrote that trash? Nineteen forty-seven. He was seventy-three. 'Brahms the Progressive.' Obviously he was going soft. Plus he was in Hollywood."

"L.A., not Hollywood," Barrow said. "UCLA."

"I know this—"

"Where Heifetz taught."

"What do I care where Heifetz taught?"

A couple of Hochschule students passed them on the sidewalk, and they both nodded a greeting—Tano somewhat stiffly. They passed a few more stores before the Romanian spoke again. "I hate this I-know-more-than-you shit."

Barrow chuckled. "It shows." Tano grunted. "Where did you learn English?"

"Champaign–Urbana. Illinois."

"No kidding."

"No kidding."

"I wouldn't have thought you'd be allowed."

"It was an experiment," Tano said. "A cultural exchange. As it happened, your government didn't like the bargain, so they shipped me back to Romania."

They arrived at the broad, interconnecting public gardens of the Schlossplatz. At the center of the gardens was a sprawling yellow palace—a German-speaking Versailles, towering and airy. It had been leveled in the war and, like everything else in Karlsruhe, restored to perfection.

"Tell me," Tano said, "for the sake of argument, what would your beloved Brahms have done in 1933?"

Barrow's first hunch had been correct—the man lived to argue.

"Well?"

"I have no idea. I suppose he would have been another Hindemith. Someone like that. An innovative traditionalist."

"This is not what I'm saying," said Tano.

They were on the crushed-stone path leading to the rear of the palace.

Barrow remembered—1933 was the year of Hitler's ascension. Hence the question.

"Brahms as Brahms. As the man he was. Would he have left the country?"

"Schoenberg left around that time, didn't he?"

"Schoenberg was a Jew. What if one didn't have to leave?"

Would Brahms have left? Barrow knew nothing of the composer's politics, except that in his study in Vienna he'd hung a portrait of Bismarck draped with a laurel wreath. But was Bismarck a good guy or a bad guy? Barrow couldn't remember.

He stalled. "Hindemith and Weill emigrated around that time too, didn't they? Kurt Weill?"

"Again, Weill was Jewish. And Hindemith left in 1937. Four years he was in Berlin, right under Hitler's nose. So what was he thinking?"

They pulled out their coffees and dropped to a bench in front of an impromptu soccer game. University students charged back and forth, sweaters marking the goals.

Tano plowed ahead. "Hitler comes to power in January of 1933—is this okay? You don't mind?"

"No, please—"

"In *months*, he consolidates control over every institution in Germany. He pulls Jews from every post, important or unimportant. Some artists, people of conscience, leave the country. Others stay—Strauss, Karl Böhm, Furtwängler, of course. Herbert von Karajan, he joins the Nazi Party."

"Hindemith stays."

"Hindemith stays. He must care, yes, that his Jewish friends are fired, are in exile? Why is he staying?"

Barrow was impressed. "You know German history."

"Welcome to Europe."

A pounding of feet had them look up. A corner kick, ten feet away.

Barrow decided to give it his best shot. "Look, I don't know why Hindemith stayed as long as he did, but what's important, it seems to me, is that he did leave eventually." He was flying blind and he knew it. "It's easy to criticize people with the benefit of hindsight."

"Yes, hindsight. Precisely who does that benefit?"

Barrow laughed. "This is just from one year? I mean your English. It's good."

Tano had been observing a figure on the far side of the grass, a woman drawing on a sketch pad. The tall trees of the Hardwaldt—an arm of the Black Forest that reached into Karlsruhe—framed her handsomely.

"They would no longer play his music," Tano said, still looking at the woman. "He was officially banned. *That's* why Hindemith left. Professional reasons."

"I'm sure it was a combination of things," said Barrow. "I'm sure he would have left when things got really bad."

"I suppose," said Tano. "*Kristallnacht* perhaps."

"Yeah, I suppose," Barrow said warily. For *Kristallnacht*, he at least had images. Shattered shop windows, Jews pulled into the streets from their beds, beaten and murdered. *Kristallnacht* was the night the Nazis gave rein to the anti-Semitism they'd been stoking for a decade, the first public hint of their genocidal intentions—with the benefit of hindsight. "Did Hindemith leave before *Kristallnacht*?" he asked, hoping he did.

"He left in 1937."

"Which was before *Kristallnacht*?"

Tano looked genuinely puzzled. "You don't know?"

"What."

"You don't know when *Kristallnacht* was?"

"No, I mean, vaguely."

"But you must. I thought—from your remark in rehearsal?"

"No."

"When you said, Today is November tenth, yes or no? of course, I assumed."

"No."

"*This* is *Kristallnacht*. Fifty-one years ago last night. Night of November ninth and again night of November tenth. Today is the anniversary."

If there was a trace of irony in the Romanian's face—a crease in the lips, a grain of light in the eye—Barrow could not find it. Just the flat, dead-pan delivery.

"To invoke such a memory to a roomful of Germans," Tano said, "I thought you must have known."

"I didn't."

The sun had dropped behind the trees, casting all of them—the soccer players, the sketch artist—in shadow.

Tano dropped his empty coffee cup to the stone path and flattened it with his foot. "You think they did not know that?"

"I don't know."

"Of course they do. All over Germany they are *busy* knowing that."

"I mentioned the day—I mentioned November 10 because of the Berlin Wall coming down."

"Not at all," Tano said, slipping the spent coffee cup into the pocket of his overcoat. "November 10 is the morning after *Kristallnacht*. It will always be the morning after *Kristallnacht*."

When Barrow finally spoke, he could only whisper. "Did I insult them?"

Tano shrugged. "We played like princes, didn't we?"

✍

The soccer players left behind a goal post, a black sweater whiskered with dead grass. Barrow stooped for it and began picking off the blades. His head swam. The coffee might be buzzing him—he'd eaten nothing all day but a cruller.

Anniversaries.

Enough time goes by, and they start backing up on themselves. It's inevitable with only so many numbers to go around.

He thought of Arnold Schoenberg, a brilliant composer and an even more brilliant mind. Schoenberg had been gleeful at the fact that the fiftieth anniversary of Wagner's death was the hundredth of Johannes Brahms' birth, Wagner's nemesis. And *that* anniversary, of course, happened to be 1933, the year of Hitler's rise, the year Schoenberg, a Jew, left the Fatherland, the year of his written tribute to Brahms. And now, fifty-one years after *Kristallnacht*—not fifty, that would be too obvious—fifty-one years later, down comes the Wall, wholeness restored. Three times seventeen, lovely pair of primes. Too fucking elegant.

He shook out the sweater and dropped it on the bench. The lights from downtown Karlsruhe glowed on the far side of the great palace, lit the clouds.

Funny that in all his cross-examination, Tano had not mentioned Ziegler.

12 A middle-aged couple approached from the lower end of Lessingstrasse, and Barrow stepped back from the door to let them pass. "She should never have gone to Paris," the woman said. He couldn't hear the man's response.

He stepped up to the door and knocked. Ziegler's curtains were drawn, but the shutters were still up and there was a light on inside. He waited a full minute. He had already taken a few steps up the sidewalk, when he heard the door come away from its seal. There it stood, cracked its regulation three inches.

No one was in the studio, no one behind the desk. The cat slept on a stack of scores, a pillow of gray stone. He closed the door behind him but remained close to it, the better to affect a manner of having stopped by on a whim. He noticed things he'd never noticed before: a banged-up flute case on a shelf behind the desk, a framed glossy of a man in tails, lancing the air with his baton.

A book lay open on the maestro's desk. A textbook. Its typography was Japanese, or maybe Chinese.

He called quietly, "Herr Ziegler," and started to take a couple of steps toward the desk just as the old man appeared from the kitchen carrying a tray with a pot of tea and two cups, thick white china of the Howard Johnson's variety.

"Please excuse me, Herr Ziegler."

The old man stopped short, just outside kitchen door. Barrow wished he would step into the light.

"I came to see if you were okay."

"Yes."

Yes, I'm okay, or Yes, I heard your question?

Like some ailing communist premier, Ziegler stepped into the room. He wore a neat blue turtleneck. His face showed plenty of color as he leaned into the lamp to set down the tray. *As you can see, the comrade is fine.*

"Tuesday, yes?" said the old man.

The time of Barrow's next lesson.

"Yes, of course," Barrow said.

But he was not ready to leave. There were questions. He wanted a reaction to his performance earlier in the day, for one. Other questions, questions of greater import. The one that had been lingering all week, about Petra's demotion. Another that had been damming up for months—*What did you do in the war?*

"Herr Barrow"—the old man's voice startled him—"the last time I heard an American address a crowd of Germans and tell them how they should feel about their country, it was in the square across from Schöneberg Rathaus? You know Schöneberg Rathaus? In Berlin?"

Barrow hesitated. "No, Maestro."

The old man had slipped behind the desk—he was arranging the tea set. "It is where your President Kennedy made a speech and attempted to inform us that he was Berliner. We also walked away at that time, as I did this morning. We left, though we loved that man, Kennedy. We were humiliated for him, grossly humiliated, not because he said 'I am a doughnut,' which is *Ich bin ein Berliner*, which he did not know he was saying and so we could not blame him, but because, simply, he is *not* Berliner, he was *never* Berliner, he was only a much adored man standing on a platform, too much adored, even by me, and we felt sick to see such forgetfulness in Germany, such response to *adored men* like JFK."

Mortified, Barrow concentrated on breathing. There was a pause and he grabbed it. "This morning."

"Yes."

"You left during my performance?"

"I stayed a few measures. I heard nothing I did not expect."

Barrow felt his jaw start to lock up. Forget sounding natural, forget *ease*. Just proceed to your next question.

"Why did you replace Petra Vogel as first oboe?"

The maestro had been warming his hands on the sides of the teapot. He looked up in surprise. "Herr Barrow, that was on your advice."

Barrow stared back; nothing visible contradicted the perfectly chosen note of protest in the old man's voice. He struggled to keep his place. "Perhaps," he said, "there was a misunderstanding of my comment about the tuning."

"I don't think I misunderstand the situation."

"Herr Maestro Ziegler, there is no situation."

"I am expecting a guest."

"*There is no situation.*"

"I am expecting a guest." Ziegler glanced at the door. "I am seeing you on Tuesday."

"There is nothing going on with the oboist."

Ziegler took his hands away from the teapot and lowered himself into his chair. "You have only one friend, Herr Barrow," he said. "And that is your ear."

Barrow loathed him. The prescriptive tone, the carefully inserted precepts. Decades of teaching, pretend-conducting—this made him an expert on life?

"Please go."

∽

At the top of Lessingstrasse he passed a woman clutching the collar of her raincoat, noticeable because she was Asian—Japanese, he judged from his brief glimpse. He turned back and watched her proceed halfway down the block. He saw her knock on the door, which fell back almost at her touch to reveal a wedge of grayish light.

There was a phone booth across the street at Mühlburger Tor. He held the receiver, pretending to dig for change in his pocket. It was as if Petra's smile, her desire for him, the soft curve of her back—memorized while listening to Bach—the lift of her breast at the start of a long phrase, they were all on the menu in a restaurant across the street, and it was his destiny to pace back and forth on the opposite sidewalk.

Wolf answered.

"She's gone."

"What?"

"Since half an hour."

"Where?"

"I don't know. School maybe. She had her oboe."

Waiting for the tram, he lost patience and started running—past windows of cheese and plumbing fixtures, past the chess shop and out to Durlacher Allee. He ran, cursing his backpack, the scores inside, the Brahms, the manuscript paper, the Beethoven's Eighth Ziegler had told them to bring to the postrehearsal session he'd failed to show up for. At Gottesauer Platz, one block short of the music school, he stopped, his lungs shrieking. He dropped into a crouch and hugged his legs. Siting up the long street, he saw a hundred shop windows and imagined them all bursting at once, a flash flood of glass on the sidewalk—how much volition would that take?

He ran again. The windows were dark on the parking-lot side of Schloss Gottesaue. Inside, the monitor was nowhere in sight—which had to be against some regulation. He took the stairs three at a time and heard her the moment he reached the third-floor landing.

She was playing long tones. Incredibly long. *How far I could swim underwater on one of those breaths.*

A name plate on the door read PROF. MESSER-EICHEN, OBOE, and affixed above it was a magazine photo of the Bavarian Alps. He leaned against the opposite wall, his breathing still coming down from the run. Petra started another note. He slid off his pack, opened his jacket and waited. She notched down another half step, and another. When she finished what he thought was the B below middle C, he tapped on the door. He was wrong—the curse of not having perfect pitch. She started another note and he leaned against the door jamb, waiting. When she was done he knocked. There was a pause—she would be worried at a knock on the third floor of the Hochschule on a Friday night—there had been an incident in October. He knocked again, not hard.

"*Wer ist das?*" she asked.

"*Der amerikanische Scheisskopf.*"

"*Wer?*"

"*Der amerikanische Scheisskopf.*"

The American shithead.

Another pause, this one swamped with dread that his instincts had failed him. He heard a bolt slip and the door fell back. The closeness of her face shocked him.

"*Abend.*"

"*Abend.*"

"I'm sorry," he said.

She wore the European uniform, blousy wool sweater and skin-tight jeans. Her shoes lay under the piano.

"You may come in."

He'd given no thought to what he was going to say, imagining somehow that she would take the lead. But the part of her that once so generously filled in for his awkwardness, his stupidity, seemed unavailable. She was in that state of mind one enters when practicing, a level of concentration that brooks no interruption, by anyone.

"I'm interrupting."

"It's okay."

She retreated to her music stand. The oboe lay on the piano bench behind her, keys up.

"I went to Ziegler's."

"Yes?"

"He disappeared during rehearsal. I thought maybe he wasn't well." He glanced out the window, the lights of Durlacher Allee angled off in the distance. "But he seemed fine."

"That's good."

He stood with one hand on the door knob while she leafed absently through a book of etudes, its pages black with sixteenths. It occurred to him that he'd never been alone with her in a room.

"I asked him about the seating change."

"Oh," she said simply. And, betraying herself, "It's been over a week."

"I know. I'm sorry."

"Why should you be sorry?"

"Because it looks like I was responsible."

"Only to stupid people."

"What do *you* think?"

Her hand dropped from the music and searched for a way into the front pocket of her jeans. "I think it is not my... it is not mine, to know why this happened," she said in English.

The language switch, the physical distance—she was delivering a prepared a statement, and his heart sank. He had underestimated his blunder by miles.

"Why not? What did Messer-Eichen say?"

She hesitated, glancing at her oboe. "That Ziegler is an asshole."

"He said that?"

"And that you are an asshole."

"He used that word? In English?"

She paused without smiling; she had disappeared behind a familiar curtain, the peculiar Teutonic literalism that, simply put, hears no sarcasm. It did nothing to protect her—her eyes still sought a place to land.

"And that you are an American," she said.

"I *am* an American."

"That you do not care for our sound. The German oboe."

"I love your sound."

"It really doesn't matter."

"Of course it matters."

"It doesn't *matter*."

There was a note of pleading in her voice—she was begging him to accept the explanation at face value, as if her teacher had bugged the place and this was the public line they both must accept.

She picked up a pencil and erased something in her music, and it struck him how she must have felt, replaced after the third rehearsal, humiliated before ninety fellow musicians, an East German among *Wessis*—the injection of doubt into the group mind, the way doubt hardens to stigma. He knew the dynamic well; Ziegler's opinion of her had even caused him to second-guess his own ear. A dangerous hurdle in her career had materialized from nothing, a mere impression, a comment he, Barrow, had made about parallel octaves with the flute. An impossibly high hurdle perhaps. Or perhaps not so important in the long run. But it didn't matter—to her, to her teacher, it had all happened on the American's watch, following *his* rehearsal with the orchestra.

She crossed to her oboe and removed the reed. "Will you wait for me?" she said. "I do not like to go down alone."

"Of course."

He watched her break down the instrument, pass the cleaning feather through its three barrels, slip the reed into a clipcase with several others. She put away her music. He turned out the light and followed her into the hallway. She bolted the door while he started down the hall.

There was no sign of the monitor—no sign that anyone else was in the building—and they let themselves out onto the story-high landing that overlooked the parking lot. He saw that Wolf's Citroën was parked in a far corner of the lot.

"They're dancing on the Berlin Wall," he said.

"Yes, I heard that." They took the stairs together, a meter between them. "Should I drive you to the tram?" she said.

A courtesy. She couldn't mean it.

"No thanks," he said.

They stopped midway across the pebble lot. He dreaded the tram ride ahead, the dry heat smelling of rubber.

"Good night," he said.

"Good night."

He looked over at Wolf's car, symbol of the little community she had with her soft-spoken roommates. When he looked back she was watching him.

"You are a conductor," she said.

He allowed a little clearing where she might add something, but she started off for the car, letting the comment hang alone in the night air. He'd read a note of sweetness, and he supposed she meant to compliment him, but in that moment he knew he would trade it all, the morning's victory on the podium, the years of preparation, Eastman, Juilliard, Brooklyn, the talent he was born with, the chance of success, all for a single glance, tossed in his direction, over her shoulder. But she climbed into the car without looking back.

13   He made use of her unavailability, the marked agony of it, by throwing himself into his work, reentering the monastery he'd furnished for himself back in September. He read scores like novels—Schubert, Schumann, Beethoven, Wagner, Brahms. He'd read them before, but this time secrets stepped forward from every corner, revelations. He prepared whatever score Ziegler assigned and read five more besides, indulging his own best instinct for what to pick up next, sniffing conquests over the horizon: Shostakovitch and the Russians, a pack of contemporaries, the Poles, the latest wave of Americans. He thought, If I can keep this up, I'll own them all.

He sank from view, ignored the newspaper—only vaguely aware of fallen governments to the East, ongoing celebrations. He chose unpopular cafés and lesser-used routes, all so he could rehearse and recount without interruption, so he would not be seen muttering to himself.

A week went by. One morning he passed a bakery he'd never no-ticed. Inside, a crowd of players from the orchestra lined up for coffee. He picked up his pace and continued to the next corner where he heard a voice behind him.

"I waved. You didn't see?"

Alexandra, Petra's roommate.

"Sorry," he said.

"Are you conducting today?"

"No."

"Too bad. We like you."

"Thanks."

They started up the sidewalk.

"Petra is running to Frankfurt a lot," Alexandra said. "Will you go this Saturday?"

"What?" The sound of her name had ripped through him.

"Wolf and I can't go. We are in Köln next weekend."

"Go where?"

"To Frankfurt. She is playing with the Radio-Sinfonie. This weekend."

They had stopped at a crosswalk. "It's busy," he said. "I doubt I can get away."

"Of course."

✍

On Saturday he stood outside Frankfurt's magnificent Alte Oper con-cert hall, ticket envelope in hand, watching the water spill from its huge pedestal fountain. The city seemed half slung from cranes. The other half gleamed under a choppy gray sky.

A small, wiry man stood above him on the steps. "A city of banks, that's what we have here," the man said in English. "A shrine to the deutsche mark."

Barrow smiled politely.

"The Alte Oper, this building, it is less than ten years old, you know this? The kaiser built it, hundred years ago, exact copy of the Comédie-

Française in Paris. You bombed it in the war, thank-you-very-much. Sat here, nothing, twenty-five years."

Barrow hadn't opened his mouth—no way for the guy to know he was an American.

"All this time we are fighting hard for a new hall, brand new, look forward, next millennium, something astounding like Sydney Opera House, glass, tall sheets of glass, Walter Gropius, I. M. Pei. We talked with many architects, but in the end we got this. Copy of something that was a copy of something French, all to commemorate one of the stupidest Germans to wear a helmet. Have you already bought a ticket?"

"Pardon?"

"I am Franz Messer-Eichen." The man carried a double oboe case. "And you are Mr. Cooper Barrow?"

"Yes."

"Someone has pointed you out to me, one of my students. I teach oboe at Hochschule für Musik in Karlsruhe."

"Of course."

"You have come to watch Werner Schott conduct Bruckner."

He caught sight of the envelope Barrow held in his hand.

"Show me your ticket." Barrow did. "I will get you a better seat. You can sell this one tonight, out here on the steps. It is lucky I have seen you."

This wasn't the plan.

"Wait here."

The plan was to observe this man's prize student, Petra Vogel, from a hundred yards, maybe approach Werner Schott and introduce himself—which would be a natural thing to do, even a smart thing to do—perhaps bump into Petra backstage in the green room—if there *was* a green room—compliment her playing, perhaps her teacher's as well, and by this routine, by this little drama, make it clear to her that he was interested, even repentant.

Messer-Eichen returned and held out a ticket. "Not the best, but better than that one."

"Thanks."

"I'm going to buy a sandwich," said Messer-Eichen. "Have you eaten lunch?"

"No."

"Join me."

They crossed the Opernplatz and entered a narrow street lined with cafés. "Here is Fressgasse," said Messer-Eichen, an apparent font of information. They stopped in an American-style deli and ordered sandwiches. The oboist flirted easily with the woman behind the counter. Their accents matched, both distinctly southern. *"Tschuss,"* he said after he'd taken his sandwich. *"Tschuss,"* she said—the parting word ubiquitous in the south.

He led the way to a table up front where they could watch the Saturday crowd. "Three weeks, this place will be crammed with Christmas. All up and down, the outdoor booths, the Santa Clauses. My students tell me you are quite talented."

"Thank you."

"Tell me what you think of Ziegler."

Caught off guard, Barrow swallowed before he was ready. "He's a fine teacher," he said.

"You have come from Juilliard to study with him."

"Yes," Barrow said, not mentioning his eight-year hiatus upstate in Fishkill.

"It is interesting. His reputation inside of Germany is not so great, but he seems to bring such talent from other countries. There was a woman from Great Britain last year."

"Pauline Lawford."

"Yes. Lawford. They did not get along. Is this what you heard?"

Antonio had described Lawford in unfriendly terms.

"I haven't heard much," Barrow said.

"Of course, she did not get along with anyone, or so I was told."

"You seem to take an unusual interest in the students."

"Not at all. I am kind of a dog for gossip, perhaps this is obvious. Life is otherwise pretty boring."

"So I should watch what I say?"

Messer-Eichen smiled, turkey sandwich halfway to his mouth. He slipped out a word—"Naturally"—and took a bite, a large one for such a small man. Barrow noticed his nails, which were immaculately groomed, cuticles pushed back, a millimeter-wide gray-white crescent tipping each finger.

They both ate.

Barrow broke the silence. "This is good."

"It is not Carnegie Deli," said the oboist. "But ... ," and he shrugged the shrug of a salesman.

"You have always been principal here in Frankfurt?"

"Always. Since I came."

"How long is that?"

"Twenty years, I think. Twenty-two."

"So you played under Raab?"

"I screwed his daughter."

Barrow laughed in spite of himself. He awaited further amplification; there was none, and he decided to seek some gossip of his own. "So are the players happy with Schott?"

"We love him. You will see tonight. He is from the newer school. Very organized beat patterns, we follow him easily. He is friendly to us. We are his colleagues. All that sort of thing."

"You don't seem convinced," Barrow said, enjoying the vertical play of Messer-Eichen's eyebrows—the way they carried more expression than the jaw.

"A colleague of mine from St. Louis sent me an article once from an American magazine. A survey of job satisfaction or some such. Very interesting. I posted it in our lounge at the Oper. Do you know what job had the least satisfaction, according to this survey in the States? The most hated job?"

"I have no idea."

"Orchestral musician. Do you know how many times I have played the Bruckner Four? Eight times. And this is not even to bring up Beethoven. You do not want to hate Beethoven, who wants to hate Beethoven? I hate Beethoven." He tore the final corner off his sandwich, leaving a round hunk between his fingers. "I exaggerate of course. Who can hate Beethoven? I am bored with Beethoven. That is more accurate. There are still moments of love. The Seventh, second movement." He swallowed. "Tchaikovsky though, I hate. Bruckner I am not so fond of either. It is why I play chamber music whenever possible. And every season I am using my entire allotment of absences. My students love me for it. They always substitute. Petra Vogel—you know her?—she is playing tonight."

"Tonight? I had not heard," Barrow said, aware that the other man had been scrutinizing him. He ignored the urge to point out that he'd had nothing to do with Petra being pulled from the Brahms.

"The assistant has a medical operation up north. Petra is in for him— at my suggestion of course. She has played before so it is not a question. Also, Schott likes her." He looked down for his napkin. "He likes her very much, actually."

The way he dropped in the last comment, the mention of Schott, the way he still searched the floor for his *Mundtuch*—all seemed patently deliberate, designed to make Barrow ask for clarification, as with Raab's daughter. Barrow felt certain he would betray himself by taking it up.

He tried changing the subject.

"Is it still hard for women in Germany? To get into an 'A' orchestra?"

"In particular a woman from the East?" said the oboist, shaking out his newly found napkin.

"Any woman."

"Very hard. If the woman gets a position and she is attractive, there will always be a question. Skepticism on the part of the other players. If the woman is attractive. You have met her? My student?"

"In rehearsal."

Messer-Eichen nodded and raised a single eyebrow—perhaps testing for fraternity—did the American agree that she was a fine piece of flesh?—reducing her to a cheese-round on the plate between them, drawing up rules of engagement before plunging in.

Barrow faked as blank a look as possible. "That's too bad," he said. "About the skepticism."

"Mm," the oboist said. "And what will you do this afternoon?"

"I thought I might see Clara Schumann's house."

"I have never been."

"On Myliusstrasse. Do you know it?"

"I am afraid I don't." The oboist snagged a leftover rind of turkey loaf and popped it into his mouth. "You should come behind the stage after the concert. I'll introduce you to Schott."

∽

Barrow watched as Messer-Eichen disappeared in a crowd of weekend shoppers. Feeling a tug on his sleeve, he glanced down to see a pretty, olive-dark face looking straight up into his, its forehead creased in supplication.

"*Bitte, bitte, mein Herr.*"

The girl clutched his hand with both of hers. Her moist fingers plied his skin—

"*Bitte, mein Herr, zwei Mark, nur zwei Mark—*"

She was selling newspapers for the homeless. She was maybe ten, fearfully canny, and a bad actress, and had he only been in motion he might have shaken her off. But she eloped with the five-mark piece that had been the first bit of change to come up from his pocket, leaving him to stand outside the American deli, conned and smiling for no good reason.

14 The principal cellist of the Radio-Sinfonie of Frankfurt was celebrating a birthday, and someone had prepared a cake for him in the orchestra lounge after the concert. Scanning the crowd for Petra, Barrow picked out Werner Schott chatting animatedly with two of the players. The conductor looked older than he had on the podium, probably fifty, shorter than Barrow, but broad, with a dense stand of orange hair.

"Come, I will introduce you." Messer-Eichen seemed to make a habit of appearing out of nowhere. Barrow followed him through the tightly packed crowd of probably forty musicians, and Schott's circle opened to include them. The two players with Schott were laughing.

Schott turned to Messer-Eichen. "Was it so awful, Franz?"

"I have a new joke."

"No thank you."

"What is shorter than a thimble, yet more inspiring than the Bible?"

"What," said Schott.

"Bruckner's dick," said the oboist. "But you should hear the man's symphonies."

"Which are long and a little less than inspiring?" added one of the other players.

"Thank you."

"Talk of uninspired," said Schott.

"Only because I made it up during the second movement," the oboist said. "The problem with you Germans, you have no sense of irony."

"Us who?" said the musician who had already spoken. Barrow tried to identify his accent—perhaps Scandinavian.

"So you, Michael, you are not German," said the oboist, "but it's all made equal when you sleep with one. It leaks out, a little at a time. Ask my ex-wife. A Londoner. One night with me—yes, technically, I am Austrian—one night with me and all that exquisite English irony, all that I married her for, is gone."

"And what is so inspiring about Bruckner's dick?" Schott asked.

The oboist shrugged. "A small imperfection in the joke. Besides, who has seen it?"

"Frau Bruckner, perhaps?"

"But none of us," the oboist said.

"No."

"So who's to say?"

There were a couple of appreciative grunts from the others. Barrow forced a smile.

"What does your American friend think of Bruckner?" Schott asked.

Once again, Barrow had not opened his mouth.

Schott addressed him directly. "What do you think?"

He hated verbalizing about music. Worse, he had no strong opinion of Bruckner. "I like him. I, uh … I like him. In passages, he is as beautiful as any. And there is something about the accumulation of sound—"

"From New York City?" Schott asked.

Barrow nodded. Once upon a time.

"Please continue."

Bullshitting in German was not his forte. "I guess, over an hour, the accumulation of such rich sonorities, which are not so complicated really, certainly not as developed as maybe Brahms, but beautiful ..." They were all looking at him, listening intently. He shrugged. "There's an elation that happens."

How fucking insipid.

"You see, gentlemen," Schott said, "we have grown cynical. No, Franz? 'Cynical.'" He repeated the word in English and Barrow nodded, unbelieving. "Go on. You have heard other performances of the Fourth?"

"Only recorded."

"Recording is death for Bruckner. You must be in the hall with him. You agree?"

"Certainly."

"Of course he agrees with you," said Messer-Eichen. "You think he is stupid?"

"Everything is better live," said one of the other musicians.

"At least with a recording you can be in the kitchen," Messer-Eichen said, "fry up some bratwurst, a little salt."

"You are from Karlsruhe," Schott said. "In Ziegler's studio."

"Yes."

"I have heard about you."

From whom—from Petra? Across the pillow of some hotel suite in Frankfurt?

"Quote, 'You do not speak of God with affection, why so with music?'"

It was Schott, addressing him. "Excuse me?"

"Has Ziegler announced this yet?"

"Yes."

"Such horseshit. I have never met someone to feel the music so deeply as Karlheinz. Especially Brahms. Brahms for him is holy scripture. It is why he will never play Bruckner or Wagner. Brahms, for him is *Mensch*. He thinks he *is* Brahms."

Someone came around with cake. Starving, Barrow took a piece and dug in. So did Messer-Eichen. Schott refused.

"It has killed his career, this obsession with Brahms. He admires him too much, never killed him. You have to kill the composer at some point. Today it is all respect for the composer. Fine, I say, but do not have too much of it. If you have too much respect for the ham on your plate, you will never want to eat it." The maestro had begun to attract a sizable portion of the room's attention, but he was oblivious to it, remaining fixed on Barrow.

"What are you doing there in Karlsruhe? Right now. What is it that you are doing?"

Barrow described the Brahms rehearsals, his forthcoming assignment to coach the *Musikhochschule*'s opera chorus—*Hänsel und Gretel* was slated for December—and the possibility of working with the new music ensemble.

"This is all?!"—he'd begun to interpret Schott's outbursts as compliments—"You should be busier. You are trapped in that school. You should do things outside. This is what Ziegler is bad at. He is no politician. No pulling strings"—*Fäden in der Hand*—"No strings to *pull*. Not for years. Not for decades. It is why no German wants to study with him. He is not a, what—perfect word in English—a 'player.' He could have been Wilhelm Furtwängler. This is not known, but I know this. He could have been Furtwängler, but he is teaching foreigners in Karlsruhe and no one will go near him. And he hates us all. He hates us because of this. People are forgetting him, and that, *that* he likes. I hate this man. I *hate* him. He is a waste of genius, this man."

Schott's face was red to the point of tears.

The room had fallen silent. In the suspense of the moment, Barrow felt someone looking at him from across the room. It was Petra in a long gray raincoat, holding her backpack in front of her. She stood by the door and held his gaze, but he couldn't get to her because Schott had grabbed him by the elbow and was steering him in the opposite direction.

He leaned into Barrow's ear. "Patricia could not come. She is practicing."

"Patricia?"

"Franz did not tell you?"

They were in the corridor.

"Patricia Levy. My, how would you say, my 'girlfriend.' She says she knows you?"

Barrow's head was a mess of confusion—Petra's sudden presence, and a name reentering after ten years, dragging a whole world behind it.

"Yes. I..."

"She cannot stomach Bruckner," Schott said. "That is the real reason she did not come to the concert. This panic thing, 'I have to practice,' it is all an excuse."

Barrow hesitated. Pat Levy? "What's she practicing for?" he asked.

"Debut recital in London. Queen Elizabeth Hall. She is doing a premiere, a new piece by Boulez."

Ↄ

Schott landed his satchel on the seat between them and gave instructions to the taxi driver. "I do not believe in limousines," he said after their doors were shut, peering over his shoulder at the small flock of concertgoers on the sidewalk. "Not for politicians and certainly not for artists."

The cab pulled away, the force of it settling them back in their seats. Schott loosened his bow tie and, in an example of exquisite, perhaps even artless, timing, dropped a brutal question, "What did you think of our orchestra?"

"Very fine."

"After wine you will tell me what you really think," Schott said, popping out his collar studs. "Remind me again?"

"Sorry?"

"How do you know Patricia?"

"From Eastman School of Music." A rush of scent from the deep past, just to utter that word, just to hear *Eastman* come out of his own mouth.

"Of course. 'Marty.' The ex."

"Martin Weissberger."

"And you liked him?"

Barrow hesitated. The judgments by which you are judged.

"Yes."

"And who else?" Schott asked.

"Did I study with?"

"Yes."

"Gil Shanahan."

"Juilliard. Who else?"

"Master classes." He'd once despised the résumé game. "Some with Bernstein. Giulini."

"Giulini," Schott said, taking up the word like a fragment from a hymn. "And now Ziegler."

"There's a lot to learn from him," Barrow said, unnecessarily.

Schott nodded. "You have a place in Karlsruhe."

"Just outside."

"Funny town, is Karlsruhe. Bit of a what-you-call 'throwback.' Stinking rich. Conservative."

Barrow let a moment go by. "Did you study with him?" he asked.

"With whom?"

"Ziegler."

"Germans do not study with this man," Schott said, gazing at the far curb where a woman in a raincoat shielded her squatting dog with a newspaper. "Look at that. Too pathetic. To shit in public *and* be rained on."

Barrow nodded.

"You do not say much," Schott said. "You are a Cleveland boy, correct?"

"My German is not—"

"Your German is excellent. I have conducted in Cleveland. You grew up there?"

"A suburb."

"Did you see Szell?"

"No," said Barrow. He interpreted Schott's silence as a reprimand. "He was already dead."

"Of course."

"But I remember it. His death."

"And, of course, Maazel. You saw him?"

Barrow hesitated, aware that he was being assembled by his opinions. "I loved him." Schott didn't respond. "I was a kid," Barrow added, in case it wasn't obvious.

"Of course, as a child, how could you not fall in love with him?"

"He was exciting to watch."

"Yes, 'exciting,'" Schott said, demoting the word to English.

The cab stopped at a light. An entire block lay under construction, the first few skinless stories of an office tower. From deep in the interior, security lamps winked back through the rain. The light changed and after another block Schott spoke. "Listen to everything he says about Brahms."

"Maestro Ziegler?"

"Everything."

The construction would not stop—another steel-girdered monster strode the next block. "You see this?" Schott said, jabbing his thumb in the direction of the window. "This is the result of our big happy embrace of democracy. Our reward. What do you think?"

"Of all the construction?"

"Yes."

"Might as well be New York."

"If only."

⁂

They walked a narrow corridor, twenty flights up. The fabric-lined walls skimmed all resonance from Schott's voice, revealing a staticky excitement. "I hated it. I never lived higher than two floors, but now I sit in the living room in the big couch and I look out the big window—you will see it faces west—and I imagine I can see straight into the living rooms of those ten-million-dollar condos on the Upper East Side. I am five minutes to the airport, nonstop to Boston and Tokyo, plane to London every ten minutes. So I love it and—stop. Do you hear?"

A noise boomeranged behind the walls, whipped past them—close, distant, close. A buzz.

"Do you know what that is?" Schott asked.

Sounds had pestered Barrow all his life; his only way of coping was to catalogue them. "Reminds me of ice breaking up on a lake," he said.

"I like that. I like that you say that." Barrow shrugged. "You have heard it? In buildings?"

"Sometimes."

"It is maddening to me."

"Yes."

"That I cannot identify it."

"Yes."

∽

Pat Levy threw her short arms around his waist. "God damn it. Coop-fucking-Barrow." He nodded, feeling too tall in the cramped foyer.

"Yeah, I'm…"

Pat wore jeans and a white cotton sweater with the sleeves pulled back, and no shoes. She'd been practicing. For all its abundance, her black hair, carelessly pinned up, barely reached his chin. She pulled away, grabbed his hands. "Look at you. You've filled out. All that schnitzel. What's it been, eight years?"

"Ten,"

"I want every goddamn detail," she said, pegging him with a fierce look he'd long forgotten. She was the first grown woman he'd ever heard tell a dirty joke, sitting in the back of a chartered bus with the guys from the brass section of the Eastman orchestra. She swamped him with America, with East Coast.

Schott yelled from somewhere inside the apartment. "Bring him in here."

"No fucking way," she yelled. "He's mine."

"Goddamn Long Island Jew!"

Pat lowered her voice. "Did you insult him?"

"I don't think so."

"He's wired. Tell him to watch out for his damn back."

"Hey, American," Schott yelled.

Barrow followed the sound of his voice around the corner and into a room that stretched forty or fifty feet before butting into a wall of glass, which was black and spattered with the Frankfurt night. He was surprised to see Messer-Eichen seated in an overstuffed white couch. "You should be careful with your back," the oboist muttered, throwing down a magazine and plucking another from a tower of *Der Spiegel*s on the coffee table. He raised a hand to Barrow without looking up. "Again we meet."

A mirror-black grand piano commanded the near end of the room, lid down, a seven-footer piled with scores, copies, and unopened mailers. Accordioned across the piano stand was a five-foot spread of music, a spray of hand-inked notes, terrifying in their density, penciled through with fingerings and pedalings. The Boulez.

Barrow crossed the room to where Schott crouched on his knees, head thrust into the bottom cupboard of a floor-to-ceiling cabinet. He had already laid out three or four stacks of old 78 volumes, thick as photo albums. "I'll help," he said.

"No no no." Schott said, emerging from the cupboard. "There is a system here." He breathed heavily, the same man who'd conjured up Anton Bruckner by way of sheer presence, the way a single smoldering cigar might scent a ballroom.

Messer-Eichen moistened a fingertip, turned back another page of *Der Spiegel*. "What are you looking for?"

"Herr Barrow has guessed."

"Actually, no."

Schott took an album from the top of the stack and handed it to

Barrow. "You know Talich? *That* is a conductor. Czech Philharmonic. This is amazing, this Mozart." Barrow hefted the Talich volume, heavy as slate. There was a grunt from the cupboard and Schott backed out holding a single volume. "*Voilà,*" he said, "*Voilà.*" He was grinning.

"*Bravissimo,*" Messer-Eichen said.

"Here," said Schott.

Barrow took possession of the second album.

"You are astonished?"

The album cover was affixed with a yellowed label, typewritten, the H's each a millimeter off-horizon.

```
      Brahms Symphonie Nr. 1
          Berliner Rundfunk
       Karlheinz Ziegler, dir.
```

Barrow was dumbfounded.

Schott seemed pleased with the effect. "You wish to hear this?"

"What is it?" Messer-Eichen asked, peeling back the cover of another magazine.

"Ziegler. Berliner Rundfunk. Brahms' One."

"No, thank you."

"I would like to hear."

A new voice in the room.

It was Petra, standing by the piano. "Does it say when?" she asked, her voice subdued. The question had been directed at Barrow.

"I think 'thirty-seven," Schott said. "You know Petra Vogel? Herr Cooper Barrow?"

"The student conductor from America," Petra said.

Barrow nodded. She crossed to shake his hand.

"We've been drying her off in the bathroom," Pat said, arriving with a tray of wine glasses.

"Where did you find them?" Petra asked. She was at Barrow's side, kneeling, peering at the label.

"I am always looking," Schott said. "This one I can't remember. First disc, please."

Barrow pulled out the top platter.

"He must have been very young," Petra said, her shoulder just grazing his. The jam-up of impressions—the 78s, the wine glasses, his own swift ascent into an apparently preexisting circle—was nothing compared to the damp proximity of her hair.

"It seems impossible that he should be recording," she said.

Schott shrugged. "Who knows? Only listen."

"Can we take a vote?" said Messer-Eichen, joined on the couch by Pat, who sat poised with a carrot, her feet up. The two looked like coconspirators.

"Shut up," Schott said.

The turntable was moving, the checkered calibration lights. The needle raged against the preparation groove, followed by a beat-and-a-half-long vacuum.

Barrow should have been prepared, but he wasn't. Brahms' terrible, full-throated opening—timpani pounding, downbeats only, incessant; and the contrary motion—upper strings, winds, the rising alarm, the orchestra's widening jaws—sounding what? Sounding invasion. And in this recording, Barrow thought, more so. There was a screaming intensity throughout the introduction, the microphones far too close to the first violins, as if strapped to their bridges. Nothing lush. (The lush sound would come in the second movement—they would stand for the whole symphony, he and Schott, a meter apart, perfectly still, almost a competition of stillness—and in the context of the first, the second movement would be heartbreakingly, perversely, sweet.) But this was intentionally ugly. Jackbooted.

In the shallows after the opening came an oboe solo, a six-bar fragment, and Barrow noticed—because he noticed everything about her, drank of her every move—an exchange between Petra and her teacher. At the level of murmur reserved for church, the two oboists uttered a name. "Blumenfeld."

Another instrument took the melody from the oboe, and Messer-Eichen, wafer still melting on the tongue, added the words, "Very good."

∽

They were suddenly alone. He remained at the keyboard end of the piano; Petra sat on the sofa.

"It was a good concert. The wind section ..."

"Thank you."

He glanced at the piano keys, the extra fifth at the bottom—it was a Bösendorfer.

"So, who is Blumenfeld?" he asked, grasping for a topic.

"They say perhaps the best oboist in the century."

"Who is 'they'?"

"People who heard him," she said.

"What happened to him?"

"He stayed too long."

"He was Jewish?"

She seemed impatient with the topic. "One of Furtwängler's Jews."

Barrow waited. "Furtwängler's Jews?"

"Hitler liked Furtwängler. He was conducting the Berlin Philharmonic which was also Hitler's favorite, so Goebbels allowed Furtwängler to keep a few Jews in the orchestra. Even after the Gestapo had removed them from everywhere else. The Jews."

"Yes."

How poorly the term flowed in German. *Die Juden.* Perhaps it could never flow again, a wrong-shaped stone in the brook. Enharmonic.

"Ziegler must also have had some privilege," he said.

"How is that?"

"To have had Erich Blumenfeld in his orchestra."

"Perhaps," she said, adding—clearly wishing to close out the topic—"It was not his orchestra, of course."

She turned, at last, to face him. A twist of still-damp hair had come loose to graze her temple.

"Good to see you," she said, and his heart sank—her deliberate air of casualness.

Pat appeared. "Phone's all yours," she said, and Petra disappeared down the hallway before he could catch her eye, communicate something, anything.

Pat picked up a tray of empty wine glasses from the piano bench and handed it to him—it was a finger to the lips. "Come," she said. She was so in command of her surroundings. A breeze off Lake Ontario, she floated across to where he was, to where he merely existed, blistered and confused, untethered by alcohol.

"He can do a lot for you," she said, backing through the double-hinged door to the kitchen.

"Who?"

"Werner, for godsake."

"He's never seen me conduct."

"So what."

"No one's seen me conduct."

"So what, he likes you."

"Who?"

"Werner. Didn't you hear me?"

"I'm flattered."

"He's stingy with comments like that. He's not a generous man. He may appear generous, but he's not. He likes you." She began tucking the leftover carrots into a drawer in the refrigerator.

He felt his forehead flush. "Why should he?" he finally asked, and it was the wrong way to phrase it. The words came out, he feared, like an appeal for more of the same complimentary stuff.

She took the tray of glasses out of his hands, set it down on the marble countertop. "You owe the world a great fucking debt, Coop." She was making no sense at all. "You are in debt up to your cheekbones, and I mean if you don't spend your life making payments, making *mortgage* payments to God or nature or *someone*, I will personally…" She jerked open the dishwasher and started putting wine glasses into a rack that already rattled with at least a week's worth. She had said nothing to him all night, and now she seemed to be in some sort of low-level rage.

He leaned against the counter behind him.

"Do you know why you owe so much?" she said. "Because you are so fucking dripping with talent."

He knew the words; he'd once heard them a lot. They made him want to cower, drop to his belly, and crawl. Submit to such sentiments and you're fucked—that was the obvious formula. Not that he didn't want to submit.

"Thank you."

"It's an observation, not a compliment. So where the fuck have you been?"

"I was at Juilliard. A little over a year."

"And?" She adjusted a sleeve further up her left arm to match the right one, letting the question hang somewhere in the close air between them, skinned and raw. "What about the other eight years?"

This was the path to avoid. "I've been doing some teaching. That's about it."

"Teaching what?"

"Violin. Up in Fishkill."

"Fishkill?"

"It's on the Hudson."

"I know where Fishkill is," she said. "It's beautiful up there. Hudson Highlands." It sounded like a concession, but it was really just another wind-up. "Tell me you've been practicing."

There was nothing to say.

"You piece of shit."

"What?"

"You're not practicing?"

"I'm not a violinist."

"Why. Because you can't triple-stop sixteenths standing on your head?"

"I wasn't going to be good enough."

"Bullshit."

"You're telling me I should go back to violin?" he asked.

"God, no. You're gonna be a famous conductor."

He badly wanted out, but the geography of the kitchen had him pinned to the corner.

"I watched Marty reel you in like one of his fucking speckled trout. I watched him tickle that goddamn male *thing*, whatever it is. One little well-placed 'Have you ever thought about con-duc-ting?' It's a tickle isn't it? It's so easily excited. You remember when he asked you that? You do, don't you." He did—third week of Marty Weissberger's Schenkerian analysis class, spring of his first year at Eastman, Weissberger's office on the third floor. "And tonight. Everyone's going on about, you know— *Werner's* going on and on—about Karlheinz Ziegler this and that, about his missed chance, all his missed chances, and it's all really about penises, isn't it?"—she was definitely drunk—"Like Ziegler is less of a man, you know, less of a mensch. He just didn't have enough dick for the really big fuck. And I see you back in Rochester, teetering on the edge. I mean, I'm sorry you're not concertmaster in your freshman year, you're not one of the stars. Deep water takes longer to boil, think about it."

"Okay."

"I mean, *we* saw it, Martin saw it, what's-his-name from the Emerson saw it. Your teacher obviously didn't, that asshole you were studying with, what was his name?"

"Souter—"

"Souter did *not* see, but Marty sees it in you and he's like, 'I'm gonna *catch* this one,' because that's part of his game, part of his fuck. And, of course, Werner. Tonight. He sees it."

"Sees—?"

"He puts together what he sees with the fact that you're down there in Karlsruhe with the Great Houdini, and he gets excited as all hell, because everyone loves watching this whole, ya know, *cloning* process."

"What cloning?"

"*Cloning* cloning. One of those mirrors where you see a hundred copies of yourself." She pushed back the hair from her face with the heels of her hands. "I've known more than a couple of them, definitely more than a couple conductors, because the fact is I'm very attracted to them, and deep down, you know, they're assholes. Conductors. Werner included. Which is why again I'm saying—why it makes me so *fucking* mad—this crying 'Shame, shame' over Karlheinz Ziegler, you know, and at the same time building him up into this sort of god."

She lowered her voice.

"And, you know, also, I'm pretty drunk."

She blushed under her white cotton sweater. A thin veneer of sweat coated her collar bone. She grabbed a bottle of mineral water from the refrigerator and crossed to the cupboard over Barrow's shoulder. She took down a couple of tumblers. "Do you want some?"

He hadn't moved, and she was standing with her left shoulder to his right so that for the second time that evening he could smell her hair, only this time it carried a heavy aspect of alcohol.

She filled two glasses with the sparkling water.

"So you gonna tell me what happened?"

"What do you mean?"

"You know what I mean."

She'd come back to it.

"It's complicated," he said.

"You wish." She was right. It was simple. "I was there, you know," she said.

"Where?"

"Saratoga."

He held the glass of mineral water in both hands, his thumb massaging the cold rim.

"You saw ..."

"I'm gonna miss it? Your name was all over the Festival. I mean both before *and* after that night." She'd meant it to be funny and he cracked a smile. "I was on one of the chamber music programs, I don't suppose you caught that."

"I didn't, I'm sorry."

"That was it, wasn't it?"

He hesitated. His night of infamy, summer of '81. Philadelphia Orchestra, Cooper Barrow on the podium.

"Hey, raise your goddamn glass," Pat said, "it's dead and buried." She clinked his glass. "To the good guys," and after they had both taken a drink she lifted herself on her toes and kissed him on the mouth with chilled lips.

She pulled back and spoke over his shoulder, *"Mineralwasser?"*

Barrow turned.

Petra's face betrayed nothing and he wondered how long she'd been standing outside the door, how long Pat had known she was there.

"Come in, come in."

"I am here just saying good-bye, and thank you for ..." she hesitated, and through that gate, that hesitation, flowed an almost excruciating vulnerability that, even now, Barrow knew to suspect. "For this." With her free hand she indicated her now dry hair, and something else as well; perhaps some dry clothes, some underthings that had been lent.

15 Relations with Ziegler improved noticeably over the next week. He added private sessions, and those he added went long by hours. There was never a mention of Barrow's rude Friday night raid. Barrow did not fail to note the coincidence between this bloom-time with Ziegler and his failure with Petra.

At the end of the fourth of these sessions, the old man stopped him on his way out the door. "Enough scores," he said. "Meet me at the garage around the corner on Sophienstrasse, tomorrow, eight a.m."

At the appointed hour, Ziegler showed up in driving gloves and a sheepskin coat, and they ducked into the garage. Ziegler nodded to an attendant and walked straight for a late-model BMW parked close to the entrance.

They were on the street before Barrow could latch his belt. Within a few turns they had joined heavy traffic on the autobahn, where Ziegler pulled into the far left lane and ran the needle up to 175 kilometers an hour, settling into a string of five or six pairs of taillights. Barrow eased into the cracked leather seat, enjoying the car's unique tonality, its busy engine barely audible at cruising speed.

"You have no radio?"

"It is dangerous for me to listen," Ziegler said, two fingers resting lightly on the gear shift. "I might as well be drinking gin from a bottle."

There was a sudden accordioning of lights up front. Their speed dropped by a third, and Barrow's heart leapt, though Ziegler's response had been faultless.

"I do not have a stereo in my car for the same reason I do not listen to Bach and to Brahms at the same time."

Inspired by the apparent lack of formality, Barrow hazarded a topic that had been on his mind all week.

"I heard your recording of Brahms One. The 1937."

"Did you?"

"At Werner Schott's apartment."

"Schott." The syllable betrayed no opinion, while carrying a ream of knowledge. "And what did you think?"

It was an astounding question.

"You are afraid to speak?"

"It was strong. It was very harsh, as if the microphones were too close."

"In the first violins."

"Yes," Barrow said. "But it was strong. I have never heard it so violent."

"What is 'violent'? This is a not a musical term."

"*Stringendo*. Almost *marcato*. Not *'espressivo e legato'*—"

"As is written."

"As is written."

"At that time I played Brahms like Beethoven." The old man was too gentle with himself—God forbid one of his students should conduct the opening as he had on the recording. "And the second movement, how did you find the second movement?"

"Beautiful," Barrow said.

"Another useful term."

"Slower than I'm used to. A lot of *rubato*."

"A lot of bad *rubato*."

"But still, beautiful. Schott admired it."

Ziegler had no further comment.

They exited the autobahn for a charmless neighborhood of ware-houses and light industry, and Ziegler pulled into a muddy lot next to a long white stucco wall. He reached a long arm behind the passenger seat, retrieved a wobbly fistful of black rubber that turned into a pair of galoshes, and tossed them to the deck at Barrow's feet. Reaching back, he pulled out a pair of black leather boots for himself.

Barrow managed to yank one of the rubbers on over his sneaker.

"For all your movies," Ziegler said, "I have never met an American who has ridden a horse."

"*Bitte?*"

"Have you ridden?"

"A horse?"

"Yes," Ziegler said, suppressing a smile.

"Sure."

He'd ridden once, at arts camp in Michigan. He was eight. He and his cabin-mates were hoisted one by one into the saddle and led around a corral on a rope—he didn't even get to steer.

Their car doors slammed as a pair of low-flying fighter jets shattered the atmosphere directly overhead. Both men stopped to watch.

"French Mirages," Ziegler said. "Reminds us whose *Besatzungzone* this is."

"Pardon?"

"'Zone of occupation,' I think you say."

They trudged through the mud along an alley of empty horse stalls—swaybacked roofs, pancakes of plaster missing from the stucco. The alley led onto a railed-off track, two or three football fields in size. Low buildings rimmed the oval. A couple of riders in black dome hats bounced along in slow motion at the far end; beyond them, more dirty stucco, and the dark hillsides of the Black Forest.

Closer at hand, two horses, attended by a young woman in calf-high boots, stood at the center of a small paddock. They grew too quickly on approach, defying perspective. One was gray and mottled-white. The other was brown and seemed sprung straight from the mud, the woman's head coming only to its nose.

"Ruthi will show you some boots."

There was a tack room at the far end of the paddock, where sky trickled through a couple of filthy windows. The woman nodded to a rack of shelves crammed with creased-leather riding boots, uppers folded uniformly to the left, smelling thickly of a much earlier time. Barrow felt disoriented. He glanced back—Ruthi stood sentry in the doorway, a mere silhouette.

Downing boots at random, he found a pair that slipped on over his jeans without too much complaint. The stiff leather met his kneecap, hugged the calf tightly, making everything below the knee as of one piece. He leaned into the balls of his feet and felt an unmistakable up-tick in excitement. His calves seemed to crave their leather shell. The sensation was new and he savored it. A whiff of power and the permission to use it.

Walking back to the paddock Ruthi spoke for the first time. "Max is very strong-willed. Very lively."

"Max?"

"Der Braune," Ruthi said under her breath. "The brown one. You should have experience." She glanced up at him with gray eyes.

Ziegler held the reins of both animals, inspecting something in the mouth of the Arabian.

"He seems large," Barrow said.

"The maestro likes them that way."

Ziegler called out, sounding a lot like a car salesman. "Are they comfortable?"

"Yes."

Barrow noted the dainty lines of the two saddles—less contour than a pair of bicycle seats. In Michigan, there'd been a giant pommel on the front of the saddle, around which he'd wrapped his eight-year-old hands. The stable hands had laughed. "Where you from, kid?" "Chagrin Falls." "Where's that?" "Ohio." "Where?" "Ohio."

Max, Der Braune, complained audibly from the depths of her impressive neck. Barrow looked hopefully at the Arabian, who stood quiet and elegant as a statue in a park. "She is beautiful."

"There is another Arabian," Ziegler said, "but she is stabled outside Luzern. We do not bring her over the mountains. Too old."

Now was absolutely the time to confess that he had never ridden, not once, ever. That he had no idea what he was doing. But he hesitated—he'd never seen such exuberance from the old man—and it was too late.

"Max has wonderful energy for a young man like you."

Radiant, he handed Barrow the reins of Der Braune, who pulled up so sharply that he knocked himself in the chin with his own fist.

With the back of his free hand, Barrow wiped the sweat that had begun to sheet his forehead. "I have never ridden this kind of saddle."

"You are used to Western. This is better. More horse under you."

Max began moving sideways, her hooves beating an irregular pattern in the mud. Ruthi had been lowering the stirrups. She came forward, took the reins, and reached up to touch the mare's cheek with the back of her hand, quieting the horse.

Ruthi caught Barrow's eye. There was sympathy there—she saw everything.

Ziegler too—not a man to be surprised by events—must see everything, must know that a kid from the Cleveland suburbs, a musical kid, would know nothing of horses.

Max groaned from somewhere astonishingly deep in her neck. Her flesh snapped back under Barrow's fingertips, and he stayed in close, his heart beating faster than he could calculate. He raised both hands to the front lip of the saddle. The stirrup danced as Max began her side-to-side stamp, and Barrow brought down his right hand to steady the strap. He slid his left boot into the stirrup, flew his left hand back up to the front rim of the saddle, and pushed off with his right foot; he pulled hard, threw his right leg over—like he'd seen countless times in the movies— and felt the saddle arrive under his groin, foreign but welcome.

But the horse was already moving. He tried slotting the right stirrup, but it was too damn low. Ruthi was running alongside, holding up the reins, but he had both hands on the pommel. He seemed to need them there. She was yelling, "Please take these!"

Max was moving beneath him, her up-and-down motion uneven and severe. He grabbed the straps with his right hand and by some reflex pulled back. But they were too long and there was no tension, no contact with the bit. They were out on the track, and he spotted the two helmeted riders bearing down on them. He dove for Max's neck as she spun out of the way and charged down the track. He had no proper hold on the reins as she kept on and on, in close by the rail, where he fixed on the source of her terror—not the riders, but another pair of Mirage fighters.

The roar became a scream as the jets split the sky in two equal parts, and he felt the entire earth lunge up into his chest through the animal beneath, his full-body grip shot to hell. All he saw was sky between the flat-back ears, then the ground, everything, falling and his chest slamming into the sharp molded leather of the saddle, which had somehow slid out from between his legs, and there was an explosion of muscle and the animal bolted out from under and his head bounced along her huge, rock-hard flank and briefly he was in midair where the mud flew up to meet him.

∞

He lay sprawled on his stomach, his left cheek to the track. One arm was stretched out in front, the other trapped under his torso, wrist pinned to the dirt. The roar from the two jets grumbled and died in the clouds while he considered the possibility of moving.

A figure knelt beside him—Ruthi. She was saying something. He rolled to his side and felt a sharp crease of pain across his upper chest where the saddle had hit. He could not see out of his left eye—a heaviness above the lid.

"I'm okay," he said and got to his knees.

"You should not move," Ruthi said as Ziegler rode up on the Arabian, leading Der Braune—Max the Victorious—who tossed her head, happy, like she'd just awoken from a bad dream.

"He is okay," Ziegler said, his voice contending with the ringing in Barrow's ears. "No one is hurt in this mud."

Ruthi was smiling. They both seemed far off, viewed through the one good eye.

"So, perhaps, a suggestion or two," Ziegler said. "But first, there is the tap." He pointed to a cast-cement trough along one side of the paddock, its tap screwed to the end of a green copper pipe.

Barrow got to his feet and walked, testing his joints along the way. He brought a hand to his face and discovered the source of his blindness—a shell of mud on the left side of his skull. Part of it fell off in his hand. He plunged his head into the icy water and his skull screeched from every constricted capillary. Ruthi was waiting with a towel that smelled powerfully of horse flesh. He pulled back the collar of his sweater to catch the water before it soaked his stomach and back, watched the mud from his face cloud up the trough. He handed Ruthi the towel, thanked her, and turned to face the center of the paddock.

"Do not move," Ziegler said.

Barrow nodded. He hadn't planned on it.

"Consider first the excellence of this horse—you are listening?"

"Of course," Barrow said. The wind stung his face and neck.

"She is called in North America a quarter horse because she runs the quarter mile faster than any other breed. You see that post"—and Ziegler pointed to a bright orange marker almost directly across the track—"that is her distance. Aaron here is half her age. He has never beat her to that post. Also, consider that while she has only six years, her breed is several hundred years old. Understand this when you compare your ages, yours and hers. She has carried dozens of riders in her life. Her breed has carried hundreds of thousands."

Max stood untethered but attentive, as if herself absorbed in the old man's discourse.

"Are you impressed?"

"Yes."

Ziegler paused, his tall frame in the sheepskin coat, stark against the broad white sky.

"Never be."

Barrow stared at the old man. Just as he thought—another lesson. With Ziegler, no wasted effort.

"And if you are impressed, do not show it. Ever. If you are impressed a second time, quit. This time forever."

Barrow caught the not-so-veiled reference to his own past. He looked down at his feet. His mud-caked jeans. "She's the orchestra," he muttered.

"Speak louder."

"Max. She's meant to be an orchestra."

Ziegler looked away, let a few seconds go by.

The Arabian flicked his tail.

"It is in the first step that you make the relationship."

There were players who insisted they knew whether you could conduct simply by watching your approach to the podium.

Barrow leaned into his riding boots, gave in to their support. Der Braune's eyes registered his movement. She stamped to the side, but otherwise held her ground.

"When you arrive you will take the reins"—the old man's tone was the consistency of warm milk—"and toss them over, so when you reach for the saddle you also pick up the reins, and when you arrive in the saddle they are in your hand. This you will do in one motion, then you pull the reins back so you feel the bit, and when there is some behavior in her, any behavior, pull the bit to the teeth, *now*, not later."

Barrow arrived at Max's nose. He touched her reins, which just grazed the mud, and the mare shifted her hooves. We're both hypnotized, Barrow thought. He grabbed the straps, perhaps a shade too abruptly, and Max jerked her head back, but stayed her ground. He drew the reins over the ears, conscious that his reflexes had been subverted by the old man's voice, that he was going up again, over the side.

"All in one motion," Ziegler said.

By some miracle Barrow's toe found the stirrup, higher than he remembered—hip high—and his hands found the reins and the curved pommel. He pulled with both arms, willed his right leg up over the mare's back. His chest was screaming, but he arrived in the saddle. Max had stepped off already, whinnying, and Barrow cinched his grip far up on the reins. The enormous head flew back in apparent disbelief. He'd arrested the mare's forward motion, leaving her hooves to pound the mud two meters below. He clamped her ribs between his legs and they flexed back.

∽

For an hour the old man maintained a steady patter of instruction, *mezzo piano*, correcting posture, explicating the horse's mind—her gullibility and her powerful instinct, and how to exploit them both. He demonstrated how to sit for the trot, the canter, and the gallop, sprinkling his explanations with Italian musical expressions, *allegro vivace, marcato*.

He set up a race for the orange post. Well before the agreed-upon "go" mark, he leaned forward and yelled something fierce, and Aaron broke into a dead run, leaving Barrow and Max ten paces back.

"Come on," Barrow said. "Come on!" and he banged his heels hard into Max's belly.

Max caught Aaron by the start of the turn, stayed abreast on the outside, and shot past at the straightaway. The orange post was just another pole for Max—she remained at full gallop with Barrow helpless to stop her. "You're a fucking quarter horse," he yelled, "slow down," and she did. Bereft of spirit, she pulled up into a hard lope and a walk, before coming to an abrupt stop just before the second turn.

Barrow hoisted his right leg across Max's rear, which gave off moisture like a sponge. He lowered himself to the track and waddled to the front of the horse. The air eddied fast and hot around her nostrils, and he applied the back of his hand to her cheek just below the eye, as he had seen Ruthi do earlier. "Good girl," he said, and, as an afterthought—though it seemed a poor translation—"*Gutes Mädchen.*"

Ziegler rode up and dismounted, his face flush from the ride. He removed a glove and skidded his bare hand along Max's shoulder-high rump, clearing a path through her sweat. They stood on the track, horses and riders alike, breathing heavily, nothing to mark the decade. It could be 1935.

Ziegler breathed heavily, cheeks red and eyes watery, lost and distant.

"Did you know Furtwängler?" Barrow asked.

"Sorry?"

"Furtwängler. Did you know him?"

"Why do you ask?"

"I once saw a picture of him riding."

Ziegler dried his hand on his coat and put his glove on. "Many people rode."

"So did you know him?" It wasn't an illogical question. The great conductor was living in Berlin at the time of Ziegler's Berlin Rundfunk recording.

"Of course."

"I was just curious if you ever rode together. Like you must ride here with your students."

Ziegler glanced at Barrow, crossed to the Arabian, and placed his left hand on the pommel. "I have never brought a student here."

✍

Barrow glimpsed the palace, the pale yellow Schloss that marked the center of downtown Karlsruhe. His heart pounded in anticipation of the question he was about to ask.

"I have wanted to know..."

"Yes?"

"I have wanted to know what you did for the war."

Ziegler didn't flinch. "I was detained."

Festgehalten.

The word rang in Barrow's ears.

Festgehalten.

On such a word turned a man's entire identity.

"I was detained like the rest, is this not what you understand? This is how it has always been given out."

Given out? By whom. *To* whom. No one Barrow knew had ever received it, if this is how it was "given out."

"Detained how?" Barrow asked, but the old man merely shrugged, whipping his prize coupe onto the exit ramp before shifting down to the politic streets of Karlsruhe.

16 The following night, Barrow left his attic at precisely seven and strode the tight lanes of center-village Ettlingen, past schnitzel joints and swinging Pilsener signs, recalling brisk Ohio evenings—his father still at work, his mother enclosed in a paperback—when Beethoven or some first-heard Prokofiev symphony propelled him into the deaf suburban streets, how he would smash his rubber-nosed sneaker into the curb, high on undifferentiated desire too vast for his violin's skinny finger board and too rough to settle for anonymity.

His want was back.

He crossed the grassy park by the station just as the tram arrived. He took a side bench in the back car and lost himself in the stream of light and rail, the endless reflections from the street thrown back and forth between black panes of glass.

By seven-thirty he stood inside the doors of the Konzerthaus lobby. He lingered by the concession line, eavesdropping.

An older man caught his eye—a handsome square face, smallish eyes matching a light gray suit, hair shock-white, skin recently tanned. He seemed to be associated with two women, both trim and attractive in matching charcoal jackets, forest-green crewelwork along the edges. One of the women spoke of a cousin who lived on the far side of the Wall. "We have sent a package—food and clothes—first Monday of every month, for twenty-six years," she said. From two meters, Barrow could see that she had a tear in each eye, just a shimmer, thickening the cornea. The man lifted two small bottles of mineral water from the concession counter, and the three dissolved into the crowd. There had been a vague resemblance to Barrow's father—perhaps in the way he stood off from the women.

He heard Antonio's voice in his ear. "An accident with the tram. Bizarre. I have never seen it. Expensive car punches right into it."

"We ran here from Kaiserstrasse," said Berndt, clearly out of breath.

Barrow pulled the envelope from his pocket.

The Italian continued, "Terrifying, something such as that, in a place where everything works so goddamn perfect." He spotted the tickets and snatched them from Barrow's hand. "Let's hope these are out on the first violin side. I want to see the old man's profile. At least some of it."

Barrow smiled, vaguely irritated. "Forward balcony. On the left."

"Excellent."

Their seats were high along the left wall of the Konzerthaus, at right angles to the stage.

Antonio hadn't stopped talking. "Karlsruhe loves him. And they forget him because he only plays one, maybe two concerts here, one or two in Belgium. I have never seen a review in the paper—why bother? One concert. So there is a silence around him. 'Imposed'—I think is the correct American word."

"'News blackout,'" said Berndt.

"Does anyone know how he is?" Barrow asked.

"He's fine," Antonio said.

Ziegler had not looked well in rehearsal that morning, spending the bulk of the session working the soprano into the Mozart songs, knocking off early without touching the Brahms. He'd had to steady himself several times by gripping the back rail with his left hand, conducting with his right. "He is opening his left side to Frau Martin," Antonio had said. "For contact. He does this with pianists as well." Barrow had been skeptical, but the Italian shrugged off the symptoms. "You have never seen him in performance. Only wait."

The players had begun warming up on stage.

Barrow spotted the man in the gray suit, his snowy head. Distinguishing mark of the male.

"He was detained before the war," he said.

The others stared at him.

"Who?" Berndt asked.

"Ziegler."

"How do you know this?"

"He said so. The other day. In a lesson." The horse business—that he would keep to himself.

"My God."

"Ziegler said he was detained?" Antonio asked.

Barrow might as well have announced the Second Coming. "He also said that it was common knowledge. That that was how it was 'given out.'"

"'Given out'?"

"Reported."

"I have never heard this," Berndt said.

"Perhaps early on," Antonio said. "Perhaps in the nineteen-sixties this was so-called 'given out.'"

"I guess people forget," Barrow said.

"Nothing is forgotten, only not spoken of," said Antonio. "So continue—detained for what reason? He is not Jewish."

"I assume in a concentration camp," Barrow said.

"They were all concentration camps."

"Jewish. Gypsy. Homosexual." Berndt ticked off the list on his fingers. "A couple of, I don't know, American religions. Communist."

Barrow's eyes drifted left to take in the fledgling orchestra, Ziegler's brood, backs straight. He felt a wave of affection, wondered if Ziegler ever felt it.

"Not Jewish," Berndt said, "certainly not Gypsy."

Barrow regretted speaking—he'd planned to keep the information to himself.

"Homosexual," Berndt said. "No?"

"Perhaps, but this would hardly fit with the reputation."

"What reputation?"

"You do not notice?"

"Oh chrissakes," Berndt said, awkwardly copping the American expletive.

"There is occasionally someone"—again, the pleasure the Italian took, second-year man among first-years—"usually short-term. But some young woman."

The house lights dimmed, and with that a smattering of applause for Tano's entrance. Petra's tuning note glided out from center stage—she was playing first oboe in the opening piece.

"For example this Korean girl," Antonio said.

"What Korean girl?"

"You have not seen?"

"*Scheisse*," Berndt said under his breath.

Applause tore down from the chandeliers.

Ziegler had emerged from the wings. He moved at no particular clip, his thin white hair blazing under the harsh light. His authority doubled with every footfall, gathering the attention of the hall. By the time he reached the podium, he was captain of the cavalry, life or death. *Few will survive, few will leave the field.*

He lifted his arms—the slightest of gestures, but it emitted heat. The fingers of his left hand were bent into a partial fist. He allowed the passage of a split second, his head lowered—and suddenly, stunningly, Mozart. The startling announcement of *Così fan tutte.*

In a concession to fairness, Petra had been asked to play principal oboe for the overture. In a brief arpeggiation, a single broken chord, she caught up Barrow's heart—there was no other way to put it. Seconds later, a quick, delicate figure, and she threaded it perfectly, mocking her demotion to second desk on the Brahms.

She traded seats for the set of Mozart songs that came next. The singer, an aging opera diva, had been saving her voice in rehearsal that morning; but it was all here, burnished and wise, fine casting by Ziegler. The students surpassed themselves, and Barrow found himself drifting into sheer enjoyment.

He was completely unprepared for the emergency.

He saw it first in the audience, a collective flinch in the first few rows. Nothing discourteous. His eyes shot to the podium where Ziegler's left hand clung to the security rail, knees bent. Tano, playing concertmaster, reached forward with his bow arm. Ziegler's hand left the rail, his legs strong again, and Tano withdrew his arm. The soprano, professionally oblivious, sang to the end of her *Alleluja*.

But Ziegler failed to appear for a single curtain call. The soprano took her bows alone, and she was still on stage when the three student conductors bolted for the mezzanine corridor, rushing for the backstage door.

The orchestra manager saw them and yelled from thirty meters, "Antonio!" Her voice carried well, sprung by the marble floor. "He wants you!" She was out of breath and her hair had come loose—her shining moment. Antonio threw Barrow and Berndt a glance and dashed off.

Barrow froze, his brain jammed, audience pouring into the hall.

"What do you think?" Berndt asked.

The way to the stage door was choked with bodies. He saw an opening through the main lobby and took it, thinking to circle the building and get in through the rear stage door. He rounded the front end and sprinted the full length of the Konzerthaus, losing Berndt in the process. A few meters shy of the loading dock, he pulled up, *Why Antonio?* ringing in his ears.

A car idled in the driveway that butted the loading dock, its parking lights on. It was a cab. The stage door swung open and a tall figure stepped out, street-length coat unbuttoned, a familiar silhouette. The old man hesitated under the spill of light outside the door, searched the deep pockets of his coat. The lamp above him hummed defectively. For these few expensive seconds they were alone.

"Maestro," Barrow yelled. His voice felt strong and frank; perhaps even American, if that meant anything. But if Ziegler heard—and he must have—he failed to show it; he found his gloves and pulled them on. The door opened again, and he was joined by a man in shirt sleeves, probably the stage manager. The cab's headlights knocked up and Barrow lost sight of his teacher's face.

"Maestro," he yelled, standing in the stream of the cab's headlights. "It's Cooper Barrow."

Others appeared at the entrance, and Ziegler parted from the group, scarcely looking up. He made the curb in three strides. The rear door of the taxi opened from the inside and someone in the back seat scooted across—a woman with dark hair. Ziegler dropped in next to her and shut the door. The cab, already in gear, gunned past Barrow, swerving to avoid him.

17 After Antonio's third curtain call, he gestured for silence and informed the audience—in accented German, molten with charm—that Karlheinz Ziegler was at home resting, that his doctors had already visited, and that there was no cause for alarm. Up went a huge, triple-size ovation. The hall emptied on a tide of good will.

Outside Ziegler's dressing room, Antonio shrugged. "The old man knows I conducted the Second once before. In Bologna, at university." His elegance in victory wanted for nothing. He insisted that Barrow and Berndt join him at a nearby *Kneipe*, where the three traditionally met to dissect the performances of visiting artists. Barrow, brain-numb, agreed. Berndt put forward his wife-and-baby excuse to which Antonio responded, "This concert should be different from any other?" When Tano, acting the good soldier, stopped by to shake Antonio's hand, the Italian invited him along as well.

Barrow left the group temporarily, searching for a safe path to some kind of post-rout dignity. His jealousy was unseemly—as a second-year student, Antonio was certainly entitled to the nod from Ziegler. But somehow that didn't matter.

He wandered back into the wings. The stage rattled with the stacking of chairs, musicians packing up. The Fulbright percussionist walked by and flashed Barrow a two-finger salute.

He noticed Alexandra chatting with Petra in the corridor, making plans. They had changed into their jeans. Petra saw him and held his glance for several seconds, enough to touch off a squall in his chest. Alexandra looked over her shoulder, spotted him too. They pressed cheeks and Alexandra started off in another direction, her coat slung over the front of her viola case.

Barrow's hands were jammed in his pants pockets, jacket swept back. He called out, "Good concert."

"You think?" She was still five meters away, a swirl of activity between them. Her face was one familiar detail after another. They both took a couple of steps forward.

On almost no breath, he asked, "What are you doing?"

"Nothing."

"We're going to find a *Kneipe*." She waited. "Will you come?"

"Okay."

"I'm just—" and he indicated the toilet.

She nodded.

✍

Antonio's entourage crossed Ettlinger Strasse and paired off for the sidewalk.

Barrow fell in next to Petra. They listened to Antonio up ahead, regaling his girlfriend with "the moment before," the shock of hearing his name echo down the corridor, the ridiculous panic over retrieving his tuxedo, the brief nod from Ziegler.

Petra spoke first. "Perhaps you understand a little."

Her cheekbones shone faintly in the blue lamplight. A black scarf hid her hair—no American girl would wear a scarf that way.

He knew what she had meant. *You see what it's like to be passed over by Ziegler?*

An unbroken chain of headlights exited the parking garage of the Badisches Staatstheater.

Petra jabbed him in the ribs with her mittened fingers. "What's wrong with you," she said. He stiffened and jerked away, directly into the path of a cyclist, humped against the cold night. With a nasal hiss of brakes, the cyclist swerved hard—an impossible angle between tire and pavement—and leaned into his pedals, spitting out a curse over his shoulder.

Someone—Antonio—yelled back, *Scheisskopf!* The others stopped to see if Barrow was okay. He was, and they continued their slow march. His hands had never left his pockets, but he felt the sweat on his forehead.

"You are so goddamn serious," Petra said in English.

She was right. He was in danger of shutting down. It was all he could do to cope with his jealousy of Antonio.

"Hello?" she said.

He granted her a glance. She had grabbed up her oboe case and was hugging it to her chest while they walked. Her scarf had migrated back from her forehead, and loose strands of hair blew back over it. They had fallen well behind the others.

"I was joking," she said. "You are passed over for Antonio. I was passed over for Magda. 'Perhaps you understand a little.' I am trying to be funny."

"Okay."

"Okay?"

"I'm an idiot," he said, watching himself back down. "I'm completely inept"—all because of her, some mysterious perfection—"I'm totally socially idiotic."

"You expect that I am without sarcasm?"

"No."

"As is said everywhere about us Germans." She pulled the scarf down around her neck, unveiling the loveliness of her face. "I know what sarcasm is."

"You've practiced," he said in a weak attempt at recovery.

She made a little noise of appreciation. When he looked, her lips were pressed together. She was suppressing a smile.

They stopped outside the *Kneipe* and she rested her chin on her oboe case, eyebrows raised. Their last encounter, in Pat Levy's kitchen, had seemed so final, but here she was—flirting perhaps, he could never tell—waiting for a signal from him.

Faces flickered behind the amber-pebbled windows of the bar. Corny, rough-hewn logs framed the door.

"Let's go to Berlin," he said.

She looked at him. Nothing showed, no surprise. With an angling of her head, she gestured for them to go inside.

∽

The entourage arranged itself like a sextet at rehearsal, coats flung wide, violin cases stuffed under the table. Petra's oboe took up a seventh chair.

Antonio knew how to command a party. He kept their mugs filled and parried their jealousy—Barrow and Berndt's. Toward the end of their first round of drinks, the conversation veered dangerously close to a consideration of his performance. Breaking the lull that followed Antonio proclaimed, "This is why God made beer." They laughed. He poured another round.

"What of this geisha of Ziegler's?" Berndt asked in the aftermath.

No one spoke, until a soft voice answered, "Her name is Marie Won. She is Korean."

It was Erika, Antonio's girlfriend, a small woman with pretty, dark features who'd not spoken since their arrival. She was a music school student who sat third or fourth stand in the second violin section.

"She was his student since ... three years, before you have come, Antonio." Clearly unhappy with English, she took another bird-sip, her mug just clearing the table.

"What have I told you, gentlemen?" Antonio said, raising his glass. "We have competition from abroad."

"She teaches," Petra said in German, presumably for Erika's sake. "At the conservatory in Seoul."

"You know this?" asked Berndt.

"I met her briefly."

"When?" Barrow asked.

"At a party at Ziegler's apartment. A small group. Some foreigners he was having over. Tano was there." She glanced at the Romanian. "Last year?"

"Of course," Tano said, angling a stream of smoke away from the group.

"I did not know about this party," Antonio said.

Petra shrugged. "Perhaps Italy is not so 'abroad.'"

"As East Germany, for example?"

Barrow placed his wrists against the side of his beer mug to cool them. It was news to him that Petra had been to Ziegler's studio. And her use of Tano's name, Tano at the Bach concert, their look just now—what was that about?

"I saw her briefly," Barrow said. "She was visiting him. He had some kind of language book on his desk. Korean, I guess."

Antonio laughed. "What did I say? Ziegler is in love."

Berndt looked unhappy. "I don't get it, how many people have *studied* with this guy? Barrow. In America, how many people?"

"Some," Barrow said.

"How many?"

"Gilbert Shanahan. Others."

"How many others? Twenty? Thirty?"

"I don't know."

"Anybody famous?"

"Levine, perhaps."

"Really," said Berndt, awestruck. "Jimmy Levine."

"And Bernstein. I don't think he studied with him, but he used to talk about his sound. How much he loved his sound, especially his Brahms."

"Ziegler hates Bernstein," Antonio said.

"What 'sound'?" asked Tano, reentering the fray.

"Right, right," Berndt said, clearly loosened up by drink, "but how would Lenny even know? How would he *know* what Ziegler's sound is? Are there recordings? Who sees his concerts? What, as a matter of fact, are we doing here at all? Who is this man?" His voice flew out across the barroom. "Ziegler is nobody and he can do nothing for us. I don't even like him. Do you like him? I, personally, do not like him."

"There is nothing essential about likability," Antonio said.

Berndt, glancing around the *Kneipe*, lowered his voice. "Naturally, it is goddamn unbelievable what he does with the orchestra. And even tonight, before he got sick. The Mozart."

"What sound?" Tano demanded.

Berndt shrugged. "Ziegler's."

"His blending of all the elements," Barrow said.

"Sure," said Antonio. "How he balances the sections."

It was Tano's turn to show his drink. "That is shit—excuse me—a famous American conductor claims Ziegler has a sound. What does he mean by that? I hear this all the time, this 'sound' business." He interrupted himself to light another cigarette. "If Ziegler cares so much for sound, why does he change the oboes."

The others glanced at Petra.

"Can I just say it?" Tano continued. "The winds were far better before this new girl. Are we allowed to say it?"

"He's right," said Berndt.

An uneasy silence followed, broken by Erika. "Pardon, but mm ... ," She was taking another stab at English. "Do you remember, since a year, Herr Ziegler did this also with someone else?"

"Fritz Poelzig," said Tano.

"Yes. Poelzig."

Barrow had heard the name once or twice at the conservatory—a Hochschule graduate who went directly from Karlsruhe to the horn section of the Berlin Philharmonic.

"And so? What happened with Poelzig?" Berndt asked.

"He also was dropped from the orchestra," said Antonio. "I had forgotten. Second or third rehearsal."

"I have said, he is not a nice man," Berndt said. "He hates talent."

"Which explains how we got here," Antonio said, to a slight chuckle from the others.

"What was on the program?" asked Barrow.

"Brahms Four," Erika said.

Antonio launched into a vocal rendition of the opening horn solo in movement two of Brahms' Fourth Symphony, throwing in a couple of cracked high notes for effect.

Barrow played his half-filled mug against the candlelight. "Any other Brahms last year?"

"How much can we endure?" Tano said.

"And the year before?"

They looked at Erika, who had been around the Hochschule for several years. She seemed to inhabit their attention with growing ease. "No."

"So, I have something," Berndt said. "Perhaps this is an explanation, perhaps not. But there was small scandal in Bruxelles, which I myself witnessed. It was that year of, what—of the Brahms Four. It was 1987. Ziegler was in town as every year, conducting the symphony because he is liked by Wesendonck. This pianist from Scotland is playing Brahms' First Concerto. And you know how in the introduction the orchestra goes so long without the piano, you are getting accustomed to this sonority. So, Ziegler is conducting, and we listen. It is beautiful, and the piano enters, and bang, it is such clash I almost fall out of my seat. The whole audience, there is a kind of gasp. Unbelievable. So the pianist, he stops, right away, and Ziegler stops the orchestra. They whisper together. Ziegler says something funny to the orchestra and they make a little chuckle, and he escorts the Scotsman off the stage. All very smooth. After a minute a fellow in tuxedo comes out and says, so very sorry, but there will be a *pause* while the piano is inspected. And out comes the piano tuner herself."

"She retunes it?"

"No one leaves the audience—it's too fascinating to watch what will happen next. And here is the mystery. According to the piano tuner—who was almost fired—it was only a few key notes in the opening passage of the piano part. And, it ends up, only one string was off per note."

Antonio shrugged. "Someone got in there with a tuning wrench, twisted a few pegs. It would take thirty seconds."

"It was never found out, who did it. It is only with this conversation that I am thinking it might have been Ziegler."

No one spoke.

The possibility was outlandish, of course.

But the thought came to Barrow, *I knew this about Ziegler already*, this capacity to cripple. Not others, but himself. And somewhere in the soundless quarter of Barrow's mind, he felt the thrill of recognition. He had something in common with the old man.

Petra was saying something in his ear.

"Pardon?"

"A song by Cat Stevens. You have heard of him?"

A girl and boy with folk guitars had begun to sing in a far corner of the bar, some vaguely familiar tune.

"Sure."

"You are funny," Petra laughed. "I know these musicians. I'll be back."

Barrow watched her cross the room, turn herself sideways to squeeze past a table.

"Antonio says that you play the violin?"

It was Erika. She had switched back to German.

Barrow nodded. "How long have you played?"

"I cannot recall a time before the violin."

Antonio had gone off for another pitcher, leaving them alone at one end of the table. Tano and Berndt sparred in the background.

"Have you always lived here?" Barrow asked.

"My grandparents left just in time to survive the Third Reich. But my grandfather was a stubborn man. He wanted to speak German, so he came back."

"You're Jewish?"

She nodded, a flicker of a smile. "You and Antonio, it's the same thing. A German would wait two years before asking whether I was a Jew."

"I'm sorry."

"No, of course, it's only an observation."

"I guess I have to ask ... I'm curious ..."

"What's it like?"

He nodded.

"Being Jewish here—my brother says the Jews in Germany are like some second- or third-rate paintings by Rembrandt. Not so very pretty, but they must be preserved. When my grandfather came back to Stuttgart, everyone was asking the same question. Why? 'It is my country,' he said." She smiled, her shyness returning. "Insanity runs in the family."

"Your grandfather sounds amazing."

"I have told this to Antonio—perhaps you would find it interesting—that he remembered Ziegler from before the war."

"Your grandfather?"

"He used to go to Berlin for business. He published textbooks."

Berndt threw a question from across the table. "He saw Ziegler conduct?"

"Yes."

"What did he say?"

"That no one ever conducted Brahms like him. That though Ziegler was not even twenty, he seemed to know the music from somewhere else, some other life. That it was a thing so holy, people were afraid of him."

She held her mug like a teacup, took a sip.

"He was happy when I told him I was going to Karlsruhe. There's never been a musician in my family, which is unusual for German Jews. He was not well, Grandpa, but he came down to Karlsruhe for a concert, the one with Fritz Poelzig, Brahms' Fourth." She paused for moment, aware, perhaps, of the intensity of their interest. "Afterward, he was very disappointed. All he said—he shook his head—'This Karl-heinz Ziegler tonight, this was not the same man.'"

∽

They parted company outside the *Kneipe*. Berndt slumped off in the direction of the Festplatz, muttering about his infant baby. Antonio and Erika left in the opposite direction.

Tano was leaning a little forward of center, but otherwise held his own against what Barrow guessed to be three or four liters of beer. "Which way are you going?" the Romanian asked.

Barrow shrugged, glancing at Petra, who stood apart from them, close to the curb. He'd been trying to read her intentions since they left the table inside.

"I go up Ettlinger to the Zirkel," Tano said. "Shall we walk a little?"

"Sure."

Tano called to Petra, "Do we walk you home?"

But something had caught her attention: a gang of five or six skin-heads progressing along the opposite sidewalk, under the zoo wall. The boy in the lead walked backwards while maintaining a muted banter with the others, fists jammed into the upper pockets of a flimsy-looking jeans jacket that was defiantly unbuttoned against the subfreezing night. His elbows punched the air.

"It is a duck," Petra said under her breath. "*Creck, creck.*"

When the pack reached the end of the second block—their leader's high voice still ricocheting between buildings—Tano, Barrow, and Petra followed, keeping to the opposite side of the boulevard.

Barrow spoke first, discontent with the silence that seemed to have closed in on the three of them. "Strings sounded good tonight," he said.

Tano responded predictably with a disapproving grunt.

Barrow tried again. "When you came to West Germany, you could have gone anywhere, no?"

"How do you mean?" Tano asked.

"To any music school."

"Possible."

"Why Karlsruhe? Why not Köln, perhaps?"

"I have never accustomed myself to the Western notion of choice."

Petra had stopped to look in a shop window, and they waited, a few feet up the pavement.

"Listen," Tano said. "If this is true ... if this *sabotage* business is true, then we own a rather big, what ... a rather big piece of him, no?"

"Of who?"

"Of Ziegler," Tano said. *"Ein Stück."*

"What do you mean?" Barrow asked, unsure whether the Romanian was pulling yet another idiomatic hat trick, or merely tripping over his verbs.

"What I mean ... that he makes flaws in all his Brahms performances."

"Maybe he does, maybe he doesn't," said Barrow.

"I'm sorry. Isn't this the right expression?"

"We own a secret," said Petra, rejoining them. "We own *one* of his secrets."

"I'm not sure what you mean."

"So we own a piece of him, is this right?" said Tano. "I have heard this somewhere. I like it."

"Die Erpressung," Petra added.

"Which is what?" asked Barrow.

"When you make them pay."

Tano shrugged. "So, we make him pay. Or we tell everything."

"Blackmail?"

"That is it, yes."

Barrow thought for a moment that the violinist might be serious, but there was no follow-up.

They continued for several blocks, each to their own thoughts, until Tano stopped. "Your neck in the woods?" he asked Petra, his English markedly degraded by drink.

"Ja," Petra said. They stood by a street sign that read Schützen-strasse.

"Shall we walk with you?"

She didn't move, glancing at Barrow. "We're going to Ettlingen tonight," she said.

"Ettlingen?"

"It's where he lives," Petra said.

"You are together?"

Petra said nothing; she was waiting for Barrow. "Yes," he finally said.

"One would not know."

"It's new," Barrow said. He searched the other man's face for disapproval. There was nothing either way, so he continued his stammering vows. "We don't want Ziegler to know."

"Ziegler? Why?"

"Because ..."—but he couldn't think why.

"Because he would use it," Petra said.

"Ahh," Tano said, joyfully elongating the words, "blackmail and sabotage."

"May we walk, please?" Petra said.

She huddled for warmth between the two men as they progressed up Ettlinger Strasse in the direction of the central Marktplatz. Far ahead rose the bright yellow tower of the palace, fully lit, attending the distance, magnetic north. Barrow's heart soared.

"You two would make good Romanians," Tano said, flicking another live butt into the street.

"How's that?" Barrow asked.

"Paranoid as hell. Of course, it is the same in East Germany, no?" It was Petra's cue and she dropped it noisily.

"What do you mean?" Barrow repeated.

Tano continued. "Look at Antonio, he is licking all over Erika in public like a dog. Of course, that is an Italian. And Berndt too, can he stop talking about his baby and his wife? But you are so silent."

"Perhaps it's Germans and Midwesterners," Barrow said, only half joking.

"Lot of places. I am only saying, in the East you make yourself vulnerable if others know what you want—what you badly want. So you keep your want to yourself. It becomes habit."

"You've thought about this."

"Not really. I just notice people in the West say what they want. At home, this same thing is not polite."

"*Unhöflich*," Petra said.

"More, I think, *unklug*," Tano said, catching Barrow's glance. "I'm sorry, but my English is much better than hers."

Barrow looked instinctively at Petra, saw her redden with anger, and he knew, slammed hard into the realization—the party at Ziegler's, Petra's behavior—Petra and Tano had been together. They had *slept* together. He reeled with the certainty of it. The Bach concert in Peterskirche, running into Tano there.

"Impolitic," Tano said. "That would be the sense of it in English." He was smiling, friendly, unaware that his secret had just passed to Barrow.

Without warning, from directly behind, came a voice, almost a bark—"*Achtung, Zigeuner!*"

Attention, Gypsy! The three of them turned and there stood the skinheads, five of them. Barrow felt instantly humiliated for his obedience. One of them—the leader, the one Petra had called Duck—lunged at Tano, and Barrow couldn't see because a wall went up, three skinheads, their blurred faces, their tight jeans and leather, separating him from the action. He heard the hollow thud of Tano's violin case hitting the pavement, and a long groan from Tano.

They had culled Tano from the herd and were beating him up.

Barrow pushed forward, but there was a sharp jab to his left jaw, someone's elbow—he felt the rough fabric, a burning. He flung his mouth open, tried to yell, but nothing came out. Again he threw himself in the direction of the struggle, but he was met by a large boy, his extended arm, fingers pressed to Barrow's chest. "Tano!" he yelled, rolling away from the boy's extended arm, charging the line, head down, against all thought. "Tano!" he yelled, just as his ankles encountered something solid and he went to the pavement, twisting to avoid hitting the slab head first. "Tano! Run!"

Petra stood in the middle of the street, screaming.

The skinheads were laughing, voices pitched high. He heard the word *Amerikaner,* and for a moment everything slowed down. He was looking up at the boys, their distinguishing features shaved clean—small eyes and baldness. They were ghosts, and this wasn't happening.

He was on his hands and knees. Tano lay in a heap beyond reach. Someone yelled "Nigger lover!" followed by another round of laughter—and dog yelps. "Nigger lover!" More laughter. He expected a blow as he stupidly rose to his feet.

Lights flashed from far up and down the broad, four-story canyon, both directions. Blue lights whipped the sidewalk and the gang dissolved—two, then all five skinheads, dodging the headlights. They vanished like they never were.

✍

An ambulance stood by, but Tano claimed to be okay. The "fucking assholes" had kept their fists low, and the heavy folds of his overcoat had saved him from serious injury. "An act of intimidation only," he said, "over before it began." The heel of his left hand was bloody, but he refused a ride to the hospital; he refused even Petra's entreaty that she and Barrow accompany him. The cops would drive him home—they would take his report on the way, they said.

Tano inspected his violin for damage in the backseat of a patrol car. He slid his bow out of its holder, his left hand partially wrapped in Petra's handkerchief. He ran two protruding fingers along the length of the bow, which quivered under the influence of his unsteady right hand. He sat hunched over the open violin case as they closed the door.

When the police asked Petra where she lived, she asked them to drive her to the train station please, with the American.

18 Petra's scream played somewhere in the back of his head as he stood before the urinal in the InterCity train's cramped bathroom. He braced a forearm against the wall and shuddered with relief. There'd been a rabbit once—behind the house in Chagrin Falls—tricked by the cat into screaming louder than a full-out E-flat clarinet, the slightest ripple of vibrato flickering inside the wail, and all from a skull you could tuck under your armpit. That had been Petra's scream, delivered from the median strip of Ettlinger Strasse.

He checked the contours of his face in the polished metal panel over the sink, the raised purple smudge on the side of his chin. He pressed a spot of cold water to the middle of his forehead.

In the corridor he counted back to their compartment. Darkened cars slid past on the next rail. The world was rolling—gliding on air. It would be night for five more hours; at daybreak they would enter East Germany.

Petra slept, stretched across four seats. He saw through the glass, hair veiling her face, feet cocked against the armrest nearest the door. No one had joined them in the compartment and that pleased him. He watched her sleep and marveled at how beautiful she was. Standing outside the Karlsruhe Hauptbahnhof she had turned to him, hesitation in her eyes, and when he said "Let's go"—a thought, merely, put to sound—the corners of her lips, dry and rough with exhaustion, had turned upward. He felt like a savior. She slept in their private chariot to Berlin, and he could walk, enjoy the metallic excitement in his chest and groin.

He continued down the corridor. The singular direction of the train gradually relieved his brain, the motion, the constant tempo—presumably a throttle stood upright in some panel, a hand nearby—the spare content of the cars, the visual repetition as he walked, of compartment-compartment-compartment-lavatory-passage; the night that was black and uncomplicated, the gradual bleeding off of too much daytime content—the concert, Antonio, the Duck—a gluttony of content. Tano, whose dark curls and olive skin should set him so dangerously apart.

He threaded his way up the full length of the train and back. In their compartment, he flipped up the armrest and lay face up. Points of light speckled the windows, or the navy blue outline of a factory or a village, and he imagined the rails slicing the dark a meter below.

When she woke him, it was still dark. She held his pack. Her oboe case was under the same arm. The train was still.

"Berlin?" he asked.

She did not respond but led him down the passageway. Passengers slept in the next compartment. In the next, a man in the shiny blue suit of a nightclub entertainer watched them pass. Barrow said nothing. She had his hand and led him through the end doors, down the steps to a deserted platform.

His visual reference was still with the train as it pulled away, and he stumbled back a few steps. She let go of his hand. She still held his pack—hers was on her back—and her oboe. She allowed him to recover enough balance to walk, and she said, "Come on."

He had been dreaming about a concert, and his arms hurt and his eyes burned. They must be in Berlin, West Berlin, some outlying district.

She seemed to be waiting for him to come to consciousness. "Why aren't you called Cooper?"

"I don't know."

"Your friend Patricia Levy called you Cooper."

"Yes."

They were both drunk on sleepiness, waiting for the sand to empty and the timer to flip before making their next move.

"I would like to find a *Pension*. I need to sleep. There was a weird guy who came in the compartment at Kassel."

"You should have woken me up."

"This is the border. Let's just find a place to sleep a few hours before we go back."

Go back?

He followed her to the end of the platform, where steps led to a small parking lot and a wider view of their surroundings. Here they stopped momentarily. A ribbon of gray ran the length of the horizon behind the buildings. Dawn. A small town. How could he have thought it was Berlin? "What time is it?"

"About seven I think." Her voice was soft and had something of the old comfort about it, like after their swim in Bad Herrenalb—or maybe it was just that it was *her* voice.

"There it is," she said, pointing. Floodlights squared off a small area about 200 meters from where they stood. A double set of fences—it could have been a prison compound with a road running through it. "*Die Grenze*," she said.

The border. Simple thing.

"Please, would you take this?" She held out his pack while he stared dumbly at the distant fence. "Hello?" she said, "Cooper Barrow?" and he took the pack. He thought she might bolt for the fence, but she didn't; she started up the sidewalk. No gazing at the border for her.

Up the street hung a small yellow sign, PENSION. A frosted lamp shone over the steps. He felt terrifically awake, but also wrapped in the wonderful thickness of muscle that comes with a fraction of the required sleep.

"You should wait here," she said, and he raised no objection. She went into the *Pension*, leaving him on the stoop.

Something had happened—she had rejected Berlin—she couldn't face it, or didn't need to.

The skin along the backs of his arms tingled with some sort of anticipation. He dropped his pack to the crook of his arm, pulled out his sweater, and wrestled it over his neck. He could probably sleep standing. It's a pattern, he thought—standing outside doors, waiting for Petra. Outside her teacher's studio, outside the rock club in Stuttgart. She deposits me outside doors. Imitation at the octave, at the fifth, at the second.

His mind was skipping badly.

The door pulled away to reveal a middle-aged woman with absurdly blond hair and a large face. "Your wife is upstairs," she said, although the word for *wife* in German also meant *woman*, one of a number of shortcomings he'd learned to accept. "Number three." She was tying on a print apron, gray and pink. "Coffee?" she asked.

"No, thank you."

She gave the back knot of her apron a stern cinch. "You have only four hours," she said, and disappeared down a hallway to the left of a carpeted staircase. He closed his eyes, pressed the lids with his fingers, and took the stairs one at a time. There was a thickening sensation in his chest, along the surface of his thighs. A yearning to collapse utterly, to give at every joint, to somehow melt into this girl who'd kissed him once, a lifetime ago. When he arrived at Room 3, Petra was cranking down the second of two shutters, the kind found everywhere in Germany, designed to seal off the outdoors with exquisite perfection. He raised no objection. They were both going to drop on the one bed with the stiff white duvet.

The door obeyed his push and clicked shut. They were enclosed in a cell, embedded deep within the host, sealed away, closed off from

judgment. A lamp warmed one corner of the bed. Petra stood by it
and took off her coat, still facing away. She dropped it to the floor. He
glanced at the narrow, freestanding wardrobe by the door. It, the table,
and the bed were the only furniture. He looked back at Petra. She lowered herself to the edge of the bed to remove her boots. He should say
something. Once she snapped off the light, it would stay black. There
would be no adjusting of eyes to the light; because of the shutters
there'd be none to adjust to. "I'm tired," he said.

"Me too."

"How long did we sleep on the train?"

"Maybe three or so hours."

"Where are we?"

"A town."

She stood again, still facing away, her feet bare, and he watched the
undersides of her fingers, where they emerged from the long cuffs of her
sweater. One set, the right, played with a loose thread of wool. "Have
you tried this before?"

"Yes," she said.

Pause.

"To go back home."

"I know what you meant," she said, not impatiently.

She turned and looked at him. She was not going to turn out the
light. She pulled off her sweater by retracting her arms from the sleeves
and pulling the collar up over her head from the inside. She wore a thin
cotton T-shirt underneath. The sudden advent of bare skin—pale and
smooth—unnerved him. The gentle hollow at her belly. Her hair crack-
led with static as it slipped through the neck hole; she smiled at the
sensation. He felt it in the back of his throat, a dry charge, a battery
terminal on his tongue. She gathered the hair in one hand, laid it behind
her neck, and looked at him.

"Please don't sleep in your clothes," she said, and he encountered
an almost brutal wave of nerves. "Unless you are going to sleep on the
floor," she continued.

"No," he said.

He had so many questions for her.

He turned away this time and took off his boots and his jeans, his sweater and shirt. When he turned back, she had removed her jeans and her bra, and as she leaned into the lamp to turn it off—she was bending over its warm light—he saw that in her breasts were gathered more colors than he'd imagined, pinks and whites, pale pale blue. The sheets were coarse as a sidewalk. He remained cold for what felt like minutes, moving stiffly. She found a way to nest herself in him; he felt the stupid desire to cry, but it passed. The briefest time elapsed before sleep caught them both, bound as they were, a single wound in the dark bed.

19 When he woke, he knew he was alone and pulled on his clothes. Petra's things were gone. A note closed into the door read, *I am taking a walk.*

He left a note of his own and retraced their early morning route back to the train station. He took the auto bridge across the tracks and spotted the border in the distance—and some kind of minor installation. It was only a hunch, but a strong one, that he should look for her there.

An unused stretch of road stopped abruptly at the edge of a wide strip of grass, marked by a sign that read simply, HALT! and a bizarre concrete post painted in bold stripes—red, gold, and black—like something out of an amusement park. Across the strip of grass ran a high metal fence. A concrete silo rose on the other side, flared at the top, with slits for windows.

Barrow looked up and down the endless stretch of fence, its wide border of mowed grass in front edged by corn fields on the West German side. Petra was nowhere in sight, but he noticed a break in the fence, a high gate of chain link. It stood open about a foot.

Ignoring the HALT! signs he took off across the field. He found a place where the grass had been beaten flat in a narrow trough ending at the gate. He slipped through and glanced up at the watchtower, half expecting shots to ring out. The silence was striking. A track led away from the gate, over a deep trench and across a narrow roadway that paralleled the fence.

He slowed down to admire the immaculate grounds—it could be a country club—when, no warning, a dog's bark shattered the horizon.

Barrow went stiff and spun on his heels. At five meters a German shepherd in full fur charged the end of its lead, white incisors flashing against a black mane. In the same instant, a sharp whistle sliced the air, two accented sixteenths, and the animal dropped to its haunches, ears at attention, tongue out, panting.

Barrow's chest was pounding.

A border guard in heavy overcoat and cap leaned against the wall of the watchtower. One hand held a cigarette, the other rested on the magazine of the rifle slung over his shoulder. He met Barrow's look with a nod of the head. Barrow nodded back and the guard waved him on.

There was a second barrier a hundred yards ahead—this one a solid concrete wall, also running parallel to the border, also with a gate. In the distance, just visible over the ten-foot wall, Barrow could see a squared-off church tower.

The gate was open.

He walked the gravel track that led to the village, and after about a kilometer he heard the sound of Petra's oboe.

He smiled. His hunch had been correct. Practicing was like milking-time. She must have awoken to its necessity, felt a slight panic in their dark little room. He knew the feeling.

He denied the urge to try the church door and instead followed a tumble-down wall that led to a tiny garden plot behind the edifice, bedded down for winter—sticks bundled, dry twigs spiraling along a wire trellis. A trio of crows rummaged for seed while Petra ran off her scales, proceeding through the circle of fifths, major, minor, drop a major third to the next signature—the pleasing certainty of it.

Give her five minutes.

He followed a wagon path up a short rise to a copse of pine and deciduous trees, from where he could take in the village and miles of Germany, East and West. He'd heard *die Grenze* referred to as a scar on the land. But there was also something elegant about the border, almost natural. Less rude than a highway, it followed the contour of the earth—the fine symmetry of the double fence, the perfectly stepped-off no-man's-land, blurring in the distance.

A segment of Bach arrived on the wind.

He surveyed the land for color and found little. The earth was brown, and the pine needles, rustling gently, were more gray than green or blue. He watched a stubby orange Fiat pull into the square, having arrived from the road to the east; a twist of kelly-green hung slack on a clothesline. The sky stood over the earth, white and without seam or rent. He thought how little warmth a soul could get by on. Every breath he drew contained the important elements—farm, dirt, pine. He needed no more heat, no more color, than he'd found in the last twelve hours.

He caught another whisper of oboe—a longer fragment, from one of the Bach cello suites, transcribed. This is the conductor's prospect, he thought, to pay out the music one page at a time. I am born for this, to hold myself atop the observatory, tend the giant landscape.

Shit. What were his echoed words in the Black Forest? He spoke them aloud for his own benefit. "Rehearsal over."

He abandoned himself to his feet—they pounded the dirt beneath him, the path to the church, and slowed only for the grassy path around to the street where he pulled open the door. Petra's oboe exploded the crack, filled the vestibule, and he saw that she had been playing in the near dark. A few brief measures and she stopped, though the sound took seconds to decay. She was bundled in a wool cap and sweater and, coming into view, her face was soft beyond all anticipation, a dime-sized circle at the center of her lips, reddened from playing.

She pulled off her cap and dropped it to the floor, and he went to her. He took her free hand and it was cold. He kissed it, and her face, and found himself wrapping her in his arms. "Wait, wait," she said, and she retreated to stand her oboe on one of the dusty pew cushions, holding the reed end. His eyes adjusted to the light, and for an instant the terror returned as he drew away from himself, saw the specter of engagement, appreciated how wrong he might be about the East German as she laid her oboe cushion to cushion, pads up, and carefully—a responsible duty-nurse—removed the reed. But then she turned on her own axis, grabbed his arms above the elbow, and pressed her open mouth into his and held him there, her lips warm from playing, while her hands fought with something that he realized was his sweater and shirt; she got her cold hands against the skin of his sides, her lips never leaving his, and in his fists he gathered her flannel pullover, the thing below her sweater, and yanked it up out of her jeans so that he, too, could get to her skin, the fat of her buttock giving under his palm and fingers. Her hands traveled his back, and his came clear round hers so that he could touch his fingertips to the first swell of her breasts, and they clasped themselves together, grasping for something that apparently could not be found between measures and measures and untold measures of music, Bach, Mahler, or fucking anyone else. He knew there would be trouble because of what he was feeling, the pressure of it, and she must have known too, because at just the right moment she simplified everything by squirreling her hand down his pants and grabbing him and thrusting her hand forward and forward until he came, which he did, on his clothes and on her wrist. She screeched when his knees gave and he staggered and just missed landing on her oboe. She went on kissing him as he reached back, embarrassed as hell, and found the wall.

Holding each other, they leaned against the stone innards of the church where, above their heads, he noticed a skinny wooden ledge running the length of the chapel, supporting small framed photos of the Holy Land—Jerusalem, the shores of Galilee—which to anyone in regular attendance there must have once seemed so very far away.

〜

They walked out under the glorious sky.

"I came here on tour with a woodwind octet from the conservatory. I had never seen the border, except of course for the Wall. I came back as soon as I could—borrowed my girlfriend's car—and the whole way from Berlin I was thinking, Perhaps they will forget today. Perhaps they will leave the gates unattended and I will just drive across. I was even working out how I would get the Trabi back to my friend in Berlin."

"Did you ever attempt it?"

"To escape? I could not get past the five-kilometer barrier, which I had not even noticed on the tour, that keeps everyone back from the border except the people who live there, like the people in this village."

She was talkative, rattling on in German. He thought she might have been quiet, reflective, it being her first day back in East Germany, but she was full of explanation, description, stories.

"Apparently, we must have had papers or something to let us past the barrier. We played in that same church, the octet. People came from miles around. A crowd waited outside and we had to perform the entire concert again. Even the border guards came in their uniforms. I have heard this happened in Israel, in those short wars, the Seven-Day, or maybe the Thirteen, that a string quartet might play in a bunker."

They were standing in the village square. It was a farm community, with stone barns that opened onto the street. He could smell the cows.

"So you—how did you learn things like that? From the West."

"Everything comes across. It's just a fence."

The small bakery on the square was closed, but there was a light on inside and they knocked on the door. They bought a couple of rolls— the proprietor didn't seem to mind being paid in West German marks. Barrow asked for a bathroom to clean himself up.

Afterward they started down the one-kilometer stretch to the border crossing, stopping at the top of a rise in the road. Before them lay the essential apparatus of West Germany, advanced implements of the

West German railway, signal towers, small-town station, the roads in and out of town, a slight haze above what might be a brewery on the distant edge of the town, all the outbuildings of prosperity. It had turned colder, or perhaps it was just the wind topping the rise.

She said, "Actually I learned it when I visited the synagogue in East Berlin."

"Learned what?" Barrow asked.

"About the string quartet in the bunkers in Israel."

"Really," he said, and he waited.

"My neighborhood in East Berlin was Prenzlauer Berg. There was a synagogue there, the Rykestrasse Synagogue, and I went from time to time." He glanced at her and she anticipated his next question. "Just out of curiosity."

"Tell me about this group that Alexandra teased you about. The young communists."

"Free German Youth."

"And you belonged?"

"Of course. We marched through the streets with torches. I got a kick out of it, I think is the English."

He watched her remember. "I thought we were going to Berlin," he said.

She looked at him, scrunching up her face. She brushed back the hair from her eyes. She took his elbow and turned him in the other direction.

∽

The boy and his mother were *Wessis* on a weekend excursion, marking history. Having entered the East German frontier at a crossing somewhere in the south, they were looking for a way back over, flagrantly ignoring the five-kilometer road barriers up and down the border, even to the extent of off-roading with their tiny orange Fiat.

They were fascinated by Petra and pumped her for more information than she wanted to give. "We have the time, mother," said the boy, wielding an East German road map. "We can take them to Berlin." Petra cupped Barrow's ear in the cramped back seat. "We have been kidnapped."

But she grew more and more agitated.

They sped east, past lowland villages and towns, active smokestacks and clumps of ugly apartment blocks. They drove under a section of the autobahn, high storm fences on either side. "That is the main route from the crossing at Helmstedt," the mother said. "Impossible to get on or off anywhere until West Berlin." She was a professor of French literature from Würzburg.

Petra held Barrow's arm with both hands, their feet and their packs stuffed in the small space between the front and back seats.

"You see, mother, we have to drive to the other side of Berlin, to East Berlin and come through the city from the *other* side."

Barrow asked to see the map. Distances were shorter than he'd imagined—between the border and Berlin, between East Berlin and the Polish frontier. They'd been crammed in the backseat for three hours when they came up on signs for Brandenburg, a small city on the western outskirts of Berlin.

"Please leave us here," Petra said.

"What?"

"Leave us, please. Perhaps you can take us to the train station."

"No, no, no, we will find a way into the city."

Petra was almost white with fear. He hadn't seen it coming, and perhaps she hadn't either, but some kind of panic had crept up on her.

"I would prefer not."

♊

They waited on the platform for a train that would take them to Ostbahnhof, East Berlin's main station. From there they would make their way through the Wall, at Checkpoint Charlie presumably, or Brandenburg Gate, and on to the main terminus in West Berlin for a high-speed train back West.

Her eyes followed a pair of armed soldiers who were strolling the length of the platform, apparently waiting for the same train.

"They're not checking passports," Barrow said. He'd read it in the newspaper the day before.

"You know we're a couple of flies in a bottle," she said. "We've flown in and can't get out. We're banging against the glass."

It was true—bizarrely—that there were few exits and entrances from or to this place, this Ohio-sized country, where every road and every railway seemed to end five kilometers shy of the border.

"I know you want to go there, to the Wall," she said. "I'm sorry."

The Brandenburg station was drab, no sexy billboards, no movie posters. A magazine rack held four or five publications. Free enterprise left a lot of sheer color in its wake.

"We won't go," he said.

He felt no need to question her fears—the concentrated presence of the Stasi in East Berlin, the geographical associations, the people who might condemn her, others who might have been hurt by her defection.

Her mood lightened.

They had an alternate plan, which was to take the train to Magdeburg in the morning, catch a bus to one of the small towns along the border and walk across. There was a town she'd heard of called Böckwitz, which had been bisected by *die Grenze*, and almost certainly, here on November 27, the way would be open.

They took a room in a hotel across from the train station—dreary but cozy. She suggested they wash out their underwear like old-fashioned tourists, he in the sink in their room, she in the shared bathroom down the hall. He left her alone to take a bath while he went back into the streets in search of a *Kneipe* where he could buy a couple of sandwiches. When he returned, she was combing her hair in the bedroom. They fed on the bread and cheese he'd found, which under the circumstances was delicious. "No bad cheese in all of Germany," she said.

He drew himself a bath, waiting seemingly forever in the narrow room for the thin stream of hot water to fill the tub. Lowering himself in was the second delicious experience of the hour. He settled back against the cold metal, terrifyingly awake, knowing she was awake in the same way, preparing. They'd avoided each other's eyes ever since he returned from the *Kneipe*.

She surprised him at the door, brandishing her comb like a baton. "You want this?"

With a resounding splash, he sat up, covering himself.

"Sure," he said, and she flipped it into the water.

She didn't leave, but sat on the side of the bath, her bare feet and jeans, her T-shirt riding up on her breasts. He leaned forward, pretending to wash.

"I've wanted to ask you—"

"Yeah?"

"About Saratoga."

"What?" He had not caught up with the fact of her presence, his own sprawling nakedness. "Saratoga?"

"What Patricia Levy was saying."

"You were listening?"

"Something happened that made you quit."

"It was a combination of things."

"Usually it's not a 'combination of things.' Usually it's one thing. And later you can say, 'It was a combination of things,' and forget."

She was smart. And beautiful, particularly now, her cheeks and nose still red from her bath. She dropped to her knees at the end of the bath, chin on her hands, hands on the rim of the tub. He didn't know what to make of her modesty earlier, about washing their underwear in separate rooms.

"So?"

He cleared his throat. "I was invited to conduct the Philadelphia Orchestra, up where they spend the summer, near Saratoga Springs in New York State. I was part of a concert with two contest winners, and I went crazy or something because I didn't bow."

"You didn't bow?"

"No."

"What did you do?"

"I walked off ."

"You didn't think you deserved it?"

"No, no."

"Then why?" She had one hand in the water, fishing around his ankle.

"I can't remember," he said.

"That's not likely."

"You really want to know?"

"Why else would I torture you like this?" Her fingers had sneaked up his calf, her chest pressing the edge of the tub. She was so vastly more experienced than him.

"Is this some sort of advanced East German interrogation technique?"

"I've had a lot of success with it, in fact."

He wondered, gazing across at her, how many secrets of actual import had been passed over a hot bath in a shabby East German hotel.

"A long tradition," he said.

She nodded.

"I didn't bow because it wasn't my performance." She looked puzzled, of course. "It was the concertmaster's performance. The orchestra was following him. I was just some puppet."

"Which happens all the time."

"I know."

"So you didn't bow? That's stupid."

"It's worse." She waited, her fingers quiet, just breaking the surface of the water. "It was Beethoven's First, which, of course, they could play with their eyes closed."

"Yes?"

He remembered the dumb rage—the stupefying rage—that had boiled up in his twenty-one-year-old self, his complete dissociation from the Beethoven. How polite the concertmaster and the other principals had been before the concert, how seldom they looked at him in performance.

"I left before it was over."

He waited for a response. She said nothing.

"Maybe twenty measures from the end. I just stopped beating and walked off the stage."

She looked at him with neither sympathy nor reproach.

"You shot yourself in the head."

He nodded.

"You must have known what you were doing."

"Yes," he said. He'd figured it out long ago. That behind the screen of his temper moved the cool hand of a chess player.

"And Juilliard dismissed you?"

"I quit before they could."

She took his foot in her hand. "What were you so afraid of?"

"Why are you asking me all these questions?"

"Because I want to know."

"The water's getting cold," he said, pretending to glance around for his towel. But she had a good grip on his foot.

He remembered his mother's response when he phoned her to announce that he was moving to Fishkill. "Great, son," she had said in a rare stab at sarcasm, "this way, if you should prove to be brilliant, they'll never find you."

Petra's thumb pressed deep into his instep. "What were you afraid of?"

"I was afraid that I wasn't brilliant."

"For good reason."

Their underwear lay on the heating grate under the bed, wrung almost dry. A slit of light came in under the door.

Her voice was low and hoarse. "Why did you stay away from me?"

"What?"

"I offered you a ride to the tram. I would have driven you to Ettlingen if you wanted."

"You were the one—"

She kissed him.

He moved only tentatively. Her body was such a gift—a further embarrassment. "It's okay," she whispered, and he allowed himself to test the pink area around her nipples, conscious of his unshaven chin. When she did the same to him, he bit down on the inside of his cheek to silence himself. He sank, gave in to forgotten sensation, lost any sense of coherence, any sense of his place in the world, any sense, even, of her presence as a separate entity in the bed—until, perhaps a little impatient, she took him, pressed him to her, and brought him inside, slipping down by millimeters, her knees grazing his sides. She stopped before going on, grinned, and they were two strangers again, one day old, reaching across an ocean and half a continent, complete unknowns, not even comfortable in the same damn language. She began to move, just a little, and according to a pact he'd made with himself, he did not cry out, his hands finding and clutching the edges of the mattress, and her slender swimmer's shoulders, and the soft shelf of her hips. Like on the train— the easy side-to-side, the quiet moan of the rails a meter below.

20 In the morning, still in bed, she sorted through his backpack, a lover cataloguing the contents of her man's wallet: one forgotten tartan scarf; one miniature score to Beethoven's Eighth; one palm-sized *Langenscheidt's* dictionary; one thermos cup, unwashed. She sniffed the cup. She counted the leads in his pencil case—the red, the blue— "Is this *kindergarten?*" she said. She pulled out a thick hardcover he'd tossed in just before leaving for the Brahms concert two nights before, idle reading for the commute. She opened the cover, found a penned inscription. "'Ah, what might have been.' What is that?" she said.

"A cliché. She is making fun of a cliché because there never could have been anything."

"Such as what."

"Such as a relationship."

"With you?"

"Yes."

"'She'?"

"A friend. A conductor."

"And 'she' wanted a love affair with you?"

Sometime in the night Petra had assumed ownership of him, and nothing rebelled.

"No."

"The other way?"

"Not really."

"'Not really.'"

"Not at all."

He had, in fact, briefly fallen for Carleton, a pianist-turned-conductor whom he'd met at Eastman. "I'll fuck you once, but I won't get involved," she'd said, divining his feelings. "I'm a lesbian." The book had been her gift to him shortly after their acceptance into Gil Shanahan's studio at Juilliard, especially unusual since they were from the same undergraduate school. "We are the chosen," Carleton said when he arrived at her door, "we are the Israelites on our way to the land of milk and whores."

Petra read something else from the title page. "'Where the fuck is Hollywood on this?' More I don't understand," she said.

"She means it would make a good movie." The volume was a source-book on the lives of Clara and Robert Schumann, a compendium of journal entries and letters to, from, and about them. And about Brahms, who was in their inner circle.

"Too melodramatic," she said. "Too pathetically romantic."

"Too German?" He was surprised to hear himself say it.

"Not anymore."

"Why?"

"We are the anti-romantics of the world, no? No more romance!"

She sat cross-legged. She'd pulled on her sweater, but was otherwise naked. He lay on his side under the covers.

"So much underlining." She read in English. "'... one whose destiny should be to express the spirit of our age in the highest and most ideal fashion ...'"

"Robert Schumann."

"Yes."

"Writing about the nineteen-year-old Brahms."

"You are a smart guy."

"I've read it a million times."

"Your friend has ... how do you say ..."

"Underlined?"

"Your friend has underlined all of this—'one who should not reveal his mastery by a gradual development, but spring, like Minerva, fully armed from the head of Jove.'"

"Such crap." He sounded less than convincing.

"Crap?"

"*Scheisse.*"

"You believe so?"

"*Ja.*"

"You speak like Tano Popescu."

"Do I?" he asked.

"*Ja wohl.*"

He hesitated. "You know Tano pretty well." He watched for something in her face, a clue.

"Nobody knows Tano pretty well. What is this?" Carleton had scribbled something in the margin. "'We all need a mentor.'"

"Protégé, mentor. She's being sarcastic."

"Ah," she said. Her face was soft in the light from the glass-curtained window.

"Schumann," he said, "who is the most famous composer in Germany, introduces Brahms as pretty much God. She's saying we could all use an introduction like that."

"Your friend likes sarcasm."

"You're catching on."

"I'm 'catching on'?"

"I think so."

"To hell with you."

She continued leafing through, on the prowl for more of Carleton's annotations. "Do you think Brahms ever made love with Clara?"

"I don't know."

"He did."

"No," he said.

"Because you yourself would not have?"

"What do you mean?"

"*You* wouldn't have slept with her."

He chose to ignore the taunt.

It had once been a matter of more than idle curiosity to Barrow— and apparently to Petra—and, he supposed, who wouldn't be at least curious if they knew the story? After Robert Schumann's death, Clara and Brahms vacationed in Switzerland, a vacation with an agenda: What's to become of us now that Robert is dead? Within days of their return, after having remained at Clara's side throughout the two-year ordeal with Robert—his intermittent insanity, his attempted suicide— after having patrolled her parlor and partnered her in all manner of chamber music, night after night, Brahms abruptly left.

"You are American, so you cannot imagine such a thing. You don't think—because they had all those large clothes on—you don't think he had sex with her? One night when they were playing the piano, his music, and she is telling him how much of a genius he is? She was a very sexual woman, you know, it is part of the musical passion, you don't think so? She was a little older than he and she had all those children, and so much the better." A new tone had crept into her voice, arrogance of a distinctly German variety—hers or the language's, he couldn't tell. "Germany is around so much longer than America. Religion knows its place here."

"I only think," he said, "besides there being no evidence that they slept together, it is in Brahms' personality to hold back and put all the feeling into his music."

"Speaking of cliché."

"His respect for Robert Schumann, his respect for her."

"Yes, of course, true. And therefore so much more *dangerous* for them."
She loved the fight. "Why do you think he left so suddenly? He would
need a reason, such a hard departure. He left because, yes, finally, after
much what you call restraint, he slept with her. He was revolted with
what he had done, and so he left her and went north to Hamburg, and
that was that."

Barrow nodded, though he was more convinced than ever that he
understood Brahms, that at the last minute Brahms had abandoned the
single most potent love of his life, fled home to Hamburg, and pro-
ceeded to write some of the greatest music of the nineteenth century.
He looked up at Petra—her face buried in the book, her scent everywhere—and he understood the temptation to find everything one
needed in a single passion. How easily a woman might replace his reig-
nited ambition.

"You have not been with a woman since—what?" Petra asked,
pretending to be absorbed in the book.

"You could tell."

"But how long?"

He shrugged. "Some years maybe."

"Jesus," she said. "No wonder you think this about Brahms."

21 They followed Petra's plan, managed to recross the border at Böckwitz, and arrived in Karlsruhe some-time after two in the morning. Stoned with sleep, they walked to her apartment on Schützenstrasse in the Südstadt district. Wolf sat at the kitchen table reading a textbook. He looked up and grinned. Barrow had wanted to ease into the territory, but Petra didn't stop. She drew him to the end of the hall-way and deposited him in her bedroom. He dropped his pack and stretched his tired frame the full length of the futon, face buried deep in the duvet.

∽

Ziegler canceled lessons for two weeks—the word was that he had gone to Switzerland for a rest—and Barrow spent his extra time browsing the well-stocked shelves of a music store called Franksmusik, while Petra practiced or rehearsed with her quintet. In the afternoons, they made love. Later, he would assessable their dinner from the bakeries and cheese shops near her apartment. Occasionally Wolfram joined him, and they cooked while Petra and Alexandra practiced in their respective bedrooms.

At night, they prowled the Südstadt quarter, talking endlessly about nothing important. She would describe her fascination with hotel lobbies, or point to a balcony where someone had stashed a dozen or so pairs of old wooden skis—"Do you ski?" "Yes," he would say, and be off describing the three days every win-ter his father dragged them up to a resort in Canada. "Poor American guy," she'd say. She wanted descriptions of everywhere he'd been in the U.S., and he told her of Michigan, the green lakes up north, the vast dunes heated by the July sun to the point where he couldn't go barefoot. "Barefoot is a fascist luxury," she laughed. He asked about the raft of paperbacks that lined her floorboards, the orange Penguins interspersed like the black keys. She summarized her favorites. "If I could only read all day, this would be fine," she said. If he disagreed, he didn't care.

They spoke little of music, and he never mentioned that, before meeting her, he had thought of little else.

Late in the week, they strolled out to the Hochschule to pick up some music Messer-Eichen had left for her. The red-brick Schloss Gottesaue rose up against the black sky, a fortress, a last line of defense. He remarked as much, and she pointed out how much more impressive it must have been right after the war, towering over the rubble of Karlsruhe. "Only point on the city's compass," she said.

The monitor knew them on sight, and they climbed the steps to Messer-Eichen's studio. The music Petra needed lay on her teacher's desk in a cardboard envelope. Barrow asked to see it: a set of first oboe parts to some pieces by Brahms for chorus and orchestra, Bernstein's *Fancy Free* ballet, and Haydn's "Surprise" Symphony.

He had forgotten that she was subbing for Messer-Eichen in Frankfurt. He felt a shot of jealousy. The hinted-at relationship with Werner Schott.

"What is it?" she asked.

"You are substituting again?"

"Yes."

"You're looking forward to it?"

"It's a good opportunity for me," she said. He sensed some discomfort. They were revisiting the scene of a crime, and he recognized her tone from the last time they were in this room together. Rehearsed and formal, as if the studio were bugged.

"Is something wrong?" he asked.

She had been facing the piano, and when she looked back at him, she wore a different look, one of amusement, a slight arch in her brows.

"Do you know Eugenie?"

He nodded. The stoop-shouldered oboist who had replaced her as principal on the Brahms.

"I came in here once," Petra said. "She was with her boyfriend. Under the piano. I was happy for her."

"Yes," Barrow said.

"In more than one way I am happy for her," Petra continued. "She was good, wasn't she?"

"In the concert?"

"Wasn't she?"

"Not really."

She looked at him more closely, and grinned. "You are thinking about it."

"Maybe."

"Like Brahms and Clara."

He held her gaze. "Come on," he said.

She locked up the studio, and he took her hand and led her up two flights to the top floor, the record library—a fish tank, paneled in glass.

"Antonio says that some teachers have access," he said, but she was already trying keys.

Inside it felt ten degrees cooler than the rest of the building. He slipped behind the sign-out counter and flipped a switch that brought up a single neon tube back in the stacks. He found the CD he wanted, led her to his favorite listening booth, and sat her on the floor. He flipped the CD into place and touched the skip key a few times. She said "Henze" and his heart jumped—that she would know the composer. Last movement of Hans Werner Henze's Seventh Symphony, alternating between restraint and madness, an orchestra in stampede—before the cutoff into the final measure, marked by the Henze, 20". Twenty seconds of silence.

Petra must have seen the score; she waited until the end, left the listening booth and returned with a CD of her own. Haydn's *Creation*, "Awake the Harp." It ended, and he left the room, returning with an LP—Mahler's Third, Jascha Horenstein, London Symphony. He lowered the needle on the fifth movement and a playground of boys sang "Bimm bamm!," emphatically reinventing the second, one sixtieth of a minute. When it was over, Petra lifted the tone arm and moved it to the previous band, the fourth movement, and they were in a cathedral because Mahler had set the words "*Oh Mensch!*" above a plagal cadence which made them sound exactly like "Amen," only these were the words of Nietzsche. "Oh man, take heed!" sang the contralto, and, "What does the deep midnight say?" Movement over.

They faced each other across the floor. Pale light milked in from outside. It was another cell, like the *Pension*, the hotel in Brandenburg, her room on Schützenstrasse. From her knees, Petra reached across and zeroed out the volume, and they listened again to "Bimm bamm" directly off the vinyl, distantly audible, orchestra and double-chorus in a tin cup.

Four minutes, and the needle slipped into the gutter. He gazed at her and she gazed back. She looked momentarily lost, curled up like something in its larval stage. She interrupted the softly motoring speakers. "There are limitations to this."

"Limitations?" He thought she meant the music, their own silly reverence for it; or music's utility as language, the temptation to let it speak one's thoughts while one stood back—*those* limitations.

"You are in love with me."

She said it in German, but he knew her meaning because he had researched the difference between *in love* and *love*. His heart sank, flattened by the implication that her feelings were not the same.

When he started to speak, she interrupted with a single shake of the head and went on gazing at him.

Then, seeing the expression he had grown so accustomed to—the tightening at the corners of her lips, and, discernible as a small shadow in the mute light, the dimpling of her right cheek—he knew not to worry. A second reversal of fortune in the space of a minute.

She pulled her knees up to her chest, pressed her back to the wall. "It's too late, isn't it?"

He waited, wondering what she meant. The turntable continued to spin Mahler in a silent, belt-driven glide.

"To hide anything from each other," she said.

He watched her face, once again inscrutable, angled down into shadow. "It's never too late for that," he said, though it sounded more like something she would have said.

∽

One morning after breakfast, he hopped the tram for Ettlingen and re-entered his attic after an absence of ten days. He pulled out his violin, tuned the strings, tightened and resined the bow hairs, and played a slow chromatic scale that took in the range of the instrument. From the first scrape of his bow he felt alive in a way he'd forgotten—the first bearing down of his right arm, the pliable resistance from the E-string, the tremors back up through his elbow, a whiff of resin rising this side of the bridge. He'd never been satisfied with his instrument, a cheap Lupot knockoff; now he couldn't care less. For three hours he played nothing but scales and arpeggios. He lost his mind. It was Petra's doing. There were clenched-up parts of him that were loosening.

At noon ten-year-old Elisabeth appeared at the top of the stairs, occupying the same spot her little brother had two months before. He stared at her, tongue-tied from overconcentration. "Home already?" he finally said.

She nodded. Her fingers clung to the top banister, her eyes angled up tentatively.

"It's loud?" he said.

She nodded, pointing at his face. "What's that?" she asked, and instinctively he touched the spot under his left jawbone and winced. Three months without playing had left his chin smooth and vulnerable. He'd been so intent on tuning intervals, one small correction after another, that he'd forgotten the need to work in a callus. He brushed a knuckle just behind the jaw bone and winced again. When he looked, there was a mosquito's worth of blood on the back of his finger.

That night Petra met him in Ettlingen. They made an excursion to the swimming pool at Bad Herrenalb, and under the tram's bright, clinical light she inspected the mark under his chin. She retaped the Band-Aid.

In the small outdoor pool, they reenacted her rescue of him. They stood in the freezing cold on the cement edge and, when they thought they could no longer stand it, backed up and sat on the low wall bordering the patio, chatting amiably in bad British accents, pretending it was a summer's day. A chilly wind evaporated the water from their skin. The hair on their arms stood straight and dry. They ignored the stares of the little boys who whispered and giggled, the others who joined them on the ledge, crossing, in imitation, their dripping, rubbery legs. They noted the hardening knot of cold in the bumps behind their ears. "Ready?" she said. "*Fertig*," he said. One last held moment, a further dare in her glance, and they sprinted for the hot pool.

22 Wolf knocked on Petra's bedroom door on Saturday morning, sometime before seven-thirty, and relayed a message from Barrow's landlady. Be at the concert hall at eight for a special session with Ziegler.

Barrow groaned.

"I thought he was visiting his horse in Switzerland," Petra muttered. In two weeks the smell of her hair, her sheets, had invaded the deepest ravines of his imagination. The task of leaving her futon on short notice held no equivalent in his life.

Wolf had a mug of coffee waiting in the kitchen. Graph paper, penciled and spent, lay strewn about everywhere. "What is a special session?"

Barrow shrugged, "I don't know."

On the street, the heat of Petra's bed clung to him. The dark wet pavement, the passing headlights, all marked him, he thought, for a man with a woman. He stopped for a paper—servicing his late-blooming fascination with Petra's homeland, with all things East. He read while he walked. There was an article about the arrest of Erich Honecker, former East German prime minister. It brimmed with editorial self-satisfaction. An inside page featured a high-angle photo of the man that recalled Karlheinz Ziegler on the podium, the bald forehead, the hawkish intensity of the eyes.

He was still reading when he entered the Konzerthaus. The corridors appeared deserted and he slipped through the stage entrance to size things up from the wings. There remained a cringing desire, despite recent events, to impress the old man with his promptness.

"Cooper Barrow?" The voice came from the shadows just back of the proscenium. "I think the maestro is ready."

"For what, *bitte?*"

A student, one of the undergraduate conductors, stepped into the hazy off-light and indicated for Barrow to step out on stage. He did, entering just behind the lower brass section. There was no one in sight, and he felt a strong complaint of adrenaline. He had the newspaper, and for want of any other business, he took off his pack and stuffed the paper inside.

More than a few seconds passed. His life seemed striped with such moments—reins grazing the mud, unattended.

"*Allo,*" he said.

The stage was lit for a concert; the rest of the hall was dark. He began to register—how long had it been there?—a sound. A full set of sounds, low, almost subliminal, then rising and unmistakable—the low drone of a milling audience. A chill ran down his spine.

"*Guten Tag!*"

Nothing.

The crowd noise came from four stage monitors dragged out from the wings. He peered up at the control booth, temporarily blinding himself in the lights.

"Herr Ziegler?" He noticed the undergraduate slip through an audience door and disappear up into the seats.

A hush came over the recorded audience, and he called out again,

"*Hallo*, Herr Maestro Ziegler!" He heard footsteps, so real that he looked in their direction. A low swell of applause was followed by the oboe's tuning note—an American's, judging by the dry quality of the sound—and the orchestra joining in. It was exceedingly real, exactly as it would be before a live concert. The brevity of the tuning session told him this was a professional orchestra.

"Take the podium."

Ziegler's voice, coming from far back in the house.

He heard footsteps behind him—they belonged to the conductor in the recording—and an abrupt storm of sound which he recognized as fierce applause, the kind reserved for name-brand conductors, the Maazels, Soltis, and Rattles.

He yelled over the applause. "What do you want me to do?"

"Take the podium!"

He clung to his baton, which he couldn't remember pulling from his pack.

He took the podium. So did his recorded counterpart, who until now had presumably been taking a gracious bow to the house. On the conductor's desk the score to Brahms' Second lay open to the first movement.

Is this my consolation for not being chosen the other night?

The applause dropped off; instinctively, he knew the count, the seconds to allow all elements of audience and air to settle, the build-up of collective permission.

Is this another lesson?

He could delay just so long. There would be a group breath from the cellists, possibly from the conductor himself, signaling the preparatory beat—

And there it was, the breath. His arms joined it, and with his downbeat came sound from the celli, or from where the celli should be, *deeya-da-daaah*. He looked out to the horns, the empty stands, and to the winds. He closed his eyes—he knew these measures well—and the professional timbre rose and fell around him.

A minute passed, perhaps minutes.

The old man appeared behind the lower brass, five rows of empty stands between them.

Barrow shouted above the recording. "What is the purpose?"

The old man gestured for him to be silent.

"Maestro, this is absurd." He had taken himself out of the beat pattern, put the baton down.

"Conduct!"

"This is choreography."

"It is the Second of Brahms, you don't want it?"

"Maestro—"

"Leave."

He stared at the old man.

"Leave!"

Sillier things had happened. He'd been thrown by a horse, for one.

He picked up his baton and jammed the butt into the palm of his right hand. He knew the place in the music. He took up the basic pattern.

"You're beating time."

He went further with his gesture, let in some feeling.

"No!" The old man stepped out into the orchestra, stood where the violas would be if there had been any violas. "*Espressivo!*" He clutched a stand for support, his high baritone soaring over the pealing orchestra. "*Espressivo!*"

Barrow dropped his shoulders and leaned into the Brahms. The music surged back to the foreground. He tried to anticipate the orchestra, whatever American orchestra it was, and the orchestra did not fail him. Whoever the conductor was, he did not stray from Barrow's own imperatives. Where Barrow wanted much, there was much; where he wanted little, little. Sheer beauty where he wanted sheer beauty. This was Barrow at age fifteen, shades pulled, slashing the air to long-playing records, jabbing holes in the universe. Uncompromising self-indulgence. Ziegler must loathe it.

The first movement ended. Two or three isolated coughs reminded him of the recorded audience—there must even be speakers set up out in the house. He waited for some sign that the exercise was over, but the old man dragged a chair to the back of the stage and sat in it, staring past him into the audience, head in one-quarter profile. With the tempo of the second movement—painfully slow—Barrow guessed that the conductor of this live recording might be Leonard Bernstein. Another clue to the old man's purpose? Which was what?

"Sostenuto, sostenuto!" The old man was up again, parading the sidelines like a football coach. "Sustain!"

Barrow tried. He propped up the sound with his arms until he was able to enter the logic of the tempo, meet its terms. The second movement became a study in *adagio non troppo*—slow, not too much—with Ziegler barking throughout, *No, you drop it, you desert the line. You abandon.*

Hold, hold.

More, more, still more.

Something was wrong. This was not Ziegler's tempo—this was a tempo he would curse and stomp through. Was it an exercise in knowing the enemy by wearing his clothes? On a particular foggy morning, sneaking behind the lines and leading the enemy's troops?

Ziegler left his seat before the end of the movement, took the steps to the audience and strode off into the artificial haze at Barrow's back. The second movement finished and the silent transition came to the third—the recorded transition, more stirring bodies in the audience—but a shorter break than expected, which caused him to miss the opening measures.

There was nothing from the old man. It had been better when he was visible, ranting. Now Barrow might be alone in the hall, flapping like a bird in the barn. He continued from memory, concentrating more on technical matters than in the first two movements, which he knew better. Avoiding errors, feeling more and more the marionette, dragged along by the recording. His arms and his back ached from trying to lead an orchestra that would not bend to him, that did not need him—

And it struck him. Saratoga. Ziegler knew.

The idea rushed through him in a shock of adrenaline, and suddenly he was wrestling with the very demon he'd met all those years before. The rage came up. The exact rage.

This is a lesson I do not need. What the fuck was eight years in Fishkill all about, if not burying this?

His wrists—all his limbs—shook severely. He threw himself into the final coda, one last effort at persuasion. He rang out the closing of Brahms' Second with his elbows flung wide; his heels left the platform. He shut down the orchestra, shut down the recording, shut down the ceremony.

But the tape was not through. There was a wave at his back and it slammed into him, knocked him into the conductor's desk. The applause. He couldn't breathe. And Ziegler was back, his voice belting out over the noise, "*Verbeug dich!*"

Bow. He wants me to bow.

Barrow turned. Ziegler stood three meters away, hollering. Applause thundered at their backs, undiminished, Niagara Falls in the Konzerthaus. *How does he know? How does he fucking know about Saratoga?*

"*Verbeug dich!*"

Barrow stood, drained of resistance.

"*Verbeug dich!*"

He stared into Ziegler's eyes, realized with horror that his own were watering up.

"You cannot, can you," Ziegler yelled.

Barrow glanced out to the empty house, bent from the waist, put himself into it, jerked forward, and back up.

"Again."

But Barrow snatched up his backpack.

He crashed through the first and second violin stands. To his horror, the escape door pulled back. A second undergraduate was operating the door. Barrow stopped, breathing heavily. The student looked at him like a minor government official. "You must go back," the undergraduate said.

"What?"

"For another bow."

Out in the house the applause continued, a tape loop of adulation, on and on. Ziegler stood by the podium, one hand in his pocket.

"Please, you must go out again," said the undergraduate.

Barrow looked into the face of the boy, an earnest player. He pushed past him, not quite intentionally catching the kid's shoulder with his own, knocking him back a foot or two. He strode into the dark wing, at last outdistancing the applause. There was an apology to be made, but he didn't turn back. He found the stage door and kicked through to the outer hallway.

23

Badly shaken, he jumped a tram for Ettlingen.

He wanted only escape.

His landlords were readying themselves for their regular Saturday outing—it was not yet ten o'clock. They were going ice skating at in indoor rink, and they wanted him to go along; Elisabeth and Johannes hung on his arms, *Bitte, bitte, bitte*. His anger had not abated and there was nowhere to go with it and he surprised himself by agreeing to join them. He threw himself at the family for the first time in three months. In the car, Renate Schwalb fed him a sandwich of brown bread and cheese and a box of juice. He rented skates and joined the kids on the ice, applauded the ten-year-old Elisabeth for her figures and laughed when Johannes rammed him at full kindergarten throttle. He rediscovered his own ice-legs and raced around the oval. He stood apart with Helmut Schwalb, the father, heard the latest family crisis, that Johannes had been hitting other children in school, had been required to attend twice-weekly sessions with a psychologist who assured them there was nothing to worry about, "but what a business." Renate was very upset about it, had Barrow noticed?

He had not, but he listened selfishly and with increasing gratitude to their troubles. The business with Johannes brought up the business with the skinheads more than two weeks prior, the beating of the young Romanian violinist, the involvement of Barrow and the girl from East Germany. The police had been carefully, methodically compiling a list of suspects—had Barrow been following this? No, he hadn't.

By late afternoon, the morning's episode was in partial recess.

At dark, he walked downhill to the tram and rode back into Karlsruhe.

⁂

That night he went to the movies with Petra and her roommates. *Batman*. German-dubbed, mindless, and life-affirming.

Wolf fancied himself a serious student of American pop culture, and on the walk home he peppered Barrow with questions, "What is this preoccupation with the *criminal* in America? For example, in this movie, who is the most interesting? The criminal, of course. Who is being cared about? The Joker. Who dominates? The city itself, this, what, *Gotham*. Which is like being stuck inside the huge skull, again, of the criminal. What is this fascination?"

Barrow—on some level, still reeling from the morning—threw the question back. "What do you think?"

"Unresolved guilt. Americans are fascinated with their own dark side—you see, here again, *Star Wars*. They cannot decide, 'Are we guilty?' 'I dunno, Jack, are we?' 'Let's look.'"

"What about Germans?" Alexandra asked.

"We have resolved this question of guilt," Wolf said.

Barrow took the bait. "How?"

"By accepting it," Wolf said, raising his hand. "Guilty."

Alexandra raised her hand as well. "Guilty," she said.

"Guilty," Petra said, and their laughter careened up the street.

∽

"What was this special session?" Petra asked the moment they split off from the others.

He told her everything. She was quiet. When they arrived outside her favorite winebar, she held back his arm from opening the door.

"I was with him. For a short time."

"With who?"

"Ziegler. I was with Ziegler. Last year. For a short time."

Barrow was certain he'd misheard.

"I was going to tell you," she said.

"Ziegler?"

"Yes."

"What?"

"I was going to."

In some sort of inversion of awareness, the music from inside the winebar took over his brain—a Bach prelude played on accordion, the popular one in C major. "Shall we go inside?" he asked, his voice sounding far off.

"It was shortly after I arrived from Paris," Petra said. "It should matter very little to you. I want it to matter very little."

He knew he should nod, but he couldn't. "For how long?"

"Couple of weeks."

He stared—still not believing—at the earnest look on her face, her hands hidden deep in the pockets of her duffel coat.

"I'm sorry," she said.

"God," he said.

"I am."

"God. What was it like?"

She broke into her characteristic quarter-smile. "Okay," she said.

"It was okay?"

"No. Okay, I will tell you."

They went inside, bought a bottle of wine at the bar, and took a table far from the accordion player.

"Do you know Gandhi?" she asked, filling his glass. "How he would sleep with the young Hindu girls? He would have them lie in his bed to test his willpower. It was like that."

He shook his head. He didn't know what the hell she was talking about.

"How old do you think Ziegler is?" she asked.

"Seventies. Early seventies."

"Don't be so goddamn serious."

"I'm sorry."

"He wanted me to make tea for him. This was in the time of the Brahms Four, last year. I was lucky to play in the orchestra—because I came late to the Hochschule, after the term began. But he liked my playing, and even though I was not principal oboist, he had picked me out, my abilities. I came to his studio on Lessingstrasse a couple of times, for a coaching. Once he asked me to stay for tea. I was a little flattered, and really, I was only in West Germany a couple of weeks and I was susceptible."

Barrow nodded, though he could not imagine her susceptible—she was the opposite of susceptible.

"He asked many questions about East Berlin, about Prenzlauer Berg, which is a district of Berlin where he used to live before the war. He plays the flute a little and we played together—he was awful, and he knew it—but I began to notice that he would think of any excuse for me to play the oboe. One night it was quite late, and I stayed. I felt some curiosity and, I will say, some affection for him. Also, I did not know— I was from the East—perhaps there would be some value for me if he liked me. I stayed in his bed. Nothing happened. I stayed again, later in the same week. Still he did not touch me, though we slept together in this narrow bed."

"Did you want him to?"

"Now you are going to get stupid?"

He smiled; she was winning.

"I am telling you all these things that I was afraid to say before ... I thought ..."

"Go ahead."

"Because I thought it would be less difficult for us."

"Which," he said, "is why you lied to me about the cat."

"The cat?"

"Not knowing that Maestro Ziegler had a cat. When we first talked. At Bad Herrenalb. Scooping up after the cat."

"Yes," she said. "Guilty," and she lifted the fingers of her right hand—just the fingers—off the table.

He gazed at her face. The smart tilt of her chin. The dark flecks in her brown eyes and the uncareful part she'd given her hair. She contained untamed stretches of wilderness. He tried to speak. "I'm really ..."

"Yes," she said. "I'm really, too."

They held each other's eyes. When they reached for their wineglasses, it was with such congruity of movement that they both laughed.

They watched the accordionist, who'd begun stumbling through a tango. Barrow poured more wine, turning the neck after the last dribble as he'd seen waiters do.

Petra took a sip. "It is simply that I do not like to see you so—there is a good English word—'debased' by him."

"*Erniedrigt?*"

"That is some of it."

"You surprise me sometimes," Barrow said. "Your English."

"One looks up the isolated phrase." Her eyes were bright, filled with humor. "When one is sleeping with an American."

That last phrase, his strong response to it, surprised him. He took a long sip of wine.

"And so," he said, "you think perhaps he is jealous of me? Being with you?"

"No."

"You don't think so?"

"I think he is jealous of *me*." He gave her a funny look. She was suppressing a smile. "Because you are the one he is in love with."

"We're talking about Ziegler."

189

She nodded.

"You're crazy," he said.

"He is a homosexual."

"What?"

"What do you call—?"

"Gay? He's gay?"

"*Schwul,* we say sometimes."

"He told you that?"

"No."

"*Also,*" he said under his breath.

She watched him, allowing the idea to settle. "There was—sometimes I felt there was an understanding. He left—one time, for example—he left some photos on the kitchen table. 'I found these,' is all he would say. They were all of"—and she hesitated, glancing at Barrow before continuing—"of a man. The same man, a publicity photo, a picture of this man and Ziegler himself, maybe twenty, in the mountains playing, with hats, you know, kind of jousting with those Tyrolean hats. Also, a photo of this same man with Wilhelm Furtwängler holding some horses, you know, holding the reins. That is the Berlin Tiergarten, I thought, and so I asked and he said, Yes, that is the Tiergarten. I asked him, Is that Erich Blumenfeld? And he said, Yes. Erich Blumenfeld."

Again, she looked at Barrow. "You remember? On the Ziegler recording?"

"Yes."

"People who heard him say he could have been the best oboist of the century. He was killed in the camps."

"That's what you said."

"Ziegler said to me once, 'You sound very much like him,' and that is when I became suspicious."

"That they had been lovers."

"Yes."

"Not simply friends? People always assume—"

She shook her head. "All the time I think, He is telling me this deliberately, leaving me these little clues. You know with Ziegler how everything is deliberate? And this was not a man who was interested in a woman's body, not even in the most, perhaps, aesthetic sense. Now he is talking of Blumenfeld, quite often, playing recordings, explaining things from his memory, teaching me even some of Blumenfeld's phrasing, 'Erich played like this,' he would say."

She took a sip before continuing.

"There is so much you can learn from a person's eyes when they are recalling someone."

In the far corner of the bar the accordion player was packing up her instrument.

"So, you think that's why he was detained?" Barrow asked. "Because he was a homosexual?"

"He told you of his arrest?"

"He mentioned it."

The bar had quieted down and she lowered her voice. "There was this Paragraph 175. It was in the criminal code. From Bismarck's time, and the first German Empire. Paragraph 175. It was still in there for the Nazis, and they loved it. It was still there, in fact, for the West Germans. Until 1969, when it was repealed."

"What did it say?"

"Homosexuality is a federal crime."

"Was Blumenfeld gay?"

"He wasn't known to be." And here, curiously, she hesitated. "He had, I think, a family, some children."

"That doesn't mean anything."

"I know."

"Either way."

"Correct. And I wasn't sure," she said, her voice remaining low. "Until you came. The student conductor from America."

He shook his head, "No."

She smiled, almost sheepishly. "You should see him watch you conduct."

"I don't ..."

"You even look a little like him. Like Blumenfeld. You have all the requirements."

"I don't believe it."

"You can be naive," she said. "I think we have learned that."

⁓

On their way back to Schützenstrasse she ticked off exhibits: Ziegler's jealousy, his punishment of her, his erratic attitude toward Barrow—the special treatment he had received, both good and bad.

"You understand why he picked Antonio instead of you for the Brahms concert?"

"No."

"To erase any suspicion."

"There is no suspicion."

"You don't think so?"

"Antonio was better prepared."

"Everyone knows you are the better conductor," she said. "Picking Antonio accomplished two things for Ziegler—and you are naive again if you don't conclude this—it proved to you and to himself, and to anyone looking, that you were in no way the favored boy. And second, it was another sabotage. It was just like ruining the tuning of the piano in Brussels."

"I'm not sure if I believe that anymore. About the sabotage."

"It is at least possible."

On the street outside her apartment, he stopped. "Is this what you meant the other night? When you said it was too late to hide things?"

She looked at him and smiled. "Yes," she said and came up on her toes and kissed him.

24

On Monday morning, he stopped to check for messages in the Hochschule office. Frau Heim, secretary to the director, spotted him from behind her desk. She called out in English, "This is an awful thing, what happened."

"*Bitte?*"

"With you and Herr Popescu and Fräulein Vogel. It is in the newspaper last week. We have been discussing it." She was a well-built woman, an Olympic skier back in the fifties, and a wearer of tight-fitting sweaters. "These neo-Nazis, we normally do not find them in Karlsruhe."

She handed him a torn piece of newsprint, a half-column from the local paper. "They are not from Karlsruhe," she said.

He caught the words, *Attention, Gypsy!* in the article's subhead.

"A terrible thing," Heim continued, "but you should know some of the Romanians look like Turks, and the Turks are not well loved here by a lot of people."

"They called him Gypsy," he said.

"Yes, because the Gypsies are from Egypt, you see, which is quite close to Turkey."

Before he could reach for the contents of his box, she had placed the clipping in his hand. "We have nothing against the Romanians," she said.

He felt possessed by a devil he usually ignored. "But you do have something against the Turks?" he asked.

"I do not personally, no," said Frau Heim. Some red blotches had come up on her neck.

"Of course."

"I, of course, have nothing against the Turks, and, anyway, we do not have so many here in Karlsruhe. I am only trying to tell you, Herr Barrow, that Tano should not feel badly that he was attacked for being Romanian, from the East. It was a mistake. We support those from the East. It is only these boys, these fascist-type people."

"Yes, I understand." He started to hand her back the article.

"You may keep it, of course."

"Thank you," he said.

He left the office and crossed the driveway to the main building. There had been two messages in his box, a call from Pat Levy, and a note from Tano requesting that Barrow meet him at the Karlsruhe police station, main branch, at ten-thirty. It was a little before ten. He stopped in the lobby to check the rehearsal schedule for the opera and hurried downstairs to the old *Keller*, now the student lounge. Pat's phone rang four times—she must be screening calls. She picked up the moment he started to leave a message. "Coop," she said.

"You're probably practicing."

"I'm terrified. It's Saturday. Boulez is coming to the recital. He's made it official. I feel like I'm auditioning."

"Are you?"

She hesitated; he tried but could hear nothing in the background. "How are you?" she said. "We haven't talked."

"Not bad." Events flashed by in a parade. The double fence. The little church at *die Grenze*. "How about you?"

"The word is that Barenboim doesn't have time to learn Boulez's new piece, the one I'm playing. Or he can't take the time or something."

"Which means ..."

"Which means Boulez might be looking for someone else to record it."

"Holy shit."

"Yup."

"Pat, that's fantastic." A couple of students were eyeing him from a café table. "Is it any good? The piece?"

"I'm too close to it. Werner thinks it's really good."

He had to remind himself that she was living with Werner Schott. It seemed like months since he'd been in their apartment. "It's Boulez."

"Of course," she said. "It's brilliant. I'm in way over my head."

"I doubt it," he said. "This is how the baton gets passed, eh? The next generation. The race, whatever."

"Funny you should say that." Another pause.

"What do you mean?"

"I have to ask you something, and this has to be pretty confidential." He waited. "You understand that?"

"Sure."

"Totally confidential. Werner especially. He cannot know we had this conversation."

Barrow was nodding. "Sure."

"Do you know the Brahms choral pieces, the stuff for chorus and orchestra?"

"Sure." As it happened, they were sitting on Petra's music stand in her room. "*Nänie, Alto Rhapsody, Song of the Fates* ..." There was a fourth.

"How well do you know them?"

He hesitated; there was only one reason to ask such a question. "How well is well?"

"Well enough to conduct them in five days."

He stopped, because this is when you lied. He knew that. She knew it too. Already his ears were pounding. "Where?" he asked.

"Just tell me how well you know them."

Shit.

"How well, Coop."

"What are you saying?"

"I'm not saying anything. It's just a question."

"I mean, are you saying 'conduct a rehearsal,' or are you saying more than that?" There was no response.

"Holy shit," he said.

"This is incredibly … unrepeatable, okay? Werner has never missed a concert in his life, let alone a broadcast concert."

"What's—it's—is it being broadcast?"

"It's an internal thing. With us. Werner and me."

"You've gotta tell me more, Pat. He's going to London with you?"

"Actually, what it'll be … he'll be like … deathly ill. Sudden flu or something."

"You're completely joking."

The line fell quiet.

He felt deathly ill himself. Sudden flu. There was nowhere to sit, exposed, smack against the wall under one of the *Keller's* catacomb arches, sand-blasted, primed white. The students right there, coffee, cheese sandwiches from the machine. "Tell me this is a joke."

"It's not."

"He's insane. He's never seen me conduct."

"Werner's funny about stuff like this. He gambles on instinct. It's a kind of drug for him."

Barrow hesitated. "What else is on the program?"

"Haydn 101 and Bernstein's *Fancy Free,* the dances."

"Pat. Listen to me. We studied the Brahms pieces with Marty up in Rochester, and again in New York. I spent months on them. I know them extremely well. Like the back of my hand. I even performed *Alto Rhapsody.*"

There was a pause, several beats. He had sounded terrible. And how easy it would be for her to check with her ex-husband. Idiot. *Idiot.*

"If this is going to happen," she said, "you'll hear from Werner on Wednesday, at the latest, Thursday. He conducts the first performance Friday night, then, et cetera." Against the rush in his ear, her voice sounded metallic, even microscopic, trapped in a can. "And I never talked to you."

"Sure." He had nothing else to say. His mind was in the next country. The choral pieces—he remembered the name of the fourth: *Schicksalslied.* Or, in English, *Song of Destiny.*

"Hey Coop?"

"Yeah."

"This is not, I repeat, *not* a long shot."

"Okay."

He gave her his landlord's phone number in Ettlingen. Renate Schwalb knew to call him at Petra's whenever there was an important message.

After he hung up he felt like something explosive—he himself was the explosive material. He should stay away from heat. The pair at the café table called across to him, and he nodded. "We have heard about what happened," the boy said in English.

Barrow looked at him, saw only the instrument he played. Second horn. "Thank you," he said.

He took the stairs three at a time. He crossed the lobby and got himself out of there—back out into the cold, bright morning.

25

He met Tano under the portico of the *Polizeirevier*, and they went in. They identified themselves to a woman seated behind a tall counter. "It is ten-thirty," the woman said.

"That is the appointment," Tano said.

"You should have come earlier. They did not know if you were coming."

Tano stared at her and the imminent prospect of a serious confrontation brought Barrow out of his stupor—reconstructing the one piece he actually knew on Schott's program, Brahms' *Alto Rhapsody*.

Miraculously, Tano backed down. "Can I smoke in here?" he asked.

"No," the woman said.

They walked away. Under his breath Tano said, "We have made her day."

They took seats in the waiting area. Tano's eyes darted about the room, drank in detail as if he were a visiting police detective from Romania, not an expatriate violinist. "Really very impressive," he said. "This is how they catch criminals so fast. In Romania, chaos."

"Really."

All Barrow could think about was getting back to the library, the scores to the Brahms, and Bernstein's *Fancy Free*, which would be hard to find.

"You are practicing."

"What?"

Tano pointed to the fresh violin callus under his left jaw.

"A little," Barrow said, and he remembered something he'd thought of on the way to the station. "Should we call Petra?"

"She won't come, I know her. She hates cops, anything cops"—gesturing—"she hates all this."

"Really?"

"Child of a police state." He leaned back, merriment in his eyes. "But you have been with her? For what, last ten days? Never left her side?" Here it was again, something about the Romanian that inspired confidence, or at least truth-telling—legs crossed, fingers laced together and pressed against his knee—something in his demeanor that said, *What you say stops here, I have no use for it.* Or, *I am friendless, you have nothing to fear.*

"We went to East Germany."

"Where?"

"We ended up in Brandenburg, actually."

"Not Berlin?"

They were interrupted. A Herr Froelich introduced himself and led them to a cramped office where he produced forms for them to sign. Tano stood at the window, pointing to the courtyard below, firing off questions: Is that a holding area? How many cells? How many arrests on a given night? Froelich paid out answers like a diplomat and handed them each a report. He tossed a third, possibly Petra Vogel's, to the desk. "Let me know if your recollection differs in any detail," he said.

On another floor, Froelich passed them along to a uniformed woman with boy-cut blond hair and blue eyes. Tano was captivated. The new officer addressed them like a flight attendant on message, hands at her sides. "There will be three groups. You may recognize more than one in each group, or there may be no one you recognize from the incident. Please do not feel you must make any identification whatsoever. You will view the suspects separately." They were to be each other's lie detector.

Tano, in love, followed her in first.

Barrow sat in the single chair across from the door.

His mind went straight to the *Alto Rhapsody* problem—the acute need to prepare.

He recalled some research he'd done while studying the piece with Weissberger, mainly that Brahms, thirty-something, was in love again—this time with Julie Schumann, Clara's third-eldest. The topic never came up between any of them, though Clara—loving the irony—apparently looked kindly on his infatuation. It was hopeless for Johannes. Two generations dangling just out of reach, one on either side, ready fruit. Clara in her forties, and Julie, a fulsome sixteen. Brahms never acted, never so much as "bespoke himself," except to his most intimate of friends, one Hermann Levi, Wagner's Jew conductor—a fearsomely significant detail, in retrospect. Young Julie, sweet Julie, remained oblivious—or maybe not—but either way Brahms waited and waited, sat on his hands like a jerk. When Julie announced her engagement to an Italian count, Brahms, knowing himself to be blatantly betrayed, fled to the Black Forest to compose his *Alto Rhapsody*, a piece of crushing beauty and redemption.

Schmuck.

Tano emerged. His expression told nothing. He was playing along, German poker.

"Herr Barrow," the officer said. Her uniform was simple, no regalia. The room they entered was darkened, like a recording booth, the "talent" visible through a one-way glass: five shaved heads, eyes and cheeks hollow, some smiling, some not, some with an early growth of beard, and not a single one familiar. Of course he couldn't be certain, and he said as much.

"Thank you," said the woman, with no display of feeling either way.

"Nothing?" said the Romanian when he emerged.

"Control group," Barrow said.

Tano sat in the chair, and Barrow backed up to the wall opposite, slumped down to his ankles.

"How are you feeling?" Barrow asked.

"Fingers all fine, you see?" The Romanian splayed out all nine for approval.

"I mean, otherwise."

"What do you mean 'otherwise'?"

"Other ways."

"Up here, you mean?" He tapped his head. Barrow shrugged. "Fine. You look like shit though."

Barrow grinned.

"How is she?"

"Fine, I think."

"Good, we're all fine. Except you." Tano took out a cigarette, held it between his thumb and middle finger, as if to emphasize the missing digit. Barrow had never seen him in such good spirits. "She has perhaps told you that we were together for a while last year."

"She mentioned it," Barrow said, attempting disinterest. Petra referred to Tano—affectionately—as one of her mistakes.

"We were only together a short while," Tano said, matching the American's tone, as though carelessly kicking aside a small obstruction that stood between them. "But she is a lovely woman, which I think I have said to you before."

"Yes," Barrow said.

"A girl with secrets, which is always compelling."

"Like you both said, it's a habit from the East."

Tano nodded.

A heavy door slammed somewhere on another floor.

"Whenever a person comes across," Tano said, "it is not without cost."

"Across the Wall you mean?"

"Iron curtain, what have you. Certainly in Petra Vogel's case, they had something on her, or they would never have let her go to Paris."

"A major sacrifice, I'll bet," Barrow said, as offhandedly as possible. He had not asked for the Romanian's political commentary. "Leaving everything behind."

"And for others as well."

"People who helped her?"

"No, that's not it," said Tano. "What I mean, they do not let you out—give you a visa—unless they can hurt you in some way if you don't come back. And since you are not there yourself, the hurt must be to someone you love. A proxy, so to speak."

"A hostage."

"Same idea," Tano said.

"So Petra has a proxy back in East Germany?"

"I don't know. She would never tell me."

"But you asked her?"

"The subject came up."

"Her mother works for East German television," Barrow said, "some very popular show, did she tell you that?"

"*Aktuelle Kamera*. Also that she did not lose her job, which is some kind of miracle."

"Things have changed perhaps."

The Romanian shrugged. He ran the cigarette past his nostrils, which, at the moment, struck Barrow as a silly affectation.

"And who was *your* proxy?" Barrow asked.

"I had none."

"What about family?"

"I have only an uncle. In Timisoara. He is a housepainter, so for him there was little to lose."

"Friends?"

"I made sure not to have any of those."

A woman's voice, "Herr Popescu?" The officer apologized for the wait, and Tano followed her through the door.

Barrow could not sit; he walked to one end of the hallway. He stared down the forty or fifty meters of corridor, thinking of Werner Schott, remembering their brief exchanges, few of them on musical matters, none meaningful. They'd chatted about Bruckner, listened to Ziegler's Brahms One. Why me? he thought. The man's never even seen me conduct. Why is he picking me? He started down the corridor, another round-trip. Muffled sounds came from the floor above.

Tano emerged unhappy, though again he said nothing. Barrow went in for his second round. Five new faces, and not one recognizable. He turned to the officer and shook his head.

"Are you sure?" she asked. He thought he read a slight tremor in her voice, a first wrinkle in the otherwise perfect composure of the Karlsruhe *Polizei*. The pressure was on. Hoping to get lucky, the cops had scooped up a handful of known neo-Nazi types. But neither the American nor the Romanian would cooperate.

"Why is this so important?" Barrow asked in a low voice, as if the suspects might hear him through the glass. "No one was hurt."

"It is, in fact, extremely important."

He wished he hadn't questioned her—his ignorance showing again. He did her the courtesy of one more sweep of the faces. Kids all, and appropriately sullen. "I'm sorry," he said.

Tano's final round took under a minute. Back out, he muttered, "See you outside," and started up the hallway, cigarette at the ready.

Barrow entered the room. For all he knew they might all be there, all five, but how had he thought he'd be able recognize them? It's called *blind* rage for a reason; it had driven him into the wall of skinheads, gotten him an elbow in the face.

Barrow shook his head. "Of course, I cannot be sure," he said.

A city seeking desperately to cleanse itself, and he couldn't help. Not a bit.

"I understand," the woman said. "Would you look again very carefully? Imagine, perhaps, different clothing."

He did.

"Number four?" she said.

"No, I don't think so."

26 Tano left him outside Franksmusik, which had scores for everything on Schott's program but the Bernstein, and that they promised in two days—Wednesday— just enough time perhaps. The Haydn wasn't necessarily a cinch, but he knew it well. For the present, he would pour everything into the Brahms.

He split the afternoon between the record library and one of the piano rooms in the "barracks," a building across from the music school. At seven, he left the compound to find something to eat, surprised to find the streets packed with shoppers. Three weeks until Christmas.

While he walked, he puzzled over a set of words from *Song of the Fates*, his own rough translation. They exited his mouth as thin vapor—

So sang the Fates;
the exile hears them deep in a cave, dark as night,
hears their songs—the old man—

imagines his children and grandchildren
and shakes his head.

He ducked into a McDonald's-style restaurant and ordered a meal and a shake, still running over the words in his head. When asked for a flavor, he looked back dumbly.

"*Schokolade?*" the boy suggested.

"*Ja, ja.*"

Food woke him from his stupor and he scanned the crowded tables, mostly kids, laughing and wolfing down fries. He glanced at a cluster of skinheads, recognized none of them.

This would be a Christmas to remember, wouldn't it? The Wall was history. The whole damned century was over. And would Brahms be pleased? Doubtful. The genius-grump loved his *Angst*, his precious romantic sense of doom and dread, and where was it today? The scorched earth had been reclaimed. The six million, their several voices, soprano-alto-tenor-bass, less and less audible, *al niente*—"to nothing." Certainly in this place, swamped by the din of the fast-feeding, well-provisioned great-grandchildren. All that other stuff was in recess—the Holocaust—it could only recede from memory, the blood in the soil seeping deeper, further from snout and mind, history disappearing. History that for Brahms loomed so large and awful—his horizon—come and gone.

Brahms would not be pleased with straws and plastic forks.

the old man,
imagines his children and grandchildren
and shakes his head.

Barrow felt a random stab of panic—the most familiar feature of performance anxiety. He pulled out a score. He had tabbed every transition in each of the four Brahms pieces with Post-its. It was in the transitions—the segues between differing meters and tempos—that his ignorance would be found out. He picked a Post-it and flipped to the spread—bar 116 of *Song of the Fates*, 4/4 into 3/4. No *ritardando*, tempo the same, *a cappella* chorus in six parts, hushed, tender, and *legato*, without seam—

> *The rulers turn their blessed eyes*
> *from entire generations* ...

He stared at the page. How could he have missed it? No loss of tempo, but the new meter's suspended, slow-dance weightlessness, hovering over the words, locking them in the imagination. The effect was utterly arresting. Brahms' perfect instinct—his brilliant design.

The idea left him breathless.

Brahms, precisely a century ago, selected—out of volumes, out of *libraries* of German poetry—these lines, written by Goethe precisely one century before his time:

> *they refuse to see in the grandchildren*
> *the once-loved, quiet eloquence of their ancestors.*

"Shit," he whispered. "The grandchildren are the Nazis."

He looked up from the score, and panned his surroundings. A restaurant, silly with Germans. A carnival.

He thought, This is wrong, this is too obvious.

But it *was* obvious. Brahms was a prophet. He'd seen it coming, seen the whole goddamned century, the children and grandchildren. Brahms, lifting words written a hundred years before his time, sensed a new century, the one to come. And now that century was over, come and gone, and Germany was—finally, for the last time?—reunifying. Ready to move on. Maybe.

Words, just flimsy words, but music catapulted them, flung them into another realm. And he, Barrow, knew how to work the machinery.

His hands shook. He closed the score and slid it into his pack, felt suddenly the burden of a secret, one he could unheft only on the podium. *Only on the podium.* One afternoon of study and already the need was so strong he thought he might die before he got there.

He left the restaurant and rejoined Kaiserstrasse and full-blown Christmas. He needed motion. The Ettlingen tram was boarding passengers on the next block and he jogged for it. He would check in with the Schwalbs, alert Renate in person that he'd be receiving an important call from Frankfurt and that she must forward it instantly to Petra's apartment.

He joined the other passengers jostling for position, work or shopping behind them—hot food, chilled wine, and a warm kitchen ahead. He dodged the closing doors, and a fragment from Brahms' *Song of Destiny* broke loose in his mind—he would never shake this stuff, not until he'd conducted it—the great poet Hölderlin's depressive plaint to the gods:

You walk up there in the light on soft ground,
blessed spirits ...
free from destiny

and on and on ...

But we have no place to rest
We waste away, we fall ...

Bullshit, he thought. It's *us* wandering up there in the light. The great-great-grandchildren. This is the soft ground.

Free from destiny, Hölderlin wrote of the so-called gods, the spirits, ever beyond reach, *up there.* Brahms and Hölderlin, gazing pathetically upward, smothering in their own envy.

Schicksallos. Free from destiny.

Only in German would that be one word.

27

The next day Ziegler set up a mid-morning meeting at his apartment, no explanation.

The old man met him at the door—an unprecedented event—and led him to the inner sanctum of the kitchen where he'd prepared a platter of cheese and wurst. Barrow said he'd already eaten breakfast. "You are sure?" Ziegler asked.

"Yes."

Ziegler indicated the platter. "Take straight from the tray if you like."

Barrow nodded, marking time by watching the cat bathe itself in a small rectangle of sun on the kitchen floor.

"I've never asked your cat's name."

"César," Ziegler said, loading up a plate for himself. "I was preparing the Franck A-major when he arrived at my door."

"Like a visitation by the composer?"

"If you like."

They were both watching the cat—the simple duple rhythm of his bath. The tiny rite had its accompanying sound, a scant rasp of the tongue.

"It is a sign of our intelligence," Ziegler said.

"Pardon me?"

"That we should take notice of rhythm, this is what separates us from them. No?"

Barrow nodded. What he really wanted was to bring the conversation around to their last meeting in the Konzerthaus, discover what the hell it had been about, explore his suspicion that the old man had heard about Saratoga. He could repair some damage, perhaps. He might even risk bringing up the Brahms choral pieces—without, of course, mentioning the concert in Frankfurt.

"Only humans choose to dance," Ziegler said.

Barrow looked up, peered across at his teacher. The word *dance*, coming from the old man's mouth, had clanged like a pot in the sink.

"You say animals dance, 'move with grace,' a mating dance. That is an idiotic projection of the human soul on the animal. For purposes of television. Only humans dance. Only humans manipulate rhythm. No dog conducts—have you seen a dog conduct? Not even a German shepherd."

Barrow forced a smile.

"Nor do they keep a beat," Ziegler said, reaching for an oval of black bread.

"Excuse me?"

"Dogs. Any animal. Cannot keep a beat."

"Of course."

"No small point, because also separating us from every other mammal is intelligence, superconsciousness, ego. Am I right? And so you must ask, what is the relationship between rhythm and intelligence?"

"I see."

"No, you do not."

Barrow took up a piece of cheese. "I am listening."

"We overlook this fact, that rhythm is as central to the psyche as intelligence. Intelligence goes out, to the stars, et cetera. Rhythm goes in, to the intestines, the stomach. And to say this is a regression to the animal, again this is irrational. The animal does not share in this. It is only human. As human as intelligence. Deeply human. And linked to emotion. In fact *intimate* with emotion. How in one minute can a song bring tears? Or how, in the 'Pastoral,' can Beethoven achieve elation in sixteen bars?"

Elation? Another pot in the sink.

The old man shifted his focus to the window, his fingertips in motion. His eyes shone intensely. He had an air of performance about him.

"And this, of course, is Brahms."

Barrow felt his face flush—did he know about Frankfurt? Was there *anything* he didn't know?

"Are you listening?"

"Yes."

"You have a weakness."

"Pardon?"

"A weakness."

Die Schwäche. Weakness. Debility. Failing.

"I've been meaning, Herr Ziegler—"

"In Brahms, one is to push with the emotion but release the feeling through rhythm, play it out there, attenuate it across the piece, in motion, horizontally—a coursing thing, yes?"

"Yes—"

"And the colors? The colors may change as you go, but never sit in one place, never hammer, never strain any one chord—only push this emotion to the utmost. Yet, at the same time, there must be an equal force—absolutely equal, pushing back—called intelligence. A, emotion, *evolving* emotion, against B, intelligence. Never outright despair, as with Tchaikovsky. Never outright eruption like Beethoven. Ebullience, yes certainly, but always this fairness"—he ground his right fist into the palm of his left hand—"this temperance, this extraordinary intelligence governing the whole, obsessively governing, but against it to push, *push* the emotion."

Barrow looked from Ziegler's hands to his face. The old man's eyes were bright with certainty.

"Where am I weak?"

"At the place where they meet."

"How do I solve it?"

"You cannot."

Barrow swallowed. The filter of language. The slight uncertainty. "You mean that I, in particular, cannot solve it?"

"That is what I mean."

"Why not?"

"It is hard to say."

Barrow glanced out the kitchen window. Across the courtyard a woman was shaking out a doormat.

"Why can't I?" he asked.

"I am not qualified to answer."

Defeat sounded in his ears—so loud, he felt cut off from his own voice. "Are you referring—what are you referring to, Maestro?"

"I am referring to nothing in particular, Herr Barrow." The old man's visage appeared amazingly calm. To be delivering such misfortune. "I am talking about personality."

"Is this why you picked Antonio for the performance?"

The question hung in the air for seconds—its horrifying ring of self-pity. "Antonio was better cast in that role."

Barrow pushed his chair back from the table.

"Where are you going?"

"You are done with me."

"I am not."

"You have described a hopeless situation."

"I have made no such description. One should simply know one's weaknesses."

Ziegler stood, reached into a cupboard above the refrigerator and pulled out a liquor bottle. Something clear. From another cupboard, he retrieved two shot glasses.

"The other day, you attempted serious injury on one of my under-graduate students. Why was that?"

Could that be what this was about? He should have stopped at the stage door, gone back and apologized to the student, to Ziegler.

"I'm sorry," Barrow said. "That was a mistake, I was upset."

"Do you know there are scientists—serious men—who believe that people, their personalities, are incapable of alteration? In minor ways, yes. But in essentials, no alteration whatsoever. Is that how you feel?"

"I think they're probably right."

"So that if one were to commit a grave error in the past, say, when one was young, that error—or the personality that allowed for that error—is unalterable?"

Saratoga.

The old man was talking around it, but he must know.

"Or put another way, does there exist the possibility of redemption?"

Barrow stared. *Redemption*—another loud word. One for the sink.

"I meant that as a question, Herr Barrow."

"Yes, of course. I think redemption is possible."

"I see. So, on the subject of personality alteration, you are with the scientists, but on the subject of redemption, you are with the priests."

"I don't know."

Ziegler's eyes felt strangely penetrating and Barrow looked down at his hands. He glanced at the liquor bottle. Aquavit, the label said.

"We have digressed from the purpose of this visit."

"Which is what?" Barrow asked, hearing the false note of insolence in his own voice, an old defense.

Ziegler poured the aquavit, bent his tall frame to check levels. He handed Barrow one of the glasses. "Please take this."

The liquor gave off a musty odor. Barrow did not look forward to drinking it.

"I have invited you this morning to say good-bye."

"Excuse me?"

"I am leaving Germany."

It had to be a joke—

"I have taken a position with a conservatory in Seoul. Which is an inconvenience for you, so I am telling you personally."

So quick, the arrival of this news. A paper cut. "Of course."

"South Korea."

"Yes."

"You are a promising student, whatever your problems."

"Yes."

"I apologize."

The old man could not have fashioned a more perfect dismissal. "I congratulate you, Herr Maestro Ziegler."

"Please tell no one."

"Naturally."

Barrow adjusted his position in the chair, fighting to hustle along the emotion. "Maestro," he said, the aquavit jiggling in his hand, "why would you leave?"

The old man smiled, raised his glass. "Here's to a most thrilling new pestilence," he said. "A unified Germany."

Without thinking, Barrow followed his example and slugged back the aquavit. He shook his head from the blow.

"Another?" the maestro asked, already pouring.

28 Barrow wandered up Lessingstrasse. He turned up Kaiserstrasse directly into the harsh rays of the mid-morning sun. Stopping by Franksmusik, he encountered a bit of luck—Bernstein's *Fancy Free* had arrived a day early. He hopped a tram for the Hochschule and stocked up on sandwiches from the machine in the basement of Schloss Gottesaue.

Here is your problem. It is unfixable. So long.

He crossed to the barracks and locked himself in a practice room. For the rest of the morning and all afternoon, he banged his way through scores on the piano, practiced beat patterns. He found that he could still command a rhythm, and when he quizzed his memory from the day before—the yellow-tabbed transitions—he passed every time. It was grueling, and by eight o'clock he needed a break and decided to replenish his supply of sandwiches from the other building.

The evening monitor greeted him by name, and Barrow asked if Petra Vogel was upstairs.

"Don't know."

He took the steps three at a time, and when he reached the wood-wind corridor, he heard, faint as a cat in the closet, the oboe solo from *Nänie*. He walked to the door of Messer-Eichen's studio and knocked. When she stopped, he called to her.

Within seconds, she opened the door. They were both startled by the sudden contact—alone all day with their habits. She stepped back, inviting him in with the swiftness of the gesture, backing up to her stand. It would be twice this distance on Saturday night.

"Can I hear?"

Without speaking, she played the solo again, twenty bars. He knew every note and sketched in the accompaniment with his ear. A simple melody, but it almost wrecked him the way she played it.

Finished, she left the reed between her lips to keep it moist. Her eyes returned to his, head angled down and hair hanging forward, some of it caressing her jaw line. Her left eye looked stressed; she too had been laying in the hours, scraping reeds past midnight while Barrow shared the kitchen table with Wolf.

As he moved into the room, he caught his reflection in the dark window—his cotton sweater and untucked shirttails, his dark hair too long. He pulled out the piano bench; one leg jammed in a wrinkle of the Oriental carpet and he grabbed the piano cabinet for balance. Petra smiled, reed still resting lightly on her tongue. He swung a leg over the bench and sat down.

"Any suggestions, Herr Conductor?"

"Yes," he said.

"Which?"

"More *staccato* throughout." The equivalent of bearding *Mona Lisa*.

"Yes. Of course. That's brilliant."

Something in her mode of address, the way she looked at him, suggested that she knew about Pat Levy's offer—though he himself had kept it from her. She took a step toward the piano, removed her reed and dropped it, tip first, into a water-filled prescription tube.

"Anything else, Herr Genius?" she asked.

"You know?"

"Yes, I know."

"How?"

"M.-E. told me this morning."

"Really."

That word had leaked to Schott's good friend—this must be good news, indeed.

Petra lay her oboe next to the reed cup and sat down opposite him on the bench. She looked tired, seemed to welcome the interruption. "You've been practicing for a while," he said.

"You yourself look like a concentration camp."

The reference seemed profane—he would never know which way to take such things. "I'll sleep after Saturday," he said. "I'll sleep all next week."

"You had your meeting with Ziegler?"

"He is leaving Germany," he said.

She smiled her quarter smile. "So what."

"You knew that too?"

"Come here," she said, and he edged forward on the bench.

"You knew that?"

"Of course not."

She leaned forward on her hands and touched his lips with hers, and their warmth spread through his body. She crossed a leg over one of his and leaned in further. She sometimes kissed the way hungry people eat, and she did so now, the fine bones of her jaw moving against his, her hands and fingers pressing the back of his head.

She released her mouth, but left her hands.

"Your eye's a little red."

"Yes," she said.

"Everything will change if he leaves."

"Everything will change Saturday night," she said, brushing the hair back from his forehead, tending him like a sister. "Incidentally, I identified the Duck."

"Really?"

"In a police photograph."

"That's good, isn't it?"

"Of course, it's good. Extremely good."

"So you went in to the police station?"

"Mm-hm," she nodded, apparently reluctant to go further with the topic.

"Tano said you don't like dealing with police."

"I had enough of them in the East."

She got up and turned off the ceiling light, leaving the desk lamp to glow in the corner. The air was close and overwarm, and she cracked one of the double-glazed windows, adding a slipstream of cold air and admitting sounds of practicing students, traffic from Durlacher Allee. She lowered herself to the carpet, beyond the curve of the piano where he couldn't see her.

"What is it?" she asked, her voice disembodied in the room.

Through the window, he glimpsed the shopping strip of Kaiser-strasse, rampant with Christmas. The great yellow Schloss off to the right.

"I'm nervous about the concert."

"Of course."

"You know the words to *Song of the Fates*?" he asked. "They refer to an exile. Like you."

"I've never seen them."

"They're from Goethe."

There was a pause.

"Come here," she said.

"I'm trying to imagine what you were like in East Berlin," he said.

"What do you think?" she asked.

"I think you must have scared the hell out of a lot of people."

"You are right."

"Marching with your flaming torches. Your Free Communist Youth."

"Free *German* Youth. Would you please come over here?"

"When did you quit?"

"One is too old at a certain point," she said.

217

"So you never actually quit?"

She moved out into the middle of the room where he could see her. "You don't want to fuck a communist? Is that it?"

Her sweater was off and her hair had gone a little wild; she wore a simple white blouse with buttons, several of them undone—he'd watched her put it on that morning. "Would you please come over here?"

There was a certain wicked delight in disobeying her.

"Why don't you answer my questions?" he said.

"Come over here and maybe I will."

"This is how you scare people."

"Ridiculous," she said. "Who is afraid of me?"

"I am."

"You're afraid of *all* women." She sat on the floor, flexing and unflexing her toes. "Not so?"

"You're probably right."

"Here's something to be afraid of," she said. She pressed her lips together—as she would around a reed—and released them.

"What?"

"Are you sure you want to know?"

"Of course."

She took a moment to study him, her eyes glowing in the light from the lamp.

"I was an informer," she said.

He wasn't sure of the German. "I don't know …"

"*Inoffizielle Mitarbeiterin.*"

"I don't know what that is."

"You do."

"*Inoffizielle Mitarbeiterin?*"

"IM," she said.

"For the secret police?"

"For Stasi."

He laughed. But she gazed up at him, her feelings, whatever they were, trapped behind a thin smile.

"Did they pay you?" he asked, not really believing her.

"Ha."

"Well?"

"Not professional. Patriotic. Keep asking me questions."

He felt at a loss. He'd been playing around and she was turning serious.

"Come on," she said.

"How often?"

"Twice. Once when I was a smart little girl."

"And the other time?"

"Just before I came here."

"Before Paris?"

"To make it possible," she said. Her voice sounded unnaturally flat. "To get the visa for Paris."

He stopped again, gathering his thoughts. Clearly she wanted this.

"What happened? I mean, that you were 'patriotic' and yet you defected."

"I detested it there. I did it to get out."

"You weren't worried about your mother?" he asked.

"She can save herself." He looked at her, puzzled. "She knows plenty of secrets, about other officials." She was shivering, her voice tight. "More."

"You are in touch with her? Your mother?"

She shook her head. "She publicly denounced me for defecting. More."

He got up from the bench, went to the window, and closed it.

"More questions, please."

He kneeled behind her and tried gently to turn her around.

"More questions," she said, resisting.

"I have no more."

Her cheeks were damp. "Yes you do." She was almost pleading. "For example, who did I inform against?"

He shook his head.

"Who did I inform against?"

"No more questions."

She was looking up into his eyes.

"All right," he said, "how about when you were a smart little girl?"

"One is a child. One wants hard to please people. Too easy, that question. More."

His hands were at the base of her scalp.

She hissed the words. "Barrow, ask questions."

"Okay, why?"

"Why what?"

"Why did you do it?"

"I told you," she said, and she switched to English, her words deliberate. "I was suffocating."

The sound of his native tongue was dazzling.

"I was suffocating."

The word snapped with electricity.

She seemed short of breath, on the verge of crying. His fingers went out to the crushed collar of her blouse, the narrow hollow above her collar bone. He held her shoulders. They stiffened, eased, then collapsed under his hands. He pulled her to him.

In ten days he'd learned a rough technique, always following her lead, but now she gave over to him and he felt the difference, the extra measure of authority, the strength in his hands. Pretending no polish, he stripped her of her jeans and turned her on her stomach. He ran his palms up her legs, separated them, splayed his fingers, explored her warmth.

When she crawled under the piano, he followed.

She lay on her back and whispered something unintelligible. The carpet burned his knees. He kissed her lips and hair. Her neck bent to watch when he guided himself inside, and her hands fumbled for the pedals behind her head. He grabbed one of the gold-painted beams above, supporting himself. He had to close his eyes, the way her breasts rose and shuddered and shuddered again, and he felt her wet palm press a spot just below his ribs, catching him up in the imperative of her cadence. She was a lesson in overwhelming need, and he gritted his teeth, his knees on fire, sometimes opening his eyes to watch her body quiver below him, the quick intakes of breath. When she suddenly groaned and thrust back, such cries came up in the room as he had never heard. He felt thicker than he'd ever felt, and it took gratifyingly long for him to exhaust himself; she seemed never to stop, her hard jerks.

He couldn't believe the happiness. She grasped his upper arms and made him lie on top of her. Somewhere on a lower floor, a string quartet wrestled earnestly with Beethoven. They lay for a long time, the heat building up between them, unwilling to move.

His clothes were an insult—the rawness of his knees and elbows, the large burn on the side of his buttock. He watched her in the window as she dressed. She pocketed her bra in her jeans, and was buttoning her blouse when he had to kiss her again, sneak his hands under her clothes.

They left Schloss Gottesaue, utterly spent. She tucked herself under his shoulder and stayed that way through the cold night until they arrived at Schützenstrasse—her bare hand under his collar, next to his skin, reminding him. They stopped on the sidewalk across from her building. The light was on in the kitchen window of her apartment, two stories up. "What will you do?" he asked.

"Go to any city that will have me," she said, and he rejoiced quietly that she knew what he'd meant, on what level he'd asked. "Germany," she said. "But also anywhere. Amsterdam. Switzerland. What about you?"

"A conductor can be happy anywhere," he said.

29 Barrow's presence was required at the first full rehearsal of *Hänsel und Gretel* late Thursday afternoon, a pointless exercise during which he sat in the last row of the theater, cramming Haydn's "Surprise" Symphony. Tano insisted on buying him a drink afterward, and since he'd been alone with his scores for the past thirty-six hours—Petra had left the day before to rehearse with the Radio-Sinfonie in Frankfurt—he thought he could spare forty-five minutes.

They took a chessboard table in the back of the *Kneipe*, where it was warm. Tano ordered a bottle of schnapps and a couple of glasses, and Barrow excused himself to call his landlord in Ettlingen, hoping for a message from Werner Schott or Pat. There was none. He returned to the table.

"Petra identified Duck the Skinhead Fascist," Tano announced, handing him a full shot glass.

"I know."

Tano seemed to have expected a livelier response. "And they have arrested him."

Barrow gulped down the schnapps. The stuff was exactly right for the moment. "No kidding."

Tano tipped another round into their glasses. "And so, the other reason for this goddamn potato liquor"—he lifted his glass, waited for Barrow to do the same—"to goddamn Saturday night."

Barrow stared across at the smiling Romanian. "She told you about the concert?"

Tano smiled slyly. "I got it out of her."

"Honor among defectors?"

"Good one, Herr Amerikaner."

"*Ich lerne.*"

Tano leaned back in his chair and took out a cigarette. "I am, of course, extremely happy for you," he said.

"Thanks."

"Are you worried?"

"Terrified. I should be studying this minute."

"Don't worry," Tano said. "This is better. Otherwise you get too wound up, and that's not good."

"It's probably not going to happen. I haven't heard anything."

"Who ever heard of a conductor canceling an appearance, anyway? I never heard of that."

Barrow shrugged.

Tano sat back in his seat, the arbiter of all worry. "How much do you like her?" he asked, and something about him, the missing finger, the pompous manipulation of moment and cigarette, the ability in a single posture to inculcate all that was absurd about a given circumstance— one or all of the above continued to inspire trust.

"Quite a bit," Barrow said.

"She likes you too, quite a bit."

"I'm not sure why you ask."

"She once told me she would only be happy with an American. I wasn't sure whether she knew what one was. I told her maybe she meant she would only be happy in America. 'California,' she said. She'd already thought of it."

"Cape Mendocino."

"She told you."

Barrow nodded. She'd shown him once, on an atlas. Furthest point west.

Tano continued. "She had a specific picture of it in her head, from some book she'd read, and this involved very high grassy hills falling way down into the sea. She tell you this? And warm too, she knew all about the temperature. She would talk about this very seriously and I would laugh and laugh."

"I doubt if it's all that warm," Barrow said. He took a small sip from his glass. The liquor followed the same hot path down his throat.

"You are reluctant?" Tano asked, referring to the drink.

"Like I said. I've got work."

"And like I said, don't worry. We all know you are going to succeed. Another, what, another Michael Tilson Thomas or something." As usual, Barrow couldn't read the Romanian either way on the topic of Michael Tilson Thomas. "The point is," Tano continued, "she wants out of Germany badly. She's never talked with you about this?"

"Not really."

"I guess I'm not surprised."

"Why?"

"Perhaps, on this subject you'd be the last one she'd talk to."

Barrow felt tired and the schnapps was removing what little fight he had left. He'd been up since before five, third day in a row, conducting from memory, conducting the CD, hoarding tempos, then entrances, entrances, entrances, back to the score for correction.

And this ridiculous opera rehearsal.

"You're trying to tell me," he said—and after nearly three weeks of dating, fucking, sitting up in her bed at night, no it had not yet occurred to him, and why should it?—"that she's only after my passport."

"Actually, no. Not only. Why would she need you for that? She can marry the timpani player, any happy Yank with a Fulbright." He looked off and smiled, as if imagining the scenario.

Barrow thought he should probably tell him to fuck off, but what was the harm?

"I don't think you know the cost," Tano said, "of crossing certain borders over here."

"How they won't let you go unless they have a hostage? You told me about that. A proxy."

"Yes, but that's only half of it. When I left Romania, all I could think was, Get me out, get me out. All the time, Get me out. The reasons to go, I won't even bother except—do you know the plays by Samuel Beckett?"

"Some."

"All one does, all one is entitled to do, is breathe and tell jokes. Or like living your life in a mirror, cutting your hair, you ever do that? You think you move the scissors this way, but it is the opposite, it has the opposite effect all the time. Life in Romania." He took a long pull of tobacco, let it out. "Wanting to know—perhaps this is the most important—what is true? What happened? Just now. Just yesterday. What *really happened*? What is history? I was going nuts, absolutely crazy, and perhaps it was just me because everybody else seemed to get along just fine. Perhaps it was just that I did not have the kind of things to sustain one through that. A good mother. Some great love. I suppose it is obvious I am no great lover, even of music."

"German music," Barrow said.

"Any music. So I wanted to get out of that world, and I did and here I am. And now, holy goddamn cow, I miss it." He knocked back what was left in his glass, poured another. "This, of course, is what I'm trying to tell you about Vogel."

"What's that?"

"If you're running like hell from something, it must still be very much alive inside you."

Barrow felt warm; he pulled down the neck of his sweater, exposing more of his throat. It was possible that Tano knew all about Petra's days as an informer—maybe he was sniffing around to see if Barrow knew as well. He thought of asking, but he dare not. Better it came from Tano. "So you think she's still running?" he asked.

"Not exactly."

"Pardon me, but what the fuck are you saying?"

"Yes, what the fuck am I saying."

"I'm sorry."

"No," Tano said, waving him off and looking away pensively.

"What else do you know about her?"

The Romanian looked back, seemed to consider the question. "My mother was German," he said, "did I ever tell you that?"

"Exactly when would you have told me that?"

Tano laughed, lifting the schnapps bottle. "You are better every time, have some more of this." Barrow shook his head; Tano poured a dram anyway. "My mother was a German who never saw Germany. An ethnic German in Romania, so this might apply to me, but really it applies to Petra so much more. This is just my theory, of course. Here is something you must not underestimate—"

"What?"

"That it is such a big thrill coming across."

"The danger."

"No. I mean, yes, of course. But that is not the thrill I am talking about. Really, to come across, for some few people—and I think Petra is one of them—it is like killing."

"Killing what?" Barrow recalled her statement in full, that she'd killed something that they will never have such opportunity to kill. "What exactly?"

"Something very—I don't know—badly subjective, if I'm saying it right. And, again I say, this is just my theory." He leaned forward, the opposite of expansive, "A sort of voice, okay, saying 'You are German, you are German, you are German,' on and on, something of that sort. 'You are German.' A sort of bottomless ... congruity with the role, congruity as a living thing, you understand, deep inside of you. There are those people who cannot stand that identification. And some of those

226

people, in their turn, resort to terrorism to kill it. Baader–Meinhof gang. Make a bomb or something. Others—Petra, for example—cross the border, and in doing this they strip it all away from the outside, as if their skin, you understand, their entire skin is caught on the barbed wire as they cross, left hanging there."

"The border is gone," Barrow said.

"Oh yes."

"Which means what?"

"Which nullifies the act."

↝

The temperature had dropped, and a cold wind tore bitterly at his face and at the fingers that dropped the coins and punched in the phone number Pat Levy shared with Werner Schott. He had already checked if there had been any calls to his apartment. Nothing.

"*Hallo.*" It was Pat.

"It's Barrow."

"He's calling someone else, Coop."

"What?"

"He's getting someone else."

"Wait—"

"He's sleeping."

Something rose up in Barrow's throat, and he couldn't speak. The receiver was a chunk of ice against his ear. He swallowed painfully.

"I'm sorry," Pat said.

"Has he already called this other guy?"

"I don't know, I'm totally out of it. I'm playing in two days. Tomorrow's all about travel. I was practicing when you called."

He shot a glance across the street to where Tano stood in the lee of an entryway; if only the Romanian could step in, his lawyer, plead his case. "Pat, I've gotta do this concert," he said, forcing his voice into a lower octave, masking.

"I don't know what to tell you. It was insane what he was doing anyway."

"What *he* was doing?"

"What?" The voice was flat, cold.

"Didn't you ... " he began. But he heard himself. He swallowed, tried again, "Didn't you put him up to this?"

"Are you crazy? What am I, Jesus Christ? The guy listens to no one. He's a fucking *Prussian*, Coop *and* he's a conductor. It was his idea. You know, give the American a grand send-off. But he backed down, what can I say."

Barrow's teeth had begun to chatter.

"I've gotta conduct that concert."

"I'm sorry, Coop. I shouldn't have called you before. It seemed better to let you in on it."

He gripped the receiver with his left hand while his right wandered the air, searching for a hold. He was trying to keep down what he knew was coming up inside him. "What happened ... why ..."

There was a pause on the other end, the kind of pause that could either save or destroy a life. He entertained a stray thought of her lips, their exact distance from the receiver, how warm it must be in Schott's apartment, the benign night view of Frankfurt.

"I guess he's worried you're not ready."

"What?"

"It's a big concert. TV and all."

His eyes were shedding water against the cold. Momentarily, he was able to blink back the flow, observe, across the street, the faint arc of Tano's cigarette as it rose, stalled in front of his face, and fell.

"Pat, listen to me. I *know* this music. For four days I'm basically eating the stuff for breakfast, lunch, and dinner. I'm up all night."

Another pause.

"It's Ziegler, Coop."

"Ziegler?"

"He gave you a bad rec."

"He ..."

"Werner called Ziegler. He gave you a bad rec."

It was like a paving stone, a cold-chinked, black paving stone, had flown up out of the sidewalk and smacked him in the side of the face. In a cartoon. The same display of stars.

"Okay, Pat," he said gruffly.

"I'm sorry, Coop."

His voice was packed full, ready to split. "Good luck with the Boulez."

"I'm sorry," she said.

She said something else, but he had to hang up. He was shaking in earnest. For a few seconds the receiver hung dead in its cradle. Until he understood he had another call to make.

30   The instant he began punching out the number, he knew the telephone was the wrong medium. He smashed the receiver into the steel cradle, heard the slight adjustment of change inside, smashed it again. "Fuck," he said between clenched teeth.

Tano approached but Barrow waved him off.

He jogged, and ran, to the nearest tram stop, formulating arguments, the Deutsch for this or that word, scratching at the borders of his fluency. How do you say—what is it, the subjunctive?—*I should like to fucking understand.* How do you approach? Two-fisted? Pounding the table, Ziegler's desk, leaning into the old man's face, hollering? Or—the less gratifying angle—explaining that he'd studied all four Brahms pieces in great depth, that he could do them, that he was capable of goddamn *doing* them.

In my sleep, I could conduct them!

He leapt off the tram at Lessingstrasse. He reached for his gloves and found that he had forgotten them at the telephone—his good ones, his leather-sheathed gloves. He ran to number 15 and knocked.

The door opened.

The Korean's presence brought him up short—her white pullover, her gray schoolgirl skirt, her gentle, civil smile. "He will be here shortly, and he was going out again," she said. There was something hypnotic in hearing German come from her wide Korean face. She invited him in and offered tea. He followed her to the kitchen, his second visit, noticing the bottle of aquavit on the counter, no longer shut away in the cupboard.

"You," she continued in German, "are Cooper Barrow."

"Yes." His hands felt out of control; if he wasn't careful, he'd spill something.

"He has pointed you out."

"And you are?" She'd used the formal, so he did as well.

"Maria Won. You were a student of Gilbert Shanahan?"

"Yes."

"I admire his work. I have seen him conduct in Seoul and in Tokyo. I could not get into his master class."

"Next time you should mention my name. Or Herr Ziegler's. That always makes a difference."

He said this for no reason, noting only that in her hands the teacup never seemed to land, but arrived all the same, water out of the kettle and into the cup without a whisper, sugar spooned without a clatter. The service of tea in the master's absence.

"Are you in Germany long?" he asked, imitating sanity.

"Perhaps not. You are here for one year?"

"Yes."

She would not sit but stood by the sink, watching him, gauging the short-term affect of her work. Her stillness filled the room, and he could see how she might draw the attention of an orchestra. He wondered where she slept.

"A Fulbright?" she asked.

"No. It's a private fellowship."

He warmed his fingers on the sides of the cup, and before he could take a sip, he heard the front door. He pushed his chair away from the table, felt the old man's presence behind him. The trap had sprung. Marie Won, by the sink, *Master, look who wandered in.*

Ziegler's voice: "I am going to the sauna. If you wish to talk, please walk with me."

Another setup—enough to make Barrow wonder if Pat Levy had called to warn the old man about his visit.

Ziegler disappeared into a room beyond the kitchen; Marie Won followed. Barrow put on his jacket and—not to appear ungrateful— downed the tea. When the old man returned, he poured himself a half-shot of the aquavit, and the two of them left the apartment without speaking.

At the bottom of Lessing they turned onto Sophienstrasse and walked for a block. Barrow, arguing tactics with himself, uttered nothing.

"You came because of Werner Schott," Ziegler said.

"Yes."

"You never spoke to me."

"I was told not to speak to anyone."

"So what is the issue?"

Barrow swallowed. "There is still time before the concert. There's tomorrow. To go over the music."

"It's too late."

"You said I wasn't ready."

"Are you?"

"I know this music if I know anything."

"You are from *Ohio*, and demonstrate how little *commitment* you have by quitting the craft for ten years to do nothing—oh yes, I am sorry, to teach the violin to children and wander about in the Hudson River—and you expect to come to Germany and after three months of halfhearted study—of laziness and distraction and going to a few concerts—you expect to lead a German chorus in the poetry of German poets, in *Brahms*, to lord over men who are twice your age and have lived through everything that Germany has lived through? You expect to do that?"

"Conductors do not lord over people." Barrow was shaking. "Not now. Not anymore." The old man had never mentioned his student's past, never betrayed one iota of knowledge of it. Barrow managed to suck in a breath before saying, "How dare you destroy a person's career. For—"

"Yes? For what?"

Barrow shook. "For your own weakness."

The old man stopped abruptly outside a bakery, its display trays empty for the night. He glanced at the curb, his lips fumbling—he seemed not to have expected such a personal attack. "You are an adolescent. You are in grammar school. Good night." He turned away and crossed the street.

Barrow followed.

The sauna's foyer was small and clean and smelled strongly of eucalyptus. The woman behind the plexiglass smiled for Ziegler; for the American, she snapped her face into neutral. Barrow filled out a membership card and passed the woman a twenty-mark note, avoiding her eyes. He pocketed the change without counting.

There was no trace of the old man in the tiled changing area. Barrow took a clean towel from the bench and removed his jacket and clothes and stuffed them into a locker. He flipped open the towel and cinched it around his naked waist. He didn't know what he was going to say, his purpose baffled by sheer geography, by strange custom—a German bathhouse—yet he knew instinctively that he had certain advantages. Surprise, for one; others that Petra had hinted at.

He went to the only door. It had a ship's porthole, and a thick, wood-gripped handle, and a thermometer above that read—translating to Fahrenheit—180 degrees.

Inside the air was edgy with eucalyptus, and Barrow's lungs pruned up on the first breath. A three-tiered rack of wood benches rose up like a section in a baseball stadium. The chamber was longer than he'd expected, lit by a couple of red-orange headlamps jammed in the far corners. Ziegler sat at one end, a couple of women at the other—he hadn't expected witnesses. The women's knees were up, their towels wrapped just above chest level; they glanced in his direction and returned to their whispered conversation.

"It is hotter the higher up you sit," Ziegler said in English. He sat straight as a chair, one towel under him, one across his thighs, butt cheeks visible. His skin was all shades of orange and yellow, and his hands held the edge of the bench. The old man's eyes were closed and his face was drawn to a scowl. But calm.

How habitual was this therapy for him? This rite? As far back as Berlin?

Barrow sat beside him on the second tier, wrapped in his towel, his back to the hot slat of the bench behind them. He glanced at Ziegler's long, bony spine and thought of ancient Greece, teacher and pupil at the baths. *You*, Petra had said, *have all the requirements*. This was his advantage—she had armed him with it—and he could not quite unfix his thoughts from the notion that his teacher might once have been attracted to him.

"You can ask," he began, stopping to clear his throat, "ask me about any of the Brahms pieces. Anything."

"I am sure you can answer," Ziegler said, calm in ascension.

"Anything."

"You have studied them. Of course."

Barrow forced himself to take a slow breath, a steady half-gallon of heat, the flavor singeing the tops of his lungs. It was an impossible place to be angry in.

"Maestro, it is unjust, what you did."

"No. What is unjust ... what *would* have been unjust would have been for you, an inexperienced amateur, to conduct Radio-Sinfonie-Orchester Frankfurt."

"And why did you take me on?"

"Excuse me?"

"To study with you?"

"Potential, or lack thereof, rarely reveals itself until after a few months, after some lessons."

Barrow noticed that one of the women had gone to her back, allowing the towel to loosen and drop, and her breasts to jelly flat against her chest.

He looked sidelong at Ziegler, who sat upright and motionless, a drip of sweat suspended from his chin. He tried swallowing to keep the adrenaline back.

The key element, the *vital* element, was control.

"Why do you hurt Brahms?"

"I'm sorry?"

"When you conduct Brahms. It's as if you," he struggled for the German, "you *damage* him."

Beschädigen.

"I would never."

"Yes, Herr Ziegler."

"Ridiculous."

"Not really."

Barrow pressed his palms into the smooth wood, found the grain.

Present your case.

"We see it. Everyone sees it. You sabotage Brahms. Deliberately. Every time. The concert in Brussels—the scandal with the tuning of the piano. Fritz Poelzig, the horn player—you got rid of him, and the player who replaced him messed up the solo in Brahms Four, just as you wanted."

His jaw was seizing up.

"That is a ridiculous idea," Ziegler said.

"Everyone sees it."

"Poelzig was not a good player."

"The Berlin Philharmonic hired him."

"Poelzig was insolent. He was a soloist, not an ensemble player. They will discover this shortly in Berlin."

Barrow had fucked up the evidence; it should have been open-and-shut.

"What about the oboist Eugenie? She has no rhythm—you know that. You intentionally have her play principal when in the same orchestra there is Petra Vogel, who is the most beautiful player, who is going to have—*will* have—an excellent career."

"Yes, some people think she is beautiful—"

"Yes, Herr Ziegler, some people think she is beautiful." He paused, for effect. *"You*, sir. *You* thought so."

He stared sidelong at the old man's profile, while his own body shivered with the audacity of what he was doing.

Ziegler stared straight ahead. "Brussels," he said, "was the worst, least responsible piano tuner in the world." His delivery was smooth as a beach. "They threw her out. I have never seen such a thing. Poelzig I have said, of course, a beautiful player, but not—*not*—an orchestral player. This you can argue if you want to. Petra, it is the same. So."

You can argue. That had to be interpreted as a concession.

Barrow continued. "We have also a reason—"

"Who is we?"

Yet another invitation.

"Antonio and Berndt"—he paused for effect—"and Tano Popescu."

Sure enough, at the mention of the concertmaster's name, something—a little something—went out of the old man. A loss of a degree or two in the angle of the chin. "Tano especially," Barrow said, "could not understand the replacement of Petra with Eugenie."

"Not his job."

"It is noticed. The irrational behavior."

The door unlatched behind him and he turned to see the two women exit the sauna, towels around their waists. One woman smiled, glanced back at him as the door shut behind them.

"To argue before strangers," Ziegler muttered.

"You removed me from Schott's consideration. I am—I feel I am entitled."

Ziegler looked at him, said nothing. He took the towel from his legs, bunched it between his massive hands, and mopped his face and the top of his head. The upper shanks of his legs were impressively long;

Barrow noticed a scar, a yellow zip from hip to knee, a burn line or a slice.

Sweat stung Barrow's eyes. He stood to remove his towel and mop his forehead, back to Ziegler. The slats were too hot to sit upon directly, so he laid out the towel, this time on the first-tier bench, and sat with his legs pulled up to his chest, feet flat on the towel, scrotum lying gently on the coarse terry cloth.

"You had a reason?" Ziegler asked from behind, his voice muted but startling. "For my so-called irrationality?"

"We thought that perhaps something in the war had happened to cause this, these actions."

He went no further. He was waiting, almost—as in a lesson—for guidance.

"For example?"

"Perhaps your reputation—especially regarding Brahms—with other conductors. For example Werner Schott, who thinks you were more promising than, really, anyone. Before the war."

"Before the shitting war," the old man said. He cleared his throat, and cleared it again—an extraordinary fragment of emotion.

Barrow wanted to turn around, observe the face, but he didn't. He should never have reestablished himself on the first tier where he could not read his adversary's face. It was rehearsal all over again, Ziegler with his back to the orchestra, Barrow conducting, utterly exposed, waiting for the mortar round, raw and mean, launched from the rear, *Nein!*

"Continue, Herr Barrow, because this is very interesting."

Barrow felt the close, humid breath of another trap.

"Leonard Bernstein told everybody that they had to hear you conduct Brahms—told my teacher, Gilbert Shanahan, that he simply had to. And also Erika—who is in the violins—her father."

"Erika's father? Who is this Erika's father?"

"Erika. Who was in the second violins. Who is Jewish. Her—I'm sorry—her grandfather saw you conduct before the war."

"And he was what, 'Erika's grandfather.'"

"Jewish."

"You said that. He was what?"—this was precisely his method, Ziegler's particular method of raking through his student's analysis—"He was a musician? A critic?"

"Not really a musician—I don't remember—"

"Then so what?"

"He said—"

"Who cares?"

"He—

"I don't *care* what he said," an exclamation hissed more than yelled.

"He never saw anyone conduct like you, as well as you, especially Brahms. He said, I think he said this, that people were actually *afraid* of you—you were that good."

There was a pause. Barrow stifled another impulse to turn around.

Ziegler said, "Has no meaning, this talk," and it was back again, a note of concession. Just a tincture and one could hear the ruination of a voice.

"And," Barrow said, softening, "that you were considered for the Pittsburgh Symphony. Before Steinberg."

He should turn. He should swing on his butt and face the old man, but he was afraid it would look like a concession, forced to angle his face upward. And if he stood to join him on the second tier, also a concession.

"Werner Schott," Barrow continued, "believes you could have been the next Furtwängler."

"Werner Schott is an ass."

"He wanted me to sub for him," Barrow said, nonsensically.

"He is an ass. *Nobody* misses a concert. You do that only if you are dead. He is doing that because of a woman, is that what you are given to understand?"

"I don't know why he's doing it."

"It is because of a woman."

Something was happening, something external having its intended effect—the prolonged heat—and Barrow's mind seemed to be calving in chunks, permitting the utterance of stupid things.

"The point is not, Herr Maestro, what Schott is doing." He heard the brittle center of his own voice, the lurking emotion. "The point is, you could have been Furtwängler. But you failed."

And that was it. Where he needed to be.

There was no response.

He pressed the point. "Why is that, Herr Maestro?"

Only after a minute—an extraordinary minute—did the creak of a plank tell him the old man was still alive, shifting weight.

Barrow had to get out, get to a coldwater hose. Start with the feet and ankles, the hard bolts of pain followed so quickly by life—rebirth, joint by joint. There was the impulse to move, and he managed to lower his feet to the cedar-decked floor. Leaning his weight over his knees, he came away from the towel and stood up, seeing Ziegler for the first time in perhaps ten minutes. Ziegler sat exactly as before, apparently—obviously—the stronger man. The large head and long limbs. A prehistoric, plucked bird. The sauna his habitat.

"Perhaps," Barrow said, his voice slurry with heat, "we should get out of here."

The old man spoke, his voice issuing forth like gravel. "Who in God's name would want that?"

Barrow cleared his throat, "Excuse me?"

"To *hell* with Werner Schott." And louder. "Who in God's name would want to be the next shitting Furtwängler?"

"I don't understand."

"Who in God's name?" Ziegler said, his eyes strikingly focused. "We loved him. Do you understand that? How we adored him?"

"I don't understand a thing."

"We *adored* him," the old man said, shoulders back. "You do not know, you American, you English, you do not understand how much we adored our conductors, how very much. And Furtwängler—we adored him above all the rest."

There was more. The old man spoke in a trance.

"Love of God was *nothing*. For others, love of Hitler, but that was nothing like this love of *Furtwängler*, because there was intelligence and perfection in this kind of love, and with the chancellor, with Hitler, not intelligence at all, simply mass stupidity, but with the maestro, all was different. We could love him because of the purity of music, above everything, we could let go of some judgment … And to be him, that was to be Jesus Christ—and I do not exaggerate—of course I wanted to *be* him. I wanted to be Wilhelm Furtwängler. Of course. *Of course.*"

Barrow felt a chill run up his chest, a final, glandular warning that their time was up.

"Maestro," he whispered, "we should go out."

The old man's body was too thin for his head—his knees, two masses of botched bone. The disorganized lap towel, the revealed pubic hair, steely and rancorous, darker than the hair on his head. "We plotted to find him in the Tiergarten," he whispered hoarsely. "He rode, so we rode. You, Herr Barrow, were right. We plotted to ride with Furtwängler, and we did. We ambushed him and rode with him every morning for a summer. We rode with God. We talked music with him and we were treated as equals and so we, too, were God. For a summer."

Barrow swallowed twice to find the liquid to speak. "What year was that?"

Not a flicker of response so he tried another question. "You and Erich Blumenfeld?"

"It was late in the regime, we knew it was late, but Maestro Furtwängler had not left Germany, so it had to be fine. It *must* be. We were building a fortress within. 'A fourth chamber in the three-chambered heart of Germany!' we said. There were Jews still in the Philharmonic, Furtwängler's orchestra. This was 1935, and outside the *Kulturbund* there were no Jews anywhere, but there *were* Jews in the Berlin Philharmonic. And Hindemith, he too was there. But mainly, mainly because Furtwängler had not left—because God *himself* had not left—we knew things could not be so bad, so bad as our own eyes were telling us. So we stayed, we stayed, we stayed, and it was too late."

He stopped. He took little half-breaths, his eyes drawn to some distant spot.

And then what?

The rides through the Tiergarten. At night, watching Furtwängler conduct. Counting the Jews left in the orchestra.

What then?

Ziegler was looking at him. "What in hell are we doing? We are going to die in here."

He thrust out a hand and Barrow grabbed it, pulled the old man to his feet, expecting frailty and finding strength, plenty to match his. He pressed the latch and pushed open the door, and the cold air rushed their faces, their skin. They stepped through.

"Here, over here," Ziegler said, indicating three black hoses along one wall. "It is better to start with the feet. Or perhaps you know this."

Barrow stood on the tiled floor, absorbing the shock of the temperature drop.

"They say it is better for someone else to do it for you, but I say to hell with that." Ziegler had a hose, already spilling water, splitting the stream across the bridge of one foot, and the other. Sounds he had never heard came out of the old man, "Ha-ha!" Aborted laughs. "Ha-ha!" Back and forth the stream went, between ankles and calves, the old man turning sounds of torture into full-bore laughter. Barrow grabbed a second hose and joined him, the excruciating pain just before the rush of blood spreads a warm wrap over the skin.

"Slowly," the old man shouted, "bring it up slowly, yes, ya-i-i-i-i-a," and he squealed as the hose found his armpits. He put the hose on the top of his head, and the water streamed over his ears and face and neck—the skin going strawberry red—streaming down his chest, off the end of his penis, sorting and resorting the scant hair of his legs, and Barrow—worrying briefly about heart attacks in the old and infirm—sprayed his own chest, and moaned himself until both their voices, their yells and laughs, careened off the antiseptic walls, slapped and spanked like dolphins through the upper reaches of the tiled chamber, and the old man turned his hose on the American, causing him to jump and both to laugh more. "God, God, God is good," Ziegler said, "oh God is good," and he dropped the hose to the floor and leaned forward, hands on his knees, the live hose playing across the tile until it lay quiet, still shooting its stream to the corner.

Barrow turned off both spigots; one black hose flipped back on itself, a final death throe. "God is good," Ziegler said again, lifting his head, straightening at the waist, the long pale body dribbling under the blatant neon of the changing room. His hair had sprung loose at the sides like a clown's, and he smoothed it back with his hands. "Do you know," he said. "Do you know who is conducting on Saturday night?" His hands dropped to his hips. A man accustomed to nakedness, a man whom Barrow had never seen before, the one he imagined in the fifty-year-old snapshot, framed by snowcapped mountains, lunging at his lover with a silly Tyrolean hat.

"I am," the old man said. "I am conducting the concert."

31 They did not walk so much as ease—coats open—through the cold night. A slow silent retreat to Lessing-strasse, which was on the way to the tram he would take to Schützenstrasse. He would sleep in Petra's bed without Petra, where—there being no scores to study, no urgency—he would lay back in her scent, perhaps take a book from her row of paperbacks, and read himself to sleep in a way he could not remember ever having done.

They passed a phone booth trimmed the color of a flower, purplish or lavender—another weird, unknowable Eurocolor—turned up Lessing-strasse, and stopped at number 15 where the shutters were down for the night. The old man faced him, his back to the door, his hands remaining hidden in his pockets. They stood like lovers, shocked by the evening's content.

Ziegler spoke, his words dropping one pebble at a time to the silent pavement.

"What did she tell you about Erich Blumenfeld?"

"That you were friends," Barrow said. "That perhaps she reminded you of him."

"Erich Blumenfeld was a far better player than she will ever be."

"I guess that remains to be seen," said Barrow.

The old man threw him a glance. He stood outside the door to his flat like he might stand on the podium, isolated, perhaps terribly so, awaiting the silvery moment during which every audience surrenders, each for the greater good of all. Their signal to start the show. Because it is the audience, after all, which begins the concert; no concert ever began before the audience signaled its readiness.

"Do you never drink a beer?" Barrow asked.

"Never," Ziegler said.

They walked toward the heart of Karlsruhe, where earlier in the evening he had ridden the tram, hovering by the door, calculating the best use of his anger. The anger was gone. Ziegler, in a brilliant combination, perfectly executed—almost certainly planned and with no apparent effort—had tossed him to the mat.

They came up on Ludwigsplatz, a small precinct of restaurants. Here Ziegler stopped. "I don't know these," he said, and Barrow suggested a restaurant across the street, called Krokodil.

It was late, with business at only a few tables. They went to the back and ordered a liter each, waiting in silence. The tables were draped in white cloths, each with a juice-glass vase, a hothouse bud probably from Holland, and a glass ashtray. It might be any decade in the century.

When the beer came, Ziegler took a long draught. He put down his mug and looked around, a kid in his first tavern. He kept his coat on.

"She did not tell you this ..." Ziegler said, not looking up from his drink.

"What?"

"I sent Erich Blumenfeld to Chelmno death camp to die."

Barrow stopped breathing.

"He was the finest musician. He was finer than you or I."

Barrow took a drink, a shallow one. He said nothing, not wanting to disturb the surface of Ziegler's memory.

"I was neither guard nor doctor, but there are more ways to kill a man, or several men. Thirty-eight men." He cleared his throat and took another sip of beer.

He must have been preparing this particular opener since Lessing-strasse 15, perhaps even since leaving the sauna. But starting with his next utterance, it became less and less clear that there was a plan. The voice ran flat, devoid of enthusiasm, though somewhere there must be a source of fuel, a crimped can and a blue flame.

"I was a conductor, you know, in the camps, in several of the camps."

"No, I did not know."

"Well, know it."

He had the drink clamped between his long hands.

"As if they wanted to hire me, and the best way, the quickest way, was to arrest me. So that is what they did. On a ridiculous pretense they arrested me. On a false rumor. They were really after Furtwängler. They were after God. Not Goebbels, of course—Goebbels would not have it, and Hitler probably not either, because those two loved God and they knew the people loved God—but Göring and his men, they were after God. Herbert Karajan, you know, Lucifer, that was Göring's conductor, and so Göring and his men wanted Furtwängler brought down so their man Karajan could rise."

Barrow started to speak, "I don't know much about it—"

"No, no. Fine. Politics. Göring, Minister of the Interior. Goebbels, the propaganda minister. They are always fighting to bring the other man down. Or the other man's men. Göring failed at many things, and one of the things he failed at was to get at Maestro Furtwängler through me. Or through Erich Blumenfeld, which they tried. They detained me to interrogate me about Furtwängler, because at the time there were those various men who met in the Tiergarten for disgusting purposes and they had discovered, in that summer in 1935, that Erich and I and God were in the habit of occasionally riding together in that park."

"Paragraph 175," Barrow muttered in the pause that followed.

Ziegler seemed surprised. "Yes," he said, "if you will. Paragraph 175. Göring's men, because of rumors, thought I could help them bring down Furtwängler with a paragraph. Of course, there was nothing. Furtwängler had fucked half of Berlin, but it was the female half." He smiled, took a sip, and glanced at Barrow. "You are hungry?"

"No."

"Help me with this, if you would."

Barrow stood and helped him remove his heavy wool overcoat. He folded it over the back of an adjacent chair. "And so they arrested you."

"Yes," Ziegler said. "I was cheaper arrested than freelance."

He gazed across the table, focusing on Barrow as if he were the prism of his memory.

"They put me first in one camp, then in another. Sometimes playing the flute, sometimes conducting the band. We would send the prisoners off to work in the mornings with some music. Some other functions we played for. I was released and living in Berlin, and a year later I was arrested again. They brought me to Sachsenhausen, where I was especially requested. 'Here,' they said. 'Conduct these such-and-such men.' They wanted an orchestra. Because I was learning about the politics—there was some rivalry, with Theresienstadt and Ravensbrück—because I knew this, after the first day I said to them, 'This is not adequate, I need some better wind players,' and they said, 'No,' and I said, 'Let me see the kommandant,' and I was amazed. The kommandant called me in the next day, because he had found out I knew Furtwängler. You see, don't you, that yes, in reality, Furtwängler was God.

"'Kommandant,' I said, 'I must have a real oboe player.' He said, 'How am I to do that?' I said, 'Find me Erich Blumenfeld,' because you see I had word—there was word—from a prisoner in this Sachsenhausen orchestra that he had seen Erich in Buchenwald, if I remember. 'Find me Blumenfeld,' I said, and sure enough, in under two weeks, there was Erich, in my orchestra. I had not seen him some years, we had lost count. He was not well. Already, there was so much damage. It had been ignored that he was the best oboist in the world. He had been assigned to a 175 barracks, and also he was a Jew. I asked him, 'What is worse, the pink triangle or the yellow star?' and he said, 'What is worse is to stand on that shitting platform and wave that little stick for the rest of your life.' We had to find him an oboe and, what was harder, some cane. They would not leave him alone with a knife. A guard had to watch every time he made reeds. It was a maddening situation, but, you see, all this time, Furtwängler, God, was watching over us.

"After some time I had my own office at the camp, a broom-and-mop closet. It had one little light and, of course, no windows, and I remained behind its closed door for as many hours in the day as they would forget my existence. I began to sleep there, though I could not fully stretch my legs in any direction, and they made no comment. One day Erich began to sleep there too, and still they made no comment. For us, considering our world, considering the situation, considering the camps, this could not be called a bad time. No, this was not a bad time."

Ziegler clamped his lips together. His eyes filled and he looked away.

He took a long drink.

"A monster named Luechner was the kommandant, another in a long line of dreadful tenors. Far too much nasal, too much teeth and no chest to speak of. Accustomed to yelling. The man loved to demonstrate his breadth of culture by according to me undue respect, which is why the mop closet and why I could get away with wearing the green triangle that the communists wore and not the pink triangle of the 175. He must have seen newsreels of the chancellor smiling at a concert, possibly of Goebbels sharing an open car with an opera soprano or conductor, perhaps sitting next to Furtwängler himself. He tried to impress me always with his reasonableness, but his voice gave him away. A coloratura does not attempt Carmen, no?"

"No."

"One day I am standing before him in his office, and he asks me why the orchestra never performs Brahms. I tell him I cannot explain, but he repeats and repeats his question until finally I say, 'I have never been able to bring myself to enjoy a single one of Brahms' compositions.' This is the first and last convincing laugh I ever hear from Kommandant

Luechner, though not from the chest, still confined to the sinuses. 'I, for one, loathe Brahms,' I say. 'You are, of course, lying,' he says. I say, 'I am happy to conduct more Wagner and Beethoven, Herr Kommandant.' 'You are happy to conduct at all.'

"That is where I should have pushed further—pushed my refusal—but I did not, and that was the great mistake of my life, greater than any other mistake, greater even than allowing myself to be arrested.

"There was a Red Cross concert in three weeks and Luechner suggested the Academic Overture of Brahms, a personal favorite of his, and 'Could the parts be got from Berlin?' which is a ridiculous question to ask a prisoner. Also, he wanted to hear the Second Symphony, 'If we are up to it, are we up to it?' We have thirty-eight in the orchestra, and two violas. No we are not up to it, but he is behaving like a concert producer, like we are standing in the foyer of Berlin Oper with the carpet and the chandeliers and I feel sick. I vow to myself at that moment—which, as I have already said, is already too late—that I will never conduct Brahms for that man.

"That night is a huge row with Erich. 'Brahms is not God,' he says. We have by now, of course, come to know that Wilhelm Furtwängler is not God, except insofar as God is extremely dangerous and extremely stupid. 'Gods are gods, and men are men,' Erich said. I say, also, 'Monsters are monsters,' which he did not even smile at. We are in the little closet, and it is always whispers between us in there, but this time he is shouting. 'Men are not gods. Gods up there, people down here,' he says. 'You are people. Conduct the shitting Academic Overture,' he says.

"The music was ordered from the RMK. The day it came, it was as if Brahms himself had arrived. Coming through the triple gates, standing there on the parade, bone-thin like us and gray and his beard all dirty and puckered and spun like wool. This is what I am picturing when the word comes that the music is here. And Schatz, who is a 175 who has been acting as orchestra librarian, Schatz came knocking on the closet door and delivering the parts. To the Second Symphony as it turned out—the Academic was too popular and not available. 'It is missing the second horn part,' he said. 'Shall I write it out?' Pathetic. So eager to be of use. He had been a violinist with the Mannheim Symphony, a rescue also from Buchenwald and the stone pits. He is, Erich and I think, servicing one of the guards."

Ziegler stopped for another pass at his beer, a long one this time, his Adam's apple traveling up and down his bedpost of a neck—how it must taste to him, meeting his lips at exactly room temperature, his first beer in who knew how long.

He returned his mug to its coaster. "She told you?" he asked, glancing at Barrow.

"Yes."

"What precisely?"

"About you and her," Barrow said, shifting the linen napkin on the table in front of him.

"And what else?"

Barrow looked up from the napkin and directly into his teacher's eyes, the blue-gray pupils, clouded with age, but active, loaded with information.

"Did she tell you about Rykestrasse Synagogue?" Ziegler asked.

"The one in East Berlin?" he asked. Ziegler nodded. "Only that she visited sometimes."

He stayed with the old man's gaze and thought he discerned the slightest pull in his cheek, just the beginnings of a smile, or maybe a wince.

"Ask her," the old man said, reaching for his beer, swirling the leftovers once or twice before taking a drink and returning the mug to the table.

The work of memory recaptured his face. "Erich was off teaching the oboe to one of the medical doctor's daughters. We had such a good arrangement, we thought, so lucky—and I was alone with the Brahms. At once I recognized some of the markings, and I knew that Weingartner, Felix Weingartner, who was a very old man and whom I had occasion to assist once in Vienna, he had used these parts last—or perhaps one of his protégés—and this, to me, was appalling and amazing, a kind of fantastic realization at the time, this realization that such music was circulating to the camps from the outside world, this network of musicians, in and out. After one month one forgets completely the outside, and here it is almost a year.

"I had the strong inclination to begin undoing Weingartner's marks—which I knew would be mostly abhorrent to me—but I also had decided, even after my row with Erich, that I was not going to conduct this, not in the concentration camp, not for Luechner, not in Germany. This is how I was feeling. But it was not easy, because there it was, the music itself. Brahms himself."

He paused. "I suppose," he said, "it is like having the girl naked there on the bed whispering your name—but you have already decided not to touch her."

He stopped, in what appeared to be a sort salute to human weakness. *Men are men, gods are gods.* He looked out through the empty restaurant to the street. It was hiatus enough for Barrow to imagine Petra in his bed. Had she tried whispering his name?

The old man cleared his throat noisily and signaled the waiter for another liter. He could not seem to keep his hands still, and when the beer arrived, he wrapped them around the mug as if for warmth.

"Luechner was informed immediately of the arrival of the music. He was anxious to get us rehearsing. Without telling a soul, not even Erich, I had already decided what I was going to do. *I will not be like Furtwängler.* This is what I decided, having studied all circumstances beforehand, having imagined it, lying there on the floor of our office, constructing this singular moment. It was to be, for me, a moment of stupendous glory.

"And when it came time, I followed my little construction precisely. I walked to the podium, which had been built by prisoners, and I stood there, you see, before this absurd orchestra, this thirty-eight–piece orchestra of pinks and mainly yellows and one or two, I think, communists. I stood there with the ceiling only a foot above my head—and there was the kitchen staff, as always, along the back wall with their spoons and what-have-you from the kitchen—and Herr Kommandant has come. He smiles. He is in tears with his pride, *Brahms Symphony Number Two at Sachsenhausen, here at my camp.* The parts—as I had arranged, to increase the anticipation—lay open on every stand. I opened to the first movement and turned to the celli. Only five, you see, two-stands-and-a-half, dear ones. This is all according to the plan I had rehearsed—thank God, because I was shaking. I glanced to the horns, which is miraculous because there are four horns—an absolute miracle—and the stick goes up, and, you see, everyone is filled with gratitude that for a few moments we leave, we go away from this place where we are wasting away, where our bodies are shriveling, where we are all insane. I will lead them like Moses, you see, into Brahms. This I had all prepared, in my mind.

"And I am, with my eyes, very deliberate—this is the moment, the stupendous moment—because when I look up from the score, it is not to the celli but instead to the back wall by the swinging door, directly to the despicable Herr Kommandant Luechner. I hold his stare for eight, ten seconds, and fifteen seconds—I count, you see, fifteen seconds—and, carefully, the stick goes down, and I leave it there, across the score. I know the men are watching and I leave the podium, you see, and I never once look at Erich, never once, because he is, I am sure, in a fury. And I walk past Herr Kommandant Luechner, turning away my eyes only at the last—and no one has moved—and I push through the swinging door, down the hall, which is two men wide, and out the door to the parade, and walk out to the middle of the parade, which is mud everywhere, but frozen mud that can crack your kneecap if you fall, and there is Johannes Brahms to greet me and I grasp his hand, this old man, and I send him on his way, out the gates, liberated."

The restaurant was silent, but for a solitary laugh from the kitchen.

"I was confined. The musicians joined the regular work parties." He reached for his beer, took one sip and returned it to the table.

Barrow spoke. "Erich?"

"The Jews went to Chelmno."

He sat for a long time, memory eddying, slipping on. Standing, he slid a bank note from his wallet and dropped it to the table.

On the street outside, Barrow insisted, but Ziegler would not be persuaded—he would walk home alone. They moved their separate ways, east and west along Kaiserstrasse.

32

Barrow trained up to Frankfurt on Friday. The original plan was for him to watch the concert, take copious mental notes, and spend the night with Petra, who was house-sitting for Messer-Eichen.

He decided to skip the concert, though it would have been enormously enlightening to hear Schott interpret the same material he had been immersed in all week. Disappointment met him at every corner, in every shop window. When, late in the evening, he caught sight of the concert hall—hunched massively, her pedestal fountain blooming water even in December—he turned and walked a block in the opposite direction.

He bought coffee at an outdoor kiosk and approached again. She was a pretty building, her two-story windows grandly arched, the wrought-iron lamps blazing around her perimeter. Inside, Schott was conducting. In the morning he would wake up ill with a severe bout of the flu. A call from the orchestra's management would go out to Karlheinz Ziegler.

Barrow took a bench that gave him a clear view of the personnel entrance, removed the lid from his takeaway cup, and warmed his nose and face with the steam. He allowed himself a stray image of Petra exiting arm in arm with Werner Schott. Not even arm in arm, but side by side in attempted obfuscation, putting on a show of professional distance even as the conductor flagged first her taxi, then his, both cabs destined for the same address. The scenario had everything going for it: inevitability, logic—Pat Levy was in London—and certainly irony. He determined the direction of his own retreat—which path, through which set of leafless trees—how he would circle back to the Frankfurt train station, maybe linger first in the red-light district.

She spotted him first, waved from outside the stage door and strode across to him. "I'm starving, where are we going to eat?" she asked. She was bundled in her scarf and her duffel coat, her black concert dress swooping to the paving stones.

"I'm not conducting tomorrow night," he said. He was still seated on the bench.

She stared at him. "Shit."

"Ja."

"Are you disappointed?"

"Ziegler is conducting."

"This is a joke." He shrugged. "Come on," she said, pulling him up from the bench.

They walked by the fountain, through the fine mist that rose into the night; the icy damp burned their cheeks. Her jolly mood in spite of his bad news, her apparent pleasure at seeing him, lifted his spirits.

She nudged him in the direction of Hochstrasse, Frankfurt's busiest shopping street, where the Christmas booth proprietors were shuttering up for the night.

"It was a good concert?"

"Yes," she said. She squeezed his hand. "So you are not so disappointed? Not to conduct?"

"I'm devastated."

"Too bad. Let's get pizza."

Even in her jauntier moods there were usually pockets of weight. Tonight she was without ballast.

They ducked into a skinny storefront that advertised New York–style pizza. They ordered, and she asked what he'd been doing. "Nothing," he said. "I tried reading a couple of your books."

"Which ones?"

"I couldn't concentrate too well." He studied the razor-thin lines around her eyes—the thought of climbing into bed with her in the not-too-distant future filled him with relief. "Did he ever tell you what happened to him in the camps?" he asked.

"Who?"

"Ziegler."

"No," she said. "Very little." She unzipped her backpack and wrestled out a pair of sneakers.

"I met him last night. He told me what happened to him in the camps. You were right about Erich Blumenfeld, you were completely right."

"Tell me."

He did, detail for detail. The horseback riding with Blumenfeld and Furtwängler. The arrest in Berlin for alleged homosexual behavior. The thirty-eight–piece camp orchestra. Barrow's storytelling was chaotic—"I've forgotten the name of the concentration camp"—but he related word for word the confrontation with the kommandant over Brahms, the Felix Weingartner scores, the broom closet, the argument with Erich. He finished by describing the fate of the Jewish members of the orchestra.

"Yes," she said, after waiting to see if he'd finished. "He feels he killed them. He is responsible for their deaths." The way she said it made him feel foolish. "It is an awful story," she said. "It is simply awful."

"You've already heard it."

"Of course not," she said. "Come, I know where we can walk, some shops that are open, even so late."

He stared at her in disbelief. "That's all you have to say?"

"Come," she said.

She led him—towed him—to the U-Bahn, riding some post-concert surge. They boarded the next train, and he dropped to a seat while she hung from a strap in front of him.

"All right, I'm sorry. But what if his ending were different?" she asked. "*Bitte?*"

"What if, in that moment on the podium in the dining hall, in the decisive moment, he *did* actually conduct the Brahms Second Symphony and a lot more Brahms after that. In the camp."

"Is that what he told you?"

"No. But what if he did? What if Brahms had been a great consolation to the prisoners for many months, to all these musicians. Then the war turns bad for the Germans and it is time to kill off the Jews who are left over in the camps and the orchestra is broken up."

"I don't understand," he said.

"Either way, the Jews are dead. It wouldn't have mattered." She was smearing the ink. Deliberately muddling things.

"That's not the point," he said. "The point is the tragedy, that a man stands up for something and it blows up in his face."

"Stands up?" She looked at him, he thought, with pity.

"Is this the wrong verb?"

"There are a lot of such survivor stories. There is not one survivor who is not convinced he did not condemn the others to death. Just by surviving. Come, we get off here."

They left the U-Bahn and surfaced on the south bank of the Main. The dark river stretched away in both directions, Frankfurt crouching at either bank, lights delicately glazing the river. "I like this," she said.

He was desperately cold and wanted only to collapse. "Where is Messer-Eichen's apartment?" he asked.

"We can walk to it."

A few meters on she said, "You will hate this coincidence. My teacher's apartment is in the area called Sachsenhausen."

That was it—the name of Ziegler's camp. He'd forgotten. "He told you?"

"What?"

"The name of the camp."

"Which camp?"

"Sachsenhausen."

"He never spoke of the camps to me."

"But you knew." She ignored him, leaning into the stiff wind that skimmed off the river.

"You just said—about the coincidence that Messer-Eichen lives in Sachsenhausen."

They approached one of the series of bridges that spanned the Main, a modern tubular construction suspended from cables.

He asked again. "Did you know?"

"You think I am lying to you? Why would I do that?"—her voice was hard-edged—"You think Ziegler told me this Sachsenhausen story? It is a coincidence that we speak of the concentration camps and the death camps tonight, so I say, 'Here is where my teacher lives.' And so, again, it is even more of a coincidence that it was the same concentration camp that he ... that you said he ..." She stopped. She must have known she was protesting too much. "What if he *had* told me this story?" she asked.

"I wouldn't care. I would just wonder why you should pretend that he hadn't."

"Perhaps to protect an old man's privacy."

"Or perhaps because secrets undo more secrets?"

She glared at him and started off again. He matched her stride.

"What happened at the Rykestrasse Synagogue?" He wasn't handling himself at all well—he was cold and he hadn't slept and he'd caught her in a lie.

"He told you about Rykestrasse?"

"Yes," he said.

"I was going to tell you," she said.

"It's okay."

"He told you everything?"

His face burned from the task of not responding.

"Shit," she said. "*Shit.*"

"I want to hear it from you."

She stopped and looked into his face, and he knew he wouldn't be able to play out the lie. He said, "Ziegler implied that something happened at the Rykestrasse Synagogue, something involving you."

She stared at him directly. "He told you everything, or he told you nothing?"

"I'd like to hear it from you."

"What exactly did he tell you?" she said.

Tears rimmed her lower eyelids.

"Perhaps I used the wrong words," he said.

She wavered, a mirage over the sidewalk.

"I'm sorry," he said. "I'm—" but his jaw locked and he couldn't speak. His own eyes had blurred up, and he cleared them with the back of his glove.

She was running up the bank to the avenue that ran by the river. The grass was stiff from the cold, and he lost his footing and brushed the ground with his glove. He saw her bolt across the avenue toward the grounds of one of the museums that lined the river. He dodged cars while she cut up a narrow street that broke off in the direction of the Sachsenhausen district.

He spotted her from the corner. She was taking quick, long strides as he came up beside her. "What are you doing?" he said.

"This is the end of us."

"No," he said.

She stopped. "You think I am supposed to kiss Ziegler's feet with this story of his, to worship him because he discovered he is a fucking idiot? A *fucking* idiot. What did he think? Was he surprised when the Nazis broke up the orchestra? Do you think he didn't know exactly what they would do—?"

"I don't—"

"*Exactly* what they would do. Of course he did. He made his stupid protest anyway. To be bigger than them. It is what you do—what you conductors do—you inflate yourself with authority. You think you have control? False, false, false, you do *not* have control. Control resides *else-*

where. They have control. They *always* have control," she said, and he saw the decision flash across her face, "I killed someone, do you know that? I *killed* someone. *That* is what he didn't tell you."

He could only stare back, bewildered.

"Fuck you," she yelled, clocking his elbow with her oboe case. The shock ripped up his arm. He froze at attention while she backed into the iron bars of the fence behind her, clutching her case.

"I have told you," she said, "I was an informer. *Inoffizielle Mitarbeiterin.* I have *told* you, and you did nothing. You didn't *ask* me."

He gazed across, stunned at her capabilities.

"I didn't want to—"

"I would have told you more, but you didn't ask."

He was shaking his head.

"Why didn't you ask?"

"I don't understand," he said, but he did. A door had opened that night and he'd ignored it. "I'm asking now."

"I informed on the Rykestrasse Synagogue."

"Why?"

"Because it was 'patriotic'—I don't know why."

"To watch a fucking Jewish synagogue?"

"No," she said, fresh tears forming.

"How was it patriotic?"

She looked down. "You cannot understand."

"You explain it to me."

"Please," she whispered, and for the first time there was real desperation in her voice.

She started up the street, and for a long time she didn't speak. They skirted an area of bars and restaurants and came to a residential street of modern flats set back from the sidewalk, clumps of evergreen behind wrought-iron fences. Passing under a street lamp, she glanced up at him; her mascara showed up dark against her white cheeks. She ducked into the next side street and stopped.

Away from the river, the air was quiet, unnervingly so.

"There was a young woman, younger than me, in the synagogue. I liked her. She played violin very well. Better than Tano. She had won a place in the conservatory in Leipzig, which is quite good, maybe the best."

She was shivering and she put her oboe case down, between her ankles, and jammed her hands deep into her pockets.

"Kathi her name was. She liked me also. She thought I was some sort of success with music and with boys. She confided to me things."

Petra stopped and looked up. In the light from the street lamp he could see the muscles of her jaws working. She was so tense that her breath whistled through her teeth.

"Her father was arrested."

Again she stopped—long enough that he thought she might be waiting for him to say something.

"Because of you?" he asked.

"Yes."

She was shivering in earnest, but she went on, her determination to confess unlike anything he had witnessed. "Kathi's mother lost her license—a children's physician. And Kathi lost her appointment to the Leipzig conservatory. And the music school in Berlin would not have her. No school would have her."

Petra groaned, working against a clenched jaw.

"She hanged herself. It was spring."

"How did you …?"

"From the balcony of a boy she was seeing."

∽

They spoke little and only of mundane things. Which towel he was permitted to use, whether there was anything in the house for breakfast.

He lay in Messer-Eichen's bed, staring through a set of French doors that led out to a second-floor landing, the dark floor-to-ceiling window beyond. He had one thought, and that was to gather his clothes, dress in the kitchen, and leave.

Petra returned from the bathroom and sat on the bed.

"Did you tell anyone?" he asked. "At the synagogue?" The questions were unending, the many closets of her crime.

"No."

"And you did this all to, what? To get a visa."

She seemed more calm, her explanations more ordered.

"I would occasionally go to the cinema with Victor, the bassoonist, who later was the Stasi plant in Paris, whom I told you of. He knew I had been visiting the synagogue sometimes, and so the topic of the visa came up. For the competition. He said, If you will make these one or two observations. He said, KGB is interested in the movement of certain ex-Soviet Jews in West Berlin. Observe this man, and I can get you a visa."

"What about your mother? She couldn't get you a visa?"

"My mother did not trust me. She knew I would defect, I had said so many things about DDR, how I loathed it."

"Instead, you observed your friend's father. For DDR. You took notes. You went to their house." She nodded.

"What else?" he asked.

"Nothing."

He waited. "Did you sleep with him?"

"Nothing else," she said and she switched off the lamp.

He continued to stare at the window, which now, in the dark, revealed the vague shapes of the trees across the street.

33 He arrived at the Alte Oper forty minutes early, hoping to avoid an encounter with Antonio or Berndt or any of the other Hochschule students. Just inside the lobby he heard Petra speak his name. "He wants to see you."

She moved quickly and he followed. Every voice in the corridor was an alarm; he could not feel his hands.

"He's going to ask you to conduct," she said.

"No."

"This is your tuxedo?" she asked, referring to his backpack. He nodded. "You must do it."

"No," he said.

"If he asks."

"He won't."

He went through a mental inventory: the dress shoes pressing into the small of his back, weighted down by the scores and the carefully rolled pants and jacket. How would he reveal that he had these things? How would he accept the position? It would not be innocent. Ziegler would know.

He followed Petra through a staff door. They passed choristers in packs of two and three, middle-aged men with violins in their fists, a large room blue with cigarette smoke.

She pulled him into an elevator. Her touch was warm. They had not spoken all day—she had left that morning while he was in the shower.

"You must do it," she said looking up at him.

They were alone on the elevator. Ordinarily, he would have pressed her against the sheet-metal paneling, opened her mouth with his. But he was numb. He'd spent the day standing outside a slew of art museums, unable to enter a single one, unable to shake a chain of images, ending with a Jewish girl and a balcony.

They were in another corridor much closer to the stage. There were sounds, a single horn player, a timpani being tuned. Timpani in the Haydn. His mind leapt ahead, reviewing—opening tempos, opening timbres, *How will I walk out?* The scores in his pack—*Will I use my own scores? Will I even use a score for the Haydn?*

She stopped before a door with a typed index card in a slot, *Maestro K. Ziegler.*

"Here."

He understood he was to knock; he did. The door, already cracked a couple of centimeters, swung back. Inside, a woman in civilian dress and an intense-looking violinist stood across from Ziegler, who sat facing the door, unjacketed, white tie, back to the mirror.

"Good, good. I hoped you would come, Herr Barrow," Ziegler said. "Here are Fräulein Schiff and Herr Glieb—the concertmaster. They are just leaving."

"Excuse me," Barrow said to the pair; he turned to watch them go, forcing a politic smile as he did, catching a glimpse of Petra's face as the door closed.

Ziegler spoke before he could turn around.

"What is in the sack? You have brought your tuxedo in the sack?"

"No, Maestro."

"If I were to ask you to conduct, since you are so very well prepared, how would you proceed with no tuxedo?"

"But you are not going to ask me to conduct, and so why would I choose to debase myself?"

"You had thoughts about this."

"If you want it to rain, you don't bring your umbrella." A ridiculous analogy, but he couldn't seem to control his utterances.

"And you want it to rain?" Ziegler asked.

"Of course."

"To conduct?"

"Yes. Of course I want to conduct."

"And so what is in the bag?" Ziegler asked. "Your scores at least."

"Clothes for staying the night."

"With her?"

Barrow chose not to respond.

The dressing room was Spartan, the counters, everything, white. It smelled of cologne or perfume—Ziegler's or one of the two other Germans', he didn't know. A large-faced clock dominated the wall opposite the sink and mirror. Twenty-eight minutes remained before the concert. "I should leave you."

"I need a gesture for the Bernstein."

"Pardon?"

"It is all I need. A gesture for *Fancy Free*, and it is possible. I have—I am quite a fool."

"This is why you summoned me?"

"It is, of course, not so difficult, but ..." and he shrugged.

"The orchestra will be fine," Barrow said, in freefall all over again. "They have played it already with Schott." Ziegler sat ramrod straight on a chrome-and-vinyl chair. They might as well be back in the sauna, the impossibility of touching bottom with this man, everything dancing in air, no reality, always a chase, always storm and retreat. "It is a cabaret band. It is Berlin in the twenties. It is Weimar Berlin."

"Thank you."

"Kurt Weill."

He hadn't thought these things while studying the piece. It had been all tempos and measure numbers, memorizing the rhythmic anomalies. Cram, cram. He adjusted his pack higher up on his shoulders; it felt heavy now that he noticed it, but he rolled forward on the balls of his feet, his body resonant with all his powers. He could conduct.

"You are lying about the tuxedo."

"Excuse me?"

"You have it. You are a fool if you do not. Is it hanging in the coat check in the lobby? Where is it?"

"I should leave."

"It's in your sack."

"You should look at the time."

"You have changed your mind? You do not want to conduct this concert?"

"Herr Ziegler."

"I am offering it," said the old man, unbowed, healthy, his back to the mirror.

"What?"

"I am offering this concert."

"I don't understand."

"You *do* understand."

Barrow caught his own reflection, supplicant in a flannel shirt, the absurd burden of his pack jutting out from his back.

"Shall I repeat? I am offering you this concert to conduct."

"No one cares about the Bernstein. No one is even here for the Bernstein."

"I don't fear the Bernstein," Ziegler said. "Bernstein is castrated Stravinsky. That is not why I offer."

"Why *do* you offer it?"

"To see if you will accept."

The door to the shower stall stood partially open; a steady *plink* came from the shower head, five or six seconds between drops. "No," he said.

265

"I am sorry to hear that."

"I can't."

"I suspect you will never be a conductor."

"It is your concert. It is right for you to conduct it."

"Poetic justice?"

"Yes." But it took the length of one breath to be sure of the translation. "Poetic justice."

"If I once admitted such sentiment, it would kill me."

"This is a stupid conversation."

"You are afraid."

And it was true. It was so on-the-money Barrow couldn't respond. He was cold and sweating and he wished he'd removed his pack when he came in the door. Not once did he consider the eventuality of actually conducting. He'd brought along his tuxedo, thinking, What if the old man should fall ill, throw me the concert? But he never answered the question.

"I am not prepared."

"And so?"

"I have not looked at the scores since Thursday."

"You protested—Thursday—that you could conduct them."

He had ironed a shirt and two ties—one white and one black—but out of some superstition he had not opened the scores.

Ziegler sat up straight, blue eyes blazing. "Have you noticed that I cannot move from where I am? It is because I cannot." It was true; he hadn't moved once. "Do you want an excuse to steal this concert from me? This is an excuse."

"You will conduct. The fear is normal."

"Shut up about normal."

"I'll get some help."

"No."

The intercom interrupted. *"Zwanzig Minuten, Herr Maestro Ziegler."* Twenty minutes, though the wall clock read twenty-two before the hour. Twenty minutes, then, before the time the conductor was expected backstage.

His anxiety mounted. He *did* want the concert. He slid the pack from his back, pretended to look for a place to stow it.

The intercom had begun monitoring the stage, the scrape of stand legs, fragments of Bernstein from the brass, a pair of tuning horns, and over everything the usual commotion of strings. And Petra, testing registers, a small run of notes high up in the throat of her oboe. Unmistakable.

Ziegler heard her too. "Has she told you that she is"—and he used a new word, *Abschaum.*

"I don't understand."

"Scum."

"Excuse me?"

"Scum of the earth, I think you say. *Ein Stück Dreck.*"

"You were together," Barrow managed to say. "As I told you."

Ziegler shook his head; there was strength in the set of his shoulders, the way he propped up his brow. This could not be the man who sat across from him in a Karlsruhe restaurant, hunched over a beer, broken.

"I know about the synagogue in East Berlin," Barrow continued. "I know about that."

"She came to me for absolution, did she tell you? Absolution."

This had always been his game, outpace the American with absurdities.

"She did not come to you," Barrow said.

"I see."

"You invited her, no?"

The old man smiled. "Go on."

"For her skill. Her oboe playing. She reminded you of Erich."

Ziegler shook his head. "I don't know what she told you. She came to me, this refugee at my door. Of course, I welcomed her."

Barrow hesitated. "For absolution?"

"Yes." It was possible. The old man's version. "Shall we absolve her now?" He reached a long arm for the intercom, held down a button, "Herr Klatte."

Barrow tried to interrupt. "Herr Ziegler—"

"I must speak with the principal oboist."

The intercom answered back, "But Maestro, she—"

"Thank you, Herr Klatte."

Barrow glanced at the clock, crossed to Ziegler's chair. "It's time to stand up. Come."

"Absolution, she said—"

"We must put your jacket on."

"I did not give it."

Barrow positioned himself behind the old man, the long, upright torso, the thinly veiled scalp. "Stand up," he said.

"Why should I give absolution?"

"Stand up, Maestro." He jammed his wrists under the old man's armpits.

"What—?"

"We're standing you up," Barrow said.

"I'm not able—"

Barrow lifted hard; Ziegler roared, "No," and swung an elbow back, launching Barrow into the shower door. The metal frame slammed against the tiles, banged loudly in the meter-wide stall. "You are no fucking conductor!" Ziegler yelled in English. "You bring a tuxedo! Every city, every fucking *Spazierfahrt!*"

Barrow wedged himself between the tiled walls. He brought his hand up to the back of his head.

"You are without ambition. A conductor cannot be without ambition. Do you know that?"

Barrow's fingers came back tipped with blood—

"You are shit, because you *could* conduct."

Barrow stood in the shower, controlling his breath. "I remind you," he said, "that you declined to recommend me to Herr Schott."

"This is your pathetic reason for having no ambition? Get out of the shower." Barrow could tell he had seen the blood.

"I have ambition."

"You are terrified."

"You want me to participate in the 'martyrdom' of Karlheinz Ziegler. 'Poor Maestro Ziegler, the once great …' that's what you want."

Ziegler glared at him, triumphant. "You are quite terrified," he said. "We await the principal oboist." He lowered himself into his chair, white hair and shimmering white tie, by all outward appearances cultured and accomplished. A sage, brilliant in understanding, and utterly insane.

Barrow stepped out of the shower and made his way to the jet-black tails hanging smooth on an open rack. The fresh blood was on the fingers of his right hand; he removed the jacket with his left.

"Put it back," Ziegler said.

"Why didn't you recommend me to Schott, if you want me to conduct?"

"I do not 'want you to conduct,' Herr Barrow. It is not a question of 'wanting you to conduct.'"

There was a light knock on the door.

"Open."

The door swung in. Petra stood in the hall, oboe-less.

"Come in," Ziegler said. "Please."

She entered, closed the door. "Is there an instruction?"

"You should go," said Barrow.

But no one moved. Even the clock seemed barely to have advanced; it read 7:44. Barrow felt the warm trickle of blood down the back of his neck.

"What is English for 'absolution'?" Ziegler asked, looking at Petra. She in turn glanced at Barrow.

"I don't understand," she said.

"Herr Barrow would like to know all about Rykestrasse Synagogue."

"She already—"

"Tell him about it."

"She's told me."

Petra pulled at her sleeves, said nothing.

Barrow said, "I'm not sure we can understand, perhaps, what it was like for her."

"So, therefore, absolve her," Ziegler said.

"It's not my job."

"You will do so by conducting this concert—with her in it."

"That's irrational."

"How badly do you want to conduct tonight?"

"I don't want to conduct."

"Another shitting lie. And you in a position to absolve her of this issue."

"That's ridiculous."

"And I say you absolve her if you take this baton. Unless, of course, you brought your own."

"How do I do that?"

"By not removing her from the orchestra. By not calling her out. By sharing the stage with her. By *rewarding* her."

"I'm not God."

Ziegler looked up abruptly. "You *are* God. Every time you take the podium. You remove the ticking heart of a composer, you lead people to their souls, you are God."

"I'm a conductor," Barrow said. "I conduct notes on a page."

"If that's what you think, you've learned nothing from me."

Barrow glanced at Petra. Her body seemed to quiver under her dress.

Ziegler went on. "Music is force. You conduct force. You know this, and this is why you are afraid, either to take a stand or to conduct this concert. You stand down. But you are a god. You open cages." He rose from his chair and turned to Petra. "Tell the conductor from America exactly what you want."

Her eyes were two voids. She was some nocturnal animal—sunlight would kill her.

"Do you want absolution?"

"No," she said, just above a whisper.

"You want punishment."

She hesitated, glancing at Barrow. "No."

"Too bad."

Ziegler turned away—a feint—because swiftly he was back, leading with his shoulder, the great pendulum of his arm swinging out—his right—a full arc, aimed at her head. But it was a choked swing. His hand shook, centimeters from her face.

Barrow couldn't breathe. She was looking at him, the student conductor from America, profoundly useless, no one's knight, a fraud by every measure. Her eyes were full and glistening. What he read, in minute quantity, was defiance—at whom, at what, he couldn't tell. She walked out of the dressing room, leaving the door open to the hall.

Barrow waited until he heard the ping of the elevator arriving to take her back to stage level.

"How dare you," he said under his breath.

Ziegler did not respond, watching only. The intercom issued low-level complaints from the wall, equipment checks between TV people, random swatches of violin and clarinet.

"I conduct this concert," Barrow said.

A slight smile crossed the old man's face and disappeared.

"For you now," Ziegler said, his voice calm, "only first measures. Drop everything else. Only Haydn, Bernstein, Brahms."

Barrow stared, the adrenaline just beginning to crest, the room spinning slowly.

"Life is not music," Ziegler said.

He was right. And Barrow hated him with everything he had.

✍

The bleeding was stanched and the hair sprayed hard over the spot. They walked out together. The stage manager was frantic because it was, he said, four minutes past eight and this was a broadcast concert. With him in the hall was the woman who had been in the dressing room before—Barrow recognized the perfume—Fräulein Schiff, presumably an officer of Hessischer Rundfunk, perhaps the TV producer, and better trained than the stage manager in composure.

Ziegler did not explain Barrow's presence—they must assume he was an assistant, a boyfriend, anything. When they rounded the entrance to the wings, the concertmaster spotted them and slipped through the panel door to the stage. Within seconds came Petra's note, the A. In the three or four seconds that it hung suspended and alone in the vast hall, not frail, dependable, 443 cycles per second, Barrow felt a rush of feeling, and an odd relief when the full orchestra joined her, tuning.

The panel door admitted a thin sheet of light from the stage.

Barrow had been riding Ziegler's resolve; he rode it clear to the cracked door, where the little party came to a halt. Only Ziegler was calm. They had spoken little in the dressing room after Petra left. At the last possible minute, Barrow realized he'd forgotten to pack his stretch socks. Ziegler handed him a pair. "Two of everything," he said. "Always."

They huddled at the door—Ziegler, Barrow, the woman, and the stage manager, who in his extreme anxiety had begun to widen the opening to the stage.

"It happens, Fräulein Schiff, that I feel quite sick," Ziegler said. "My colleague will take the podium." The door to the stage had been backed off a foot, room to get through, and visible to the entire audience as a dark slash in the paneling. There was no outflanking maneuver left to Fräulein Schiff. No words. She stood, utterly nonplussed. Ziegler turned to Barrow, his face catching the light, his jaws working against some stray emotion. He held the baton. "Remember," he said, clumsily pressing his hand to Barrow's chest, "the beat is here," and pressing the baton into Barrow's right hand, "not here."

"Yes, Maestro."

Voices clipped back and forth in the stage manager's headset.

"One other thing."

Barrow nodded. Ziegler's hands were trembling.

"Kill your teachers."

The old man's eyes, and his short, almost courtly bow, were the last things Barrow saw before the applause met him, and the cluttered path between the second and first violins, and the look of shock on the concertmaster's face, and the intense clarity of the lights, and the already long-since ticking of the Haydn symphony's opening meter in his head, which he held to like a solid thing, planted back in the dressing room by Ziegler.

He forgot to acknowledge the audience's applause, and it was only later, measures into the opening *Allegro*, that he would realize, fleetingly, that most of the house and much of the orchestra were thinking he was Karlheinz Ziegler, the last-minute replacement for Werner Schott.

Kill your teachers.

He did not, as he'd always imagined, hit the podium and lift his arms in one breath, flooding the hall with sound before the applause could taper off. Instead, he left his hands at his side and allowed the sound behind him to die. He looked deliberately at Petra, sought to burn a message with his eyes, *Please, just get through this.* She stared back, lifted her reed to soak it between her lips.

The concertmaster looked to be his own age. He could not be certain of the man's eyes because of the thickness of his glasses, but, in the purest, never-rehearsed gesture, a lifting of both hands, lightly fisted, palms up—a gesture of the reins—he said *This is a duet. You, Herr Concertmaster, and I.*

He glanced at the score and realized instantly that he didn't like Ziegler's tempo—too slow. He had, perhaps, more of the orchestra's attention than he would ever have again—they had to be so much on edge—and it was a great advantage. The new tempo greeted him the moment he raised his baton. He established it for the orchestra in a single upbeat, and they came along, every one of them, an astoundingly responsive group, and they would be—professionals, groomed by Schott.

His memory and the concertmaster's proficiency served him well on the Haydn.

For the Bernstein, he was to his surprise a performer, dancing as he thought Bernstein would dance, even flipping the pages of the score with aplomb, laughing at the orchestra, trying to dirty up the brass with his antics; and by the end they were all, everyone on both sides of the proscenium, smashed. The applause hit his back, a solid wall of it. He gestured with both arms for the members of the brass section to stand up, the orchestra to follow. He turned, smiling for the audience, and dropped from the waist. He took his bow deep, left the stage before the ovation peaked, and returned once again, insisting the orchestra stand before taking his bow.

At intermission, he fled to the dressing room. Ziegler was gone, his personal effects swept from the wardrobe rack. There was no note.

He threw up in the toilet.

Over the intercom the stage manager asked if he would care to address the full chorus in the rehearsal room before they went out on stage. Barrow apologized, but he would rather not. There was a knock on the door, a light one, and his heart leapt—Petra, he thought. But it was the contralto soloist for *Alto Rhapsody*, an opera singer from Berlin, who greeted him with the outsized cordiality preferred by the famous. He was grateful for her visit, he said. He would be all hers on the podium, he said. She left somewhat abruptly, and he feared he'd been rude, perhaps having overlooked some obligatory ritual.

Two or three musicians were already back on stage; he heard the chorus file out, the squeak of risers over the intercom monitor.

He thought there might be enough time for him to slip out and find Petra, but there was another knock, a hard rap, and Fräulein Schiff, the TV producer, entered the dressing room. She was friendly. "Maestro Ziegler has assured us that you are an excellent conductor, and, of course, we see it with the Bernstein."

She didn't mention the Haydn.

"Thank you," he said, "and where is the maestro?"

"He asked for a seat in a box, and we have put him in the control booth. He looked quite ill." She had papers for Barrow to sign, a contract. "I am sorry, Maestro Ziegler said you are not with a manager?"

"Quite right."

"I wonder, would it be acceptable if the arrangements are as with the maestro?"

"Do you mean my fee?"

"Yes," she said, "fee and travel and accommodations and rights, et cetera?"

He said it was acceptable and asked for the signature page without stopping to look at the amount, which he knew would only spook him further. "Could I be alone for a moment?" he said.

"Of course, of course," she said, and left.

She was good—she could not have been more nervous.

He looked around the room. The empty clothing rack. The mirror. The very floor tile where Petra had been standing.

He heard her, or thought he did, over the monitor among the other players, the brief oboe solo from *Nänie*. He recognized her sound, and she must have known he would—known that he would not expect her to play a solo, a simple lyric, as a warmup.

His hands were shaking. He loosened his cuffs and paced the small room, avoiding the mirror. *Drop everything else*, Ziegler had said. Ziegler, who mixed discipline and madness in the same glass. Intelligence and emotion.

Where am I weak?

Where they meet.

How can I solve that?

You cannot.

Neither could Ziegler.

Barrow spotted his backpack hanging from a chair, flaps unzipped.

Ziegler had known about the tuxedo from the start, hadn't he? He knew his student, he knew outcomes. But had he known what would follow? Had he planned to summon Petra? Had he planned to humiliate her, or was he driven by the feelings of the moment?

The old man had seemed in control—right down to the near slap—but couldn't that easily have been an illusion?

The questions would not stop.

He turned on the cold water and splashed it on his wrists, neck and face.

The intercom squawked to life—*"Herr Maestro Barrow."*

"Ja."

Drop everything else.

The choir was on stage. Over the monitor he sensed its sheer size, the shifting of weight on the risers and the muffled, throat-clearing coughs. He'd made a huge error. He should have appeared before the choir, publicly shaken hands with their director. He'd strayed too far from the music. He glanced around for the scores to the Brahms, but, of course, they were on the podium.

An intern escorted him to the wings. She was respectful and silent and too slow. At the stage door he stooped to retie his shoes with trembling fingers.

There was a signal from the stage manager, and he stepped into the light—the applause seemed distant. Rain on a tin roof. All he could think was how he needed the opening measures, how he craved them, because their exact execution could be his only cure. He mounted the podium and looked up. The chorus was grand and innumerable, stretching wing to wing behind the orchestra, an entire people, the human race. Every pair of eyes was on him; the electricity was overpowering. He put down his baton and clasped his hands. He offered them to the chorus, and he meant it—I am for the music, for the sound and how it can lift the words, coax them from the page. A sweeping gaze and he met them all, including Petra, the glint of light off her glasses.

The score was open. A downward glance rooted him. Of the four Brahms pieces, Schott—God love him—had programmed *Song of the Fates* first, with its opening *fortissimo*, a brutal D-minor chord joined by every instrument on the floor, majestic, certain, and redolent with fury. He lifted his arms. With him came the rush of a hundred instruments being raised, the rustle of fabric. He heard the collective breath that conductors crave—the incantation—and he knew that he was equal to the moment. On cue, the orchestra exploded, obedient and terrifying.

And the chorus.

Let the race of man fear the gods!
They hold the power and can use it as they please.

34 Petra was awake. He couldn't see her face in the pre-dawn light, but he felt the descent of her hand to his forehead. Her fingertips brushed his temple. It could easily have been a dream.

He'd stayed with her out of convenience, or so he'd told himself. But in the morning, watching her sleep—hearing the slight stir of air through her nostrils—he knew it was more than that.

At her request, they left Messer-Eichen's house, trained to Mainz, and boarded a steamer for a trip down the Rhine. They booked a one-day excursion to Koblenz and back. She made no demands on him, and at first they spoke little. But the spectacle of water and towering cliffs seemed to drive them from hiding. When she put a brochure in his hands and said "Please read me this?"—pointing to the poem printed on the back panel—he did.

It was Heinrich Heine's "Die Lorelei."

They'd come to the river's swiftest passage, and he hammed his way through the ballad of the blond siren who lured boatmen to certain death along the reefy banks of the Rhine. The sound of Petra's laughter snapped his resistance. She sang snatches of Wagner's *Rheingold*. It was idiotic. They were capable of that, of idiocy, alone, the two of them, on the bone-chilling deck of a chugging tourist rig.

They found another boat, one that would take them clear upriver to a small town only a short drive from Karlsruhe. They called Alexandra, made sure she could pick them up at the other end, paid for a cabin, and lay down on its narrow, three-inch mattress. She kissed him tentatively, and he kissed her back. At first she seemed content with his lips, and he with hers. Then, without trying, without knowing or thinking, they made love.

At midnight they stood on the freezing deck, pressed to the rail under the lee of the pilothouse, wrapped in a cabin blanket for extra warmth. They watched the silent race of lights along the shore, the slumbering beauty of an otherwise unexceptional city like Mannheim. The wind sucked diesel exhaust from the stern back up the length of the deck.

"It's cold," he said.

"You don't know about cold."

"Yes I do."

"No, you don't."

"Rochester is cold."

"Berlin is *fucking* cold."

She had performed flawlessly in the Brahms despite everything, shone where she should, blended elsewhere. She could do anything— if a symphony orchestra were a river, she could fly, belly to its surface, dive to swim along the bottom, break for the surface, defy the current, dive again. During the performance, without her looking, he returned recklessly to her face, again and again, checking for damage. She waited in the green room through all the congratulations. Wordlessly, they wandered down Hochstrasse before flagging a cab.

The Brahms, he would later realize, had bought them another day.

She was yelling above the engines. "Perhaps they are cutting off my leg and I don't even know it."

"What?"

"I have so little feeling in my body."

He could not find the key to their cabin; it turned out she had it in her coat pocket, and she let them in. She dropped to the edge of the narrow bunk, where earlier she had groaned and shaken under him. Sitting on the floor in front of her, he pulled off her mittens and tried to warm her hands with his, but she pulled them away and looked down at her palms, the short kid's fingers, curling up.

The cabin was too warm; he peeled down to his T-shirt.

"We could go to East Berlin," he said. "You could show me everything. We could get tickets for one of the Bernstein concerts and you could take me to the Rykestrasse Synagogue. You could speak with the rabbi."

She paused before speaking. "In Judaism, do you know who can forgive you?"

He shook his head.

"Only the victim," she said, hesitating. "That is the problem with murder."

"You didn't murder anyone."

"'Is your blood redder than his?'" Her voice had grown hoarse.

"What?"

"A saying. In the law. It is forbidden to murder, even to save your own life."

"It wasn't murder."

"It was a consequence."

"Which you couldn't foresee."

"Which *anyone* could have foreseen."

They fell silent. Ship sounds came forward—the thudding engines, a single low blast of the horn. He wanted to touch her, run the backs of his fingers over her cheek, but he was without jurisdiction. Her eyes stayed on his until her lids grew heavy and she rolled to her side on the bunk.

"I was going to tell you everything," she said, her voice tired, muffled by the pillow.

He waited, rose to his knees—there she lay, unabsolved, unpunished, a light trail of perspiration matting her forelock to her temple. He kissed her lightly. Her familiar smell came with a hint of diesel exhaust. She was so beautiful, the sum of her. He'd found that his love could spiral, disappear below the clouds, and come sputtering up again, just clearing the tops. Did that make him an accessory to her crime? He supposed that it did.

He waited a long time, listening to her breathe.

He removed his wet shoes and socks, switched off the cabin light, and felt his way back to the bunk, where he crawled into the narrow space between her and the bulkhead.

✍

On Monday, he returned some of the messages that had begun to arrive in the music school office, two agents—one British, one German—and an offer to guest conduct a radio orchestra in the Netherlands. He had a prearranged lunch with Antonio and Berndt, and an early-afternoon session with the *Hänsel und Gretel* chorus.

When he returned to Schützenstrasse, she was gone. Her oboe, the vise she used to make her reeds, some clothes, and judging from the gaps, ten or twelve paperbacks from her baseboard library. She had not even stopped to open the shutter. It was the disappearance of the vise that worried him most. He sat on the futon with his back to the wall until Alexandra and Wolf returned in the evening. When they claimed ignorance, he believed them.

35 He crossed the Wall at Brandenburg Gate. His first encounter on the east side was with a man wearing fingerless wool gloves, performing the Mozart Clarinet Concerto accompanied by a cassette player at his feet. He wore a black suit jacket over a thin gray sweater, and his ears were bright red from the cold. *Ossi* or *Wessi*, Barrow couldn't guess; he dropped what change he had into the man's clarinet case.

He'd done some reading that caused him to seek out Scheuenviertel, the old Jewish Quarter. The war was everywhere. Shrapnel scars in the sandstone, empty lots and broken buildings. He visited a well-kept lawn where once stood a Jewish old-age home. The Gestapo had turned it into a clearinghouse for tens of thousands of Jews on their way to the death camps. And there he caught sight of his first Petra Vogel doppelgänger.

His heart leapt. He knew within seconds that the brunette with the blue duffel coat was not Petra, but he followed her anyway. Another Petra stood beneath the angry columns of the old Volksbühne theater. He picked up her scent on a street called Kollwitzstrasse, which led past a huge Jewish cemetery.

It was dark before he reached Rykestrasse, a street of dilapidated tenements. He found the sign he was looking for next to a wrought-iron gate. There was an arched entryway and a small courtyard on the other side. The gate was open.

The building was splendid, a rising expanse of Romanesque arches. In a city where few structures could be trusted no matter what the impression of age, where past, present, and future had all risen from the same rubble, the Rykestrasse Synagogue, he'd read, was the genuine article.

A light was on in a ground-floor apartment. He stopped mid-courtyard, dropped his pack, and worked his shoulders to loosen the stiffened muscles there. He'd been unable to work out a final approach, thinking, If I can just *see* the place, I'll know what to do.

"*Kann ich Ihnen behilflich sein?*"

The voice came from the shadows, and Barrow's hands flew up. "*Bitte, entschuldigen Sie.*"

"Can I help you?" the man demanded in English. He wore a large overcoat and house slippers.

Barrow struggled for the right words.

"What are you doing here?"

"I'm sorry."

"You are American?"

"Yes."

"You have come a long way just to stare through my office window."

"I apologize for the intrusion," Barrow said, turning away.

He had arrived at the gate when the man called across, "Where from?"

Barrow turned back. The man had not moved.

"Where are you from in the United States?"

283

"A town called Fishkill." He should have said New York City. "Not far from New York."

There was a pause. "Hudson River, no?"

Barrow cleared his throat. "You know Fishkill?"

"Across from Newburgh."

The light from the window fell across the man's shoulder—he still had not moved.

"I know Newburgh."

"In Newburgh I have a niece. She is a rabbi."

Barrow took a couple of steps into the courtyard. "I am not Jewish," he said.

"Strange beasts this falling Wall lets in. Somewhere in the apartment block adjacent to the synagogue, a shutter rattled down. "Would you care for some coffee?"

At the head of a passageway that ran the length of the building, the man pushed through a door into a room stacked with books. A desk was piled with red-bordered magazines, copies of *Stern* and *Der Spiegel* and *Time*. There were two or three Russian titles. Photographs covered one wall, all of people, many grouped in the courtyard outside, people of all ages going back, Barrow thought, to the fifties and sixties, family groupings, some huddled around babies, some around—presumably—thirteen-year-old boys.

"I'm sorry, I missed your name," Barrow said.

"Josef Broder. I am a secretary for this *shul*. I am also photographer, which is why you do not see me in any of the pictures." He was drawing coffee from an aluminum urn into a porcelain teacup. He looked fiftyish. "I have been staying here often because we are having so many visitors in the last weeks or so. Who are you?"

"Cooper Barrow."

"This is not normal, of course, to invite you in. But nothing is normal in these times."

"I understand."

"So for you, this is, what, a matter of curiosity?"

"No."

Barrow's eye had been drawn to a starkly different photo off to one side of the wall. In a courtyard, possibly the one outside, two men in jodhpurs and knee-length boots stood by their horses. They smiled broadly. One man had his hand raised in a fascist salute. They both wore unbuttoned World War II army jackets.

"For a reminder," Josef Broder said. "Our synagogue was used for a stable in the war. You should sit."

Barrow sat in one of two straight-back chairs across from the desk, and Broder handed him his coffee. The flavor reminded him of how few hours one could sleep in a week and still function.

"Tell me what are you doing here."

"I don't know."

The photographer drew himself a cup of coffee, slumped down in the swivel chair behind the desk, and looked across at Barrow.

"I knew someone who visited here," Barrow said, "perhaps two years ago."

"What is the name?"

"A woman. A musician."

"Name please?"

He would say it. He would say her name and know instantly, reading Broder's face, how much he knew.

"Petra Vogel."

"No. Means nothing."

Barrow stared in disbelief. He fought to stave off the rush of relief—the surprising *volume* of relief—that came up instantly. His thoughts flew, even as he sat calmly across from Broder's desk. *So it was another story, a survival story, one of a trail of stories—*

"What did she look like?"

Barrow found he couldn't speak.

"A musician, was she?"

"An oboist," Barrow said.

And he saw it. The interest in the other man's face.

"From the Musikhochschule?" Broder asked.

"Yes."

"Marta Strebel."

"Who?"

"It is probably Marta Strebel. Quite attractive? Brown hair?" Barrow nodded. "Your age? Little bit younger?"

"Yes."

Broder rummaged through a bottom drawer and withdrew a gray envelope. He bent up the two wings of the clasp and shook out four black-and-white photographs. They lay atop the pile of red-bordered magazines. He had a collector's reverence for the prints, and with great care he picked up the top one and passed it to Barrow.

It was Petra.

She stood in the courtyard next to an elderly man in a black suit and yarmulke. Her hands were held in front of her and she looked shy before the camera. She would. She was a treacherous combination of the worldly and the reticent.

"May I ask, what is your interest?"

"There was another young woman," Barrow said. "A violinist?"

The photographer studied him. "Marta spoke of her?"

Barrow nodded and Broder looked at him intently. He seemed deliberately close-mouthed—according Barrow the opportunity to pursue his next question, while at the same time counseling him not to.

"How are her parents?" Barrow asked.

"They left DDR with the first or second wave. Through Prague, I believe."

"But were they in prison?"

"He was. For a while."

Another silence. Broder held his gaze for every beat of it. "Why do you ask these things?"

Barrow watched his face. "Do you know," he asked, "of Marta's ... involvement?"

Broder eyed him from behind his cup. "You are a musician yourself?"

"I am a violinist, and I conduct."

"So what is your interest in this matter?"

Barrow looked down at his coffee. Truth must be so plain to this man—this photographer of weddings and funerals and bar mitzvahs, the key rites and their attendant feelings.

"Do not be deceived by the size of our edifice, Mr. Barrow. This is a small congregation."

Barrow glanced back at the photo. He knew the sweater she was wearing. She must have taken it to Paris, maybe even worn it to the West German embassy.

"Who is this man she is with?"

"Kantor Blumenfeld. He died shortly after her defection. Perhaps you have heard of his brother, Erich. He, too, was an oboist. Quite a good one before the war. Marta may have mentioned him."

"Erich Blumenfeld?"

"Her grandfather."

"Pardon?"

"She did not mention this?"

Barrow felt lightheaded. "No."

He gazed at Petra's image, willed her downturned eyes to look up at the lens. Had Ziegler known? He must have. Her body stretched out next to his. Or earlier. The moment he heard her play.

Broder spoke. "Being Jewish is passed through the mother, and her mother is not Jewish. If that is what you are thinking."

He held his cup in both hands.

"She is gone?"

Barrow nodded, unable to take his eyes from the photo.

"Do not look for her here, Mr. Barrow."

✍

They spoke of Newburgh. He learned that Broder's sister had left East Germany in the late fifties, when it was still possible to walk across the border. She'd emigrated to America and settled in the old factory town on the Hudson River, where Barrow had played a handful of Jewish weddings.

The two men stood in the shul's lofty auditorium, Broder in the role of tour guide. "The lights are being replaced in the renovation," he said, "but you get some idea." He pointed out the wide aisles where the Nazis had stabled their horses, explained how the synagogue had been spared on *Kristallnacht* because it shared its outer walls with the apartment blocks on either side. "Nevertheless, there was com-plicity with the Nazis, everywhere, on all sides."

"But—and please excuse me—you came back. Your predecessors."

"Yes," Broder said, adjusting his eyeglasses, "it is our home."

Barrow nodded. He gazed up at the high arches that were the main architectural feature of the auditorium.

"Understand," Broder said, "I speak for myself." He, too, stared up at the ceiling. "But if we cannot forgive the foot soldiers, how can we live with our neighbors?"

They made their way back to the office in silence.

Barrow had two tickets to the symphony that evening—the festival concert celebrating the fall of the Wall—and he offered them to Broder. He'd been carrying them around for a week, fooling himself with the idea that he might run into Petra, stupidly mixing life, yet again, with sonata form, the classic formula so unshakable as to seem practically universal, wherein each subject is revisited one final time before the coda. Broder politely declined the offer, saying that he loved Beethoven and he loved Leonard Bernstein but that he tended to get too emotional with the Ninth. Now was not a safe time for getting too emotional, he said.

He accompanied Barrow to the front gate. A light drizzle had dampened every surface—the stone posts and the high stone wall. The ironwork glistened.

Broder drew up his collar. "It is cold. I must go inside."

They finished shaking hands. Broder made no move to leave.

"One thing, please," he said.

"Of course."

The street was quiet and the mist from their breath was the only thing that moved.

"When you find her ..."

"Yes?"

"Tell her about the foot soldiers."

∾

At the lower end of Rykestrasse, Barrow dropped his head back and closed his eyes, abandoning himself to the night. The drizzle on his nose and cheeks, the distant traffic, the low moan of the city—he felt small, shrunk down, vastly underage in an ancient, damned world, but his mind ranged up over the city, up over its two halves and the hammered Wall between. He thought of the two displaced persons who had breached his soul. What a strange sensation it was, wind bearing him up, his arms outstretched, a stammering intelligence at either fingertip—one far to the east, and one, almost certainly, far to the west—and him, kneeling on a cracked sidewalk, in a reborn city, in a reborn country.

ACKNOWLEDGMENTS

Early work on this book was generously supported by a James A. Michener Fellowship from the Michener Center for Writers, University of Texas at Austin, and by a James Fellowship from the Heekin Group Foundation. Warmest thanks to William Hauptmann for his guidance in the earliest stages; to James Magnuson, mentor of uncommon patience and wisdom; to the readers who influenced the final manuscript in countless ways, especially Rick Ehrstin, Molly Giles, Joseph Skibell, Steven Thomas, and John Walch; to Americans abroad, Laura Paulu, Karen Adams-Rischmann, and Rachel Tucker; to the two editors who so manifestly improved this book and my understanding of writing, Fred Ramey and Aimee Taub; and to my agent and ally, Amy Williams, for her unflagging enthusiasm.

And finally, to my wife, Amy Herzberg: thanks for your goodness, your patience, and your unfailing instinct for truth.

ABOUT THE AUTHOR

Robert Ford earned a master of music degree from Yale and an MFA in writing from the Michener Center for Writers at the University of Texas at Austin. An award-winning playwright, he has published fiction in *American Short Fiction*, and he has been awarded a James Michener Fellowship and a James Fellowship from the Heekin Group Foundation for *The Student Conductor*. Born in Edinburgh, Scotland, he lives with his wife in Fayetteville, Arkansas.